SHIP OF GOLD

JAMES LEASOR, who has written many successful factual books and novels, several of which have been made into films, was born and brought up in Kent. He now has homes in Wiltshire and Portugal, which is where part of *Ship of Gold* is set. He has particular interests in motoring and property, both of which played an important part in his previous novel *Open Secret*. He is married with three sons.

By the same author

Open Secret

JAMES LEASOR

Ship of Gold

FONTANA/Collins

First published by William Collins Sons & Co. Ltd 1984
First issued in Fontana Paperbacks 1985

Copyright © James Leasor 1984

Made and printed in Great Britain by
William Collins Sons & Co. Ltd, Glasgow

CONDITIONS OF SALE:
This book is sold subject to the condition that
it shall not, by way of trade or otherwise, be lent,
re-sold, hired out or otherwise circulated without
the publisher's prior consent in any form of
binding or cover other than that in which it is
published and without a similar condition
including this condition being imposed on the
subsequent purchaser

for Ted and Mary

When a ship sinks, gold weighs down its possessor.

PETRONIUS, Fragments, no. 80

one

THE SHATTERED HOUSE stood suppurating in the shimmering African sun.

Mortar fire had pocked its walls, and the dried mud beneath the whitewash showed like diseased scabby wounds. Looters had attempted to strip away the corrugated-iron roof, but the guns of one side or the other had disturbed them, and rusty sheets of metal flapped like the wings of a grotesque and frightened bird. For a moment, the lieutenant leading the army patrol regarded the house suspiciously, wondering whether it was booby-trapped. Then he shot away the lock with his Smith & Wesson and kicked open the front door.

A sour stench of sweat and dung and death erupted through the doorway like fumes from a charnel-house. He choked at the smell, and behind him his troops fell back nervously. They were all conscripts; only a few weeks previously they had been in their villages. Most had never seen a dead body or fired at a living target. Now, having sworn allegiance to their emperor, they were taking part in a revolution against him; it was all very puzzling.

The lieutenant beckoned them to follow, and walked into the hall. It was totally dark. He searched for a light-switch, but the current was off; a stray shell had hit the capital's only generating station. He gave an exclamation of disgust and came back into the doorway to examine his hands where they had groped along the wall. The palms were damp and slimy with blood.

He shouted for a torch, shone it down the hall. Here and there, on once white walls, people had scratched their names and the date of their arrest – all meaningless now, but at the time the only farewell they could give.

The officer led the way to the main living-room. As far as the beam from his torch would carry, he could see black bodies, some chained, some manacled, others with hands and feet bound by ropes, all dead. Their faces were fearfully disfigured: rodents had eaten eyes and noses and ears. The smell of putrefaction was so intense he could not breathe, and he led his troops briskly back into the outer air.

Here, they stood sweating, breathing deeply, unnerved by their discovery. Their three weeks basic training had not dealt with a situation like this. A corporal carried out a pile of ledgers he had found and tripped over a broken step in his haste to reach fresh air. Papers scattered like confetti across the dusty ground. The lieutenant picked up a page headed simply: *Executions*. Two columns were typed on it: *Names* and *Crimes*. Against every name, in careful handwriting learned in a mission school long since looted and its teachers murdered, were inscribed two words: *Not specified*.

He picked up the last page in the ledger, numbered 314. He counted twenty names on it, so this file alone bore witness to 6280 pointless murders. How many other files, in other houses and commandeered garages, contained details of thousands more? The thought bemused him. His mind felt fuddled, unable to accept let alone understand murder on this mass scale. He had worked as a clerk in a bank before he was conscripted; the worst that could happen in that safe, predictable world was that a client might default on an overdraft. Civil war and revolution were totally alien to him.

The lieutenant left two men to guard the entrance of the house, and ordered the others back to their truck, which trundled slowly up the main street. In colonial times this had been called King George Road. Now it was Independence Way, a wide strip of potholed tarmac with broken pavements on either side, and open drains clogged with purple, putrefying filth. Rows of single-storeyed buildings on either side had once been the capital's main shopping-centre. They were now empty rooms with fronts open to the street; not looted, for there was nothing left in them to steal. They had been bare for months before the revolution. Emperor Odongo's ruling Personal Freedom Party had seized millions of dollars of aid that richer countries had given to his country of Menaka; the poor had nothing to buy and no money to spend.

Here and there, at the roadside, lay the shell of a car, burned out and rusting, stripped of tyres, lights, anything anyone could carry away to sell or barter for food. Small crowds of children waited on street corners, some sullen and afraid, others waving flags half-heartedly at every car that passed, hoping for news of better times. It was difficult to be drilled at school to cheer Emperor Odongo one day, and to be ordered to revile him the next.

The white walls of Freedom Palace, the capital's largest building (Government House when the officer was a schoolboy), were heavily scored with graffiti. Sentry-boxes had been overturned, and on each upright of the iron boundary-fence a bleached human skull had been spiked – by whom no one now knew or cared. Today's revolutionaries were tomorrow's despots; the winners always took all, and first the lives of those who opposed them. Vultures had picked the flesh away; only a few tufts of hair trembled in the wind. The lawns, once sprinkled constantly and cut twice a week, and the pride of the colony, were now ridged and pitted by tyre-tracks. Emperor Odongo had used the gardens as a racecourse for his ministers and himself. The lieutenant had often seen them drive commandeered cars like dodgems at a fair, deliberately smashing into trees and each other with shrieks of laughter, stupefied by heat and whisky and the heady prospect of perpetual power.

The main bank building where the lieutenant had once worked was smashed open, and black streaks of soot reached up above broken windows. A crowd had forced its way in impatiently as soon as they had heard that the Emperor was overthrown. But others, better prepared, had been there before them with the same intentions. Late arrivals found the vaults already open and empty.

Grounded helicopters, rotors smashed and hanging like broken wings, stood crammed together in a school playground.

Russian tanks and personnel-carriers with damaged tracks were abandoned in a bamboo grove. Clenched fists defaced an advertisement hoarding; the Cubans Odongo had brought in as advisers had carried the stencils with them. The lieutenant mentally totted up a figure for the waste and ruin and misery he could see, but guessed that the true amount must be ten times, a hundred times as large.

A crowd of refugees, pushing prams or bicycles laden with their belongings, or trotting barefoot with bundles on their heads, padded away to the north and a vague hope of new beginnings. They carefully looked the other way as the soldiers overtook them, not daring to meet their eyes. Under Odongo, men had been killed for less – much less.

The radio crackled in the officer's ears. He adjusted his headphones and picked up the microphone. A voice said crisply and metallically: 'Grid 14, 175348, south-west corner of airport. Prevent by any means departure of unauthorized aircraft containing chief target.' He tore off his headphones, shouted new orders to his driver. Tyres squealed as the truck backed and turned.

Five miles to the south, the runways that Cubans and North Koreans had built for the international airport which Odongo had claimed would be the largest and busiest in all Africa lay like a vast white concrete cross amid vivid green mangrove swamps. A giant orange windsock fluttered in the sky. The radar aerial was still turning above the control-tower, although the controllers had fled hours before. Two black Mercedes, white curtains drawn discreetly over rear windows because of the heat, raced from the welcome shade of the airport buildings towards a parked aircraft. Its engines were already running, thrust from the jets bending and burning palm-fronds on the edge of the runway.

The cars stopped, and an aide next to the driver of the first sprang out to open the rear door. He saluted the imposing figure of Emperor Odongo, Lord of the Central Hills, Ruler of Middle Africa, Liberator of the People.

Odongo towered above the others as they hastily piled out of the second car to line up in front of him. Everything about Odongo was on a massive scale. He was not so much a man as a giant, a grotesque, swollen, over-inflated figure. His appearance alarmed lesser men; his reputation and his temper always confirmed their fears. Despite the heat, Odongo wore a dark-blue Huntsman suit and a black Homburg hat from Lock.

'You will wait here,' he told his followers in his deep sonorous voice as he shook hands solemnly with each one. 'Sit in your cars. I will be back within fifteen minutes, when I have made an aerial reconnaissance. Then we will drive the insurgents from our land as the Egyptians drove out the Children of Israel in ancient days.'

'And then, Your Royal Eminence?' someone asked nervously; he had heard such promises before – and he knew how close the insurgents were. Some said the capital, Mandana, had already surrendered.

'And then we shall smite the enemy as the Christians smote the Infidels in the great Crusades. As the sons of Ebu smote the Hittites in the Good Book. Victory is ours, saith the Lord. Now it is *I* who say this, it is *I* who will bring this to pass. Only believe, and all will be as I say.'

They saluted respectfully as Odongo removed his hat. Wind from the screaming jets ruffled his thick black hair. Then he climbed slowly up the steps into the aircraft. He was not in retreat; he was simply changing one defensive position for another. Like MacArthur in the Philippines in another war, in another world, he would return. A white-overalled mechanic closed the door, removed the steps, pulled away the chocks. The whine of the jets increased.

The men the Emperor had left behind now hurried back to the cars, fingers in their ears, and sat in a comfortingly cool rush of air-conditioning while the aircraft taxied up the runway and took off. He had saved them before from several near-disasters. Why should he not be able to do so again? They clutched at this hope because it was their only one.

As the aircraft gained height, Odongo looked down at the

cars. The cross of the runway reminded him of the cross in the old mission church where he had briefly served as an altar boy until the priest had caught him trying to sell the brass candlesticks in the bazaar. The two cars diminished rapidly to the size of toys. The cross dwindled, and empty green swamps stretched to infinity on every side. He pressed a button to speak to the pilot.

'Alter course,' he told him. 'Fly due south at your highest economical cruising speed. I will tell you where to land.'

'Very good, Your Royal Eminence.'

Emperor Odongo switched off the intercom, removed his hat and placed it gravely on the seat beside him as though it were an important passenger. He liked that hat; he felt it had a personality of its own. As a boy, he had once seen a British politician in a newsreel wearing such a hat and had envied him his appearance. The hat was to Odongo as symbolic as his crown: his badge of honour and office, as important as the medals he had awarded himself and which Spink in London had designed to his exact instructions. The hat was his ju-ju, his lucky talisman. Without it, who could guess what catastrophes might befall him?

He smoothed it lovingly with one hand and then took from an inner pocket of his jacket a small black box. A tiny spring-like antenna protruded from one end. In the centre was a round red button like a bell-push. Looking out of the window, Odongo could now barely see the cars, they were so small. Approaching them at great speed was a truck the size of a toy. He pressed the button gently at first, and then he crushed the plastic box to fragments in his hand.

Far beneath him, beyond the reach of all sound, and now almost out of sight, the airfield erupted in a huge orange flash. Smoke from the detonated cars, as oil and petrol exploded, billowed up black and thick, and then drifted across the green swamp and forest.

Ten men destroyed at his whim, at the touch of a button. Ten potential witnesses who, despite all his caution, all his shrewdness in never giving written orders, only verbal instructions, might still have somehow testified to his enemies against him.

And he was surrounded by enemies; only his skill, his abilities and the advice of the Englishman had saved him – and would continue to do so.

Emperor Odongo might be temporarily deposed, but such misfortunes were a hazard of all monarchs. He knew this from the history books he had ordered his English companion to read to him because he found difficulty with longer words. His mind was a rag-bag of anecdotes about past kings and emperors – 'Pricks and princes', as the Englishman crudely dismissed them. Charles I. King Zog of Albania. The Kings of Portugal and Italy. Haile Selassie of Ethiopia – a brave man. He had met him once, but the Lion of Judah had been a small man physically; Odongo could have broken his back with one hand. No one would break his – or even bend it. He had a plan. The Englishman's plan. As he had promised his staff, now dead (may their souls rest for ever), he would return.

Odongo was above all laws, for he was the embodiment of law; what he said, what he wished, that was law enough. Happy with this thought, he contemplated the smoothness of his expensive hat. Then he frowned, and his yellowish animal eyes clouded with regret. He had killed his driver down there, a man of his own tribe, who had brushed this hat for two hours every day while in his employ. To his efforts Odongo owed the fine sheen that marked out this Homburg as the headgear of a king. Then his irritation eased; he would find another of the same tribe. Difficulties were all made to be overcome. Relaxed, at ease and content, Odongo sat back in his seat and dozed. The aircraft droned on through the burnished sky.

Two thousand miles due north, on a grey windswept beach at Castelejo, on the south-west coast of Portugal, a man stood under the shelter of the cliffs. Giant boulders, porous with holes and slatted edges, the pockmarks of centuries of fury from the sea, faced a wide bay littered with stones the size of skulls. To his right, a row of gigantic rocks, broken teeth in a mammoth mouth, stretched into the Atlantic rollers. To his left, two small, dome-topped hills, streaked with different-coloured strata, red and blue and grey, stood like burial mounds, shrouded in an early-morning mist. Farther along the beach, almost out of sight, a fisherman waited with his long curved rod, patient, unmoving.

The man beneath the cliff turned towards the streaming rock-face and lit a cigarette, cupping the match-flame in his hands against wind from the sea. He had already been there for three hours. He would wait for a quarter of an hour more; and then, if the person he was expecting had still not arrived, he would leave. He had a busy day ahead elsewhere.

He was tall, in his late thirties, well built, but just beginning to thicken at the neck and waist. He wore faded jeans, an old blue yachting-cap and a thick sweater against the early-October chill. As he put the box of matches back in the pocket of his jeans, his fingers encountered the folded newspaper he had bought to read and then forgotten.

He opened it, began to read the report he had been told about. It described the last days and escape of the self-styled Emperor Odongo who had ruled the small West African state of Menaka ruthlessly for the previous ten years.

The writer declared that Odongo's rise to power had proved even more damaging than Idi Amin's rule in Uganda or Bokassa's years in the Central African Republic. Originally, Odongo had been a corporal in the British-officered African Defence Regiment. Because of his impressive size and his prowess as a boxer, he had become sergeant in charge of the presidential guard. Then, on the eve of his country's independence, he had hastily been commissioned as lieutenant. After all, the country needed black officers and he was a fine physical specimen. The few whites remaining felt certain they could keep him on the rails, tell him how to behave, and take any important decisions. That, at least, was the theory. The facts soon proved them wrong.

Odongo's first move to advance himself was to replace troops of different tribes in the presidential guard with men of his own tribe. Soon he had a small private army of his own, composed of men who owed their promotion and loyalty entirely to him.

Next, he persuaded a relation in the Army Ministry to advise all officers and non-commissioned officers of a certain rank to take a month's leave in lieu of pay which they were owed and had still not received. The President was out of the country at the time, and so was ignorant of these strange orders. Odongo then copied Idi Amin's tactics. When Dr Obote, the President of Uganda, had once been out of that country, Amin had seized the radio station in the name of the people, and ordered troops to occupy the banks and the country's only newspaper office, saying that, as guard commander, he was acting on the President's orders.

In short order Odongo did the same, and then promoted himself colonel, general, field-marshal and finally not president, but emperor. With him, up the rungs of the ladder of power, he took his tribal colleagues from the old presidential guard. Some started that day as privates and were colonels by sundown. With Odongo's hands on all levers of power, with his creatures at every level, and death the fate of all who opposed him, Odongo led his country into ten years of deepening darkness, which for him became a decade of immeasurable wealth.

He acquired homes in Britain and France, bank accounts in Switzerland and the Bahamas, but the wheel of fortune finally turned against him. The army he had tried to rule, whose loyalty he had bought so assiduously with crates of whisky and other bribes, followed the call of another. Odongo fled his capital only minutes ahead of his pursuers. But where had he gone? Was he alive or dead? Had he made a successful emergency landing in some other part of Menaka – or had his personal aircraft crashed in rainforests too thick and remote for any rescuers to find it?

The man on the beach folded the newspaper thoughtfully, put it in his jacket pocket. From another pocket he took a pair of miniature binoculars and scanned the stretch of empty sea. Morning mist hung like lace on the far horizon. Waves broke with white and distant smiles against the surging green of the sea, and then he saw what he had been expecting: a bobbing black speck that slowly grew larger; the head of a man, swimming in.

He was aiming for the only stretch of sand between the rocks. If he missed that narrow strip, if a wave carried him too far to the left or right, his flesh would be ripped from his body by the surge of waves against the jagged rocks. From the sea, the swimmer could only guess his direction, as a wave lifted him briefly and then he plunged down into the swirling deep trough behind it. Beyond the boiling surf on the saw-toothed rocks, he could see cliffs soar black against the sky; but, as one wave larger than the rest lifted him, he felt too weary to ride it. Tons of water cascaded over him, and threw him forward on to the beach.

As the water receded with a roar, a torrent of small stones and sharp-edged shells scoured his hands. He dug his fingers desperately into the hard damp sand, gasping for breath as another wave broke over him. Then, slowly, wearily, but with the strength and determination of despair, he began to edge himself inland by his toes, inch by painful inch.

Wave after wave pounded him with hammer blows. Once, the undercurrent almost drew him back into the swirling, foaming sea, but with finger and toe-holds he just managed to keep his position. Finally, he left the sea behind him, and the waves thundered harmlessly and impotently out of reach. He lay spread-eagled, sobbing for breath, lacking the strength to stand upright. He fainted or he slept, exhausted by the long, almost impossible swim. Suddenly, he was aware that within inches of his eyes lay the detritus of the twentieth century: incongruous plastic bottles, aerosol cans, blobs of solidified tar. The morning sun was drying the huge smooth stones, and he felt its welcome warmth on his sodden back. Behind him, waves boomed on the beach like distant cannon. He stood up, flexed his muscles and began to walk slowly across the sand. As he reached the bigger boulders, still slippery with dew and spray, he crouched, keeping his balance with his fingertips on some of the larger rocks. He had reached the base of the cliffs before the man who was waiting for him detached himself from their shadow.

'Thank God you made it,' he said fervently.

The swimmer saw him for the first time. His eyes were raw from the salt and difficult to focus.

'What the hell are you doing here?' he asked, his amazement tinged with relief. 'How did you know I'd come ashore in this bloody place?'

'I'll tell you when we're in the car. It's parked on top of the cliff.'

The swimmer glanced up at the almost sheer wall of rock that faced him, and shook his head.

'I can't climb that,' he said with finality.

'You will. There's an easy way up. I'll help you.'

The man handed him a flask of whisky. The swimmer drank greedily, coughing and choking as the spirit burned his throat. A huge bird circled in the empty sky: a buzzard, the bird of death. He shivered, despite the whisky. Well, he had fooled that bird, although there had been several moments out at sea when he wouldn't have put money on survival. But now, thank God, all that was behind him. He was ashore and safe and with a man he knew.

Until he began to climb he had not realized just how exhausted he was. Slowly, steadying themselves against rocks, they clambered over boulders at the base of the cliff to a flagstoned path. A strong smell of thyme and sage sweetened the air. The sun was now coming up strongly. Out at sea, beyond the false hazy horizon, as the swimmer turned and rested against the face of the rock, he thought he could see the hills of Africa. It was a total illusion – only clouds that diffused the sun.

Suddenly, the sun was above the clouds and turning the drab patch of sand to gold. Boulders glowed as though lit by inner fire. Beyond the path he saw the rudimentary outline of a building, made of huge stones cemented together; an abandoned municipal wash-house, a row of concrete steps cut painfully into the cliff and then a turning-space for cars.

This was a part of Portugal which tourists rarely visited. The country was cruel here, and the beach dangerous as waves constantly shifted thousands of tons of shingle with a harsh roar each time they broke. There were no pedalos here, no canoes for hire, no windsurfers, no beach-hut selling iced drinks. The vegetation was sparse and green; even the plants had rough leaves with razor-sharp edges. This was the uttermost part of Europe, which Europeans in search of the sun could conveniently forget. Beyond this lay the ocean and the New World.

They climbed the steps slowly. A car was parked facing the road up through the hills.

'I've got a blanket,' said the man who had met the swimmer. He reached in to the back seat, picked up a rough blanket, wrapped it around his companion's shoulders. The swimmer shivered. The car was small and already becoming warm with the swiftly increasing heat of morning, but he still felt chilled, his bones cold to the marrow. At this time of year, the Atlantic was like liquid ice. He sat, hunched up, shaking with reaction.

The other man started the engine and they set off. The road wound up between green gorse and spiky grass, no more than a single track. The swimmer thought that the scent of herbs, pines and eucalyptus trees smelled like aftershave; one of those fancy lotions, Cedarwood, Pine Forest. Why not Castelejo? The road cut into the hills, and above the distant landscape clouds were moving swiftly before the wind.

They drove in silence.

'But how *could* you know I'd be here?' the swimmer asked his companion.

'I worked out that this was the only place you could land.'

'I might have been carried miles away by the current, though.'

'So you were very lucky.'

'I don't believe in luck,' the swimmer replied slowly. 'That's too easy an explanation. I believe in consequences. You take this or that action – and one or other reaction occurs.'

'Maybe you're right. But what the hell? You took the right action – and one or other reaction occurs.'

The swimmer said nothing, but sat, still shivering slightly, staring out at the road ahead. Why did he feel so uneasy, when he should be thankful he had survived?

Suddenly, the engine faltered and the car stumbled and jerked. The driver cursed. He dropped down a gear, and then two gears.

'This bloody petrol,' he said irritably. 'God knows what it is. They must put water in it.'

The car blundered to a stop. He twisted the ignition key angrily. The starter spun the engine. It did not fire.

'Know anything about motors?' he asked the swimmer.

'Not a lot.'

'Nor do I.'

They both climbed out. The driver lifted the bonnet. The engine was covered with dust; it was a hired car.

'Any tools in the back?' the swimmer asked him. 'There might be an instruction book or something.'

'I'll have a look. You don't get much these days.'

He opened the boot.

'Only a spanner,' he said, picking it up. 'And a wheel-wrench.'

The swimmer came round to the rear of the car.

'There's a toolbag.'

'Where?' the other man asked him.

'At the back.'

As the swimmer leaned in to pull it out, the driver brought down the spanner on the base of his skull.

The swimmer sagged, gave a long sigh of acceptance, and fell forwards into the boot. Then, as his legs folded beneath him, he rolled back on to the road. The driver threw the spanner into the car, picked the swimmer up under his armpits, and dragged him into the gorse. He walked backwards, gasping and panting with the effort. He'd had no idea the man would be so heavy.

The gorse was up to his shoulders before he reached the point he had reconnoitred on the way to the beach that morning. He let the man fall and then began to drag him slowly towards the edge of a steep cliff, where the ground had fallen away in a maze of cracks and horizontal fissures. The strata were reddish brown and grey, flecked here and there with metallic deposits. Sunshine made them twinkle like fool's gold. The leaves of some of the bushes were sticky and reflected the light as though they were lacquered. He sweated with heat and exertion and the fear of being observed.

He put the man down on the ground and turned him around slowly, pivoting him on his buttocks. A gold ring with a strange crest caught the sun. On impulse, he bent down, removed it, slipped it into his pocket. Then he gave the unconscious body a sharp push and let it roll. The man bumped downhill slowly at first, and then gathered speed.

The watcher heard his head crack against one of the rocks as the body somersaulted and then landed on its back. A powdering of red dust fell from the edge of the cliff, where the movement had disturbed a mass of earth and small stones.

The swimmer's body was still visible from the top, but in any case it was unlikely that anyone would come that way. The man glanced involuntarily up at the sky. A buzzard swept above him in a wide circle, watching him, head and beak down. If too many followed, that might give away the position of the body, but this was a risk he had to take.

He began to walk back towards the road, and had almost reached the car when he heard the put-put whirring of a little bean-can motorcycle. He dropped down into the gorse, hoping that the motorcyclist would not stop. He raised himself cautiously; he could see a blue crash-helmet, a man in shirtsleeves with two enormous fishing-rods strapped vertically to the rear mudguard and swinging in the wind, like long radio aerials. He must be the fisherman from the beach. The man wondered whether he had watched them walk up the steps together. He had looked behind him and had seen no one. Anyhow, what could he prove, even if he *had* seen them?

He waited until the sound of the engine died and the blue helmet disappeared up the long winding road. The smell from eucalyptus-trees was very strong now. He hurriedly covered the last few yards to the road, climbed in behind the wheel. He saw no other traffic, no other people until he reached the main Lisbon road, running south into Vila do Bispo.

There was a fair in progress in the town, stalls piled with local woodwork, lace, linen, tablecloths. Music blared from loudspeakers tied to lamp-posts. He took the road leading east along the coast. Only when he was certain no one was following him did he relax. Then he reached up behind the driver's mirror and took down the piece of chewing-gum he had parked there on his way to the beach. He never threw away a half-chewed piece of gum. He hated waste in all its forms.

two

CARTER SURFACED SLOWLY through diminishing layers of sleep.

He opened his eyes, and horizontal slats of light, sharp as polished knives, blazed at him cruelly through the shutters. Although he had seen them every morning and on most afternoons throughout that summer, and from the same position in bed, he had drunk so much that he still took a moment to realize what they were, and where he was. As always, he found no pleasure in the answers.

He glanced around the little room, whitewashed in the local Portuguese style with *cal*, a solution of white lime dug from a quarry off the Sagres road, and spring water. He recognized familiar prints of Cries of London, which represented the tastes of the absentee English landlord. The plump, blowsy woman selling ripe strawberries always reminded him of the wives of Midlands car-dealers who rented some of the more expensive houses along the Algarve coast, and whose obese, spoilt children he was hired to teach to swim. He saw the faded white rugs, the folding wooden chairs sold to tourists in Lagos market, and then he saw the woman, still asleep, next to him. Her face was damp with perspiration and her long dark hair spread out across the pillow like a careless fan. She slept with her mouth open, a habit he disliked.

He looked at her without love or tenderness, trying to remember her name. Was she Sandra or Samantha or Helga? Not that it mattered; not that anything mattered very much now.

Carter eased himself out of bed, walked into the bathroom on tiptoe in case he should awake her and she should want him again. He closed the door, examined his face in the mirror. He was thirty that day: a milestone in a man's life, the first step to middle-age. He was tall, broad-shouldered, still narrow-hipped in spite of the amount of Portuguese brandy he drank every night, usually alone, in the Nautilus bar in São Sebastião. What had his old company commander, a passed-over major, told him sadly in the mess one night? First, you drink to remember; then you drink to forget. So why was he drinking – for one reason, or for both?

Already he could see a slight puffiness around his eyes, the faint and soft beginnings of a stomach. If he continued with this life, just passing time, somehow dragging through each day, his whole appearance would change as irrevocably as his life and outlook had changed. Then he would be over the hill, with no hope of any comeback, like so many other people of indefinite age, who lived here in the sun all the year round, complaining about their neighbours, their servants and the rapacity of local taxation, but with one important difference: he would have no income to tax.

Carter ran some cold water, doused his face in the basin, shook his head violently to drive away these gloomy thoughts, towelled and went back into the bedroom.

The woman was awake now, sitting up in bed. Her sagging breasts that had attracted him mildly earlier in the afternoon now produced a feeling of revulsion. But was it of her or of himself – or for his whole pointless existence?

'You're awake early,' she said almost accusingly, and he remembered her name. This was Shauna, and she had a flat south-London accent.

'What's the matter? Got the runs?'

He tried to smile but could only produce a muscular reaction on his face.

'Not really,' he said lamely.

'Come on into bed again,' she said. 'It was good that way. I enjoyed it.'

'It's nearly four o'clock,' he reminded her.

'So what? Dan's got the kids on the beach. He won't be back till five. I asked him.'

'He might be,' said Carter cautiously, seeking any excuse not to climb back into bed with her, but not wishing to offend her. He had made too many enemies already.

'Scared, then, are you? You could finish Dan with one hand.'

'That's not the point,' replied Carter. But what was the point? Surely, that he was pouring his life away, teaching swimming and snorkelling to children out here on holiday with parents from Sweden, Germany, France, Belgium, Holland, even the States – and was grateful to have the job.

More often than not, he went to bed with one of their mothers each afternoon: a completely double life, as devious as it was shallow and aimless. Each morning he would be waiting down in the pool, in the shallow end, to explain to the children how to relax, how they shouldn't fight to keep afloat, but breathe naturally. And then a new child would arrive, seven, eight or nine, perhaps shy, perhaps confident, and invariably with his or her mother. Fathers tended to stay in the background; taking children for swimming lessons seemed to be a mother's job.

The child would join Carter's course, and Mother would watch fondly for a few minutes, and then either stroll over to the bar for the rest of the lesson or go down to the beach. Sometimes she would stay for the initial lesson and afterwards would approach him, again like the children, perhaps shyly, tentatively or confidently.

'I hear you give private lessons, Mr Carter,' she would say.

Lessons in what? he was often tempted to reply, but of course he never did.

'Yes,' he would agree. 'It sometimes helps.'

'Well, I think my little boy' – or girl, Ronnie or Jason or Jean – 'would benefit from a few private lessons. Give him' – or her, or them – 'a bit more confidence. Know what I mean?'

I know, Carter would think to himself. Too right, I know. But he would reply correctly: 'I usually hold private lessons in the early evening. It's cooler then, and the pool is less crowded. And parents often like to sleep in the afternoons.'

'When would it be best to see you about private lessons?'

'Come back now. I've all the details in my villa.'

(How odd that what in Britain would be only a modest bungalow was immediately elevated to the Edwardian status of a villa in any warmer climate!)

'Oh, that's not very convenient,' the mother would reply hastily, as though drawing back from a step that both knew could be compromising. 'Actually, we're just going out to lunch,' she would explain. Or: 'I've promised their father to meet him in the beach café for drinkies first. I'll come at three o'clock.'

With almost invariable regularity, by half-past three – four o'clock at the latest – they would be in bed together. Sometimes, as today, he was not even certain of the woman's name. Again, the dialogue would follow predictably.

'I hope you don't think badly of me? I don't do this sort of thing often. In fact, I've never done it before,' she would say. Or, more crudely, that she had heard that Carter had screwed every woman in São Sebastião. Carter would shake his head, and smile and say: 'No, only every other one.'

And then the young mother would laugh and say: 'Go on. You are a one, you are.'

And he would go on. Later, she would cry and tell him he couldn't imagine what it was like to be married to a boring man you couldn't respect, couldn't even like, let alone love. And Carter would sympathize and look over her head at the prints on the wall, or at the sea if the shutters were not closed, and wonder whether she could imagine what it was like to be like him – a man who could no longer respect himself?

It seemed incredible that he had sunk so swiftly to be little better than a gigolo, teaching children an art about which they knew little in the mornings, and their mothers an art about which he knew rather more in the afternoons. Yet for how long? Already the summer was all but over; time swept by on silent shoes. Children who had been in São Sebastião on holiday for two or three weeks would come one day and say goodbye and shake his hand; he had thought they still had a week to go. He would give them all a certificate to prove they had swum one length of the pool, or two or five, or whatever they had achieved. Their mothers would also visit him for the last time to give him addresses and phone numbers where they could be reached; not usually their own, but offices or the homes of married friends. Carter tore up these pieces of paper as soon as they had gone: he did not want to be reminded of them; he did not wish to see any of them again.

But, while they moved on, he remained, almost a fixture of the place. His body was now deeply tanned by the sun, and the skin on his legs was dry and brittle and beginning to crack because of so much sun and sea-water. He had only been engaged for the summer season, and summer was ending, so what happened now? Through autumn and winter, there would be no children to teach, no mothers to seduce in an attempt to forget his own failures, his own inadequacies. There had been the hint of another job, but a hint was only a hope, not an offer.

'I'll be going, then,' said Shauna sulkily.

She looked around the room. It wasn't at all her sort of room. The decorations were different from her living-room with china ducks on the wall, and the rented television with its loop aerial, the bar alcove and birthday cards displayed on the imitation-marble mantelpiece. But, then, Carter was different from anyone she had met, so maybe he liked white empty rooms. She saw a brightly coloured carved wooden cock on a side-table.

'What's that?' she asked him, to delay departure.

'The cock of Barcelas,' he explained.

'Never mind his, I'd rather have yours,' she replied and giggled. 'Go on. Tell me about it.'

'It's a legend really. After a banquet years ago, the host realized that he had been robbed, and accused one of his guests so vehemently that no one would believe the man's protests that he was quite innocent.'

Carter paused, remembering the officers in the mess who had seen him driving Akbar's Ferrari. They had only said what they had seen. They hadn't added anything – but neither would any of them accept his account of the accident.

'So this chap was committed for trial in the county court at Barcelas, up north. Someone in court had brought chickens and a cock in a basket on their way to market. The magistrate heard both sides of the case and then he summed up.

' "I don't know who to believe," he admitted to the defendant. "But if you *are* innocent, then that cock will crow." And it *did* crow. So the accused man was released.'

'Do you think I'm awful?' Shauna asked Carter, not really listening to him.

'No,' he told her dutifully. 'I think you are very pretty and very nice.'

The truth was, he didn't think anything at all about her – or much about anyone else, even about himself.

'Well, that's that, then,' she said with a sigh. 'Now I know about his cock.'

He said nothing, watching her as she began to dress. Shauna wore the almost uniform underwear of other young mothers: white Marks & Spencer pants and a white bra that contrasted with her sun-tanned skin. She pulled on a sun-suit, ran a comb hastily through her hair, shook it free again, examined her face critically in a handbag mirror. Husbands were not usually very observant, but smudged lipstick or eye-shadow seemed an unnecessary risk to take.

'I must say, you don't have many manners,' she said sharply. There had been plenty of time; now she would have to hang about on the beach on her own. She hated men.

'I'm sorry,' Carter told her. 'I was thinking.'

'Don't be thinking with me in bed, dear. *I* never was a thinker. I'll say that for my old man. *He* never took me for a thinker, either.'

She crossed the carpet towards Carter, kissed him, paused. He smelled garlic on her breath, scent on her hair. For a moment he thought of undressing her again and taking her as she liked to be taken, naked, spread out, half on the bed, half on the floor, but almost immediately the thought and the mood passed.

Shauna sensed this and picked up her beach-bag.

'What will you tell your husband?' Carter asked, wondering how she would explain her absence for two hours.

'That you weren't as good as I was told you were,' she retorted, and then smiled. 'Well, goodbye, ducky.'

Her unsuitably high heels clicked on the red polished tiles of the floor as she went out of the door. He watched her walk down the steep road to the beach, wave to another woman on her package tour, then stop and talk. He wondered whether they were comparing notes. He didn't care; he didn't care a fish's tit.

Carter sat down in a chair, poured four fingers of Borges brandy into a glass, drank them greedily. He had two more private sessions on the two following afternoons, and then nothing for the rest of that week. His swimming class had already shrunk from thirty children to ten. It would be down to three by Monday morning, and he had no new bookings. By this time next week, he could be the only person in the pool – and then what? Carter put his head in his hands, pressing his eyes with his palms, trying to erase from his memory the sequence of events that had brought him to this level of hopelessness.

Only months ago he had been an officer in the British army, Captain Anthony Carter of the Golds. The regiment had taken its name from a little-known battle in the Burmese War of 1885. For reasons that now escaped him, despite all the lectures on regimental history he had given to recruits, a platoon had been detailed to protect a golden pagoda outside Mandalay.

This was not a natural defensive position, for the pagoda stood on flat ground surrounded by a scattering of houses and hutments, and the huge golden *chinthes* that guarded its gates gave cover to any enemy. But the platoon had obeyed orders and fired volley after volley, until finally, out of ammunition, and without any hope whatever of reinforcements, they had been overrun. Five men and one corporal had somehow survived. The attacking Burmese not only respected their courage, but also rejoiced that their sacred place was unharmed.

'It was a matter of bad communications,' Carter would explain in his lectures. 'They thought *we* wanted to destroy the pagoda. We thought that *they* did. In this sense, we were on the same side, although we were fighting each other. That's how important it is to know your objectives, and to let everyone else know theirs. Be sure you know who your friends are, and who are your foes.'

It was a simple enough lesson, but had he learned it? Was he not his own worst foe? He poured another brandy. He had been drinking a more expensive brand in the mess that night: a Martell five-star. It must be all of six months ago, but it might have been six centuries, six aeons. He had been celebrating because Akbar Mohammed Khan, whom he had known at Oxford before going on to Sandhurst, had arrived unexpectedly; they had not seen each other for years, and now they were both on special attachment, in a country house that the Army maintained in south Dorset.

The aim of the course was like the purpose of Carter's lectures; to reach the value of communications between people of different creeds, colours and nationalities, whose countries had once belonged to the Empire. Now vanished and crumbled, the old British Empire was in Carter's opinion like a ruined and ancient city glimpsed far beneath the sea. Some parts stayed firm – a house here, a tower there, the outline of a street – but in other areas most traces of the past had vanished. Rebels and revolutionaries were so often in control, vehement in attacking any who could conceivably offer a threat to their own new-found personal power and prosperity, their mistresses, their Mercedes, and all the other joys that flowed with the wine of power.

The officers on the course came from many regiments and corps and countries. Carter had never met any of the others before. Akbar was the only familiar face, and so all the more welcome. They celebrated their reunion in the mess.

'I would have thought that as a Muslim you wouldn't drink alcohol,' said Carter as they toasted each other.

'You think too much,' retorted Akbar. 'And you shouldn't have to in your business. Let the politicians do that. They're not much good at anything else. In any case, I believe what followers of the old Aga Khan in the 1930s used to say when people expressed surprise that he drank champagne: "Whenever alcohol touches my lips it immediately turns to water." '

'That's the only miracle you get nowadays, turning wine into water.'

'You may have a point,' Akbar agreed.

'I have so many,' replied Carter. 'Mostly good.'

They had another brandy each on that.

'Come out and see my new car,' said Akbar as he drained his glass. They walked out into the floodlit courtyard. Among a row of Escorts, Golf GTIs, Alfasuds, a red Ferrari 400i stood like a lion in a line of llamas.

'How did you get that?' Carter asked with a mixture of surprise and envy.

'Bought it, my friend.'

'But it costs about forty thousand quid.'

'You have forgotten my allowance.'

'I never knew you had one.'

'It *is* rather generous,' admitted Akbar with a rather embarrassed smile. 'You see, my father was poor when he was young. He didn't want me to be the same. I totally share that view.'

'What does your old man do, that he's so rich?'

'He's hereditary chief of Abukali, Africa's smallest country – but potentially it's one of the richest. Your government is keen to keep on good terms with him. So are most other Western governments – and several on the other side of the Iron Curtain. They all pay highly for the right to search for mineral deposits. There's also oil and uranium there. Or so the experts say.'

'And everyone wants a share?'

'Of course. But, you see, my father was a sergeant in what was the King's Royal West African Rifles in Burma during the Second World War. He is proud of that. He liked serving in what was then an Empire regiment. It made a great impression on him. He admires the qualities of your country and your people – so he prefers British companies to have first go.'

'I'm glad to hear it,' said Carter.

The conversation showed signs of becoming serious. To change the subject, he said: 'Let's see if this thing really motors.'

'It does,' Akbar replied. 'Try for yourself.'

He tossed the ignition key to Carter, who climbed in behind the steering-wheel with its prancing-horse emblem on the horn button. He smelled the rich, evocative scent of oiled black leather, soft as a silk purse, watched the dials light up as he pressed the switch, heard the rumble of twelve cylinders beat like surf on some celestial shore when he turned the key. How lucky to be rich! Akbar climbed in beside him.

They drove off slowly down the long drive, and then, as Carter swiftly grew accustomed to the car, rather more speedily. He stopped at the gates and turned to Akbar.

'You take over,' he said. 'I've had four brandies, so I can't do justice to machinery of this class. We could end up upside down with our legs in the air.'

'Best place for a pretty woman,' replied Akbar, with the air of a man uttering one of life's eternal truths. 'Legs in the air.'

'Possibly. But not for us. Not in this barouche. And we're not pretty women.'

Carter climbed out. The engine was still running with the purr of a man-eating tiger that has just devoured ten men as *hors d'oeuvre* and is wondering what's for the main course.

'I've had as much to drink as you,' said Akbar accusingly as he changed places.

'I don't think so.'

'Well, anything you say. Now, I'll show you how this thing goes.'

Akbar settled in the driver's seat, fastened his safety-belt and blipped the accelerator. The rev-counter needle fled around the dial, and the car surged forward with a squeal of tyres.

There is never a lot of traffic in south Dorset after dark in February, and on this particular evening there was almost none. The Ferrari's headlamps bored amber tunnels of light through the trees, and when Carter lowered his window the scent of an English country evening poured in, damp and fresh and cool. The hum of the engine, the muted crackle of its four exhausts, provided a lullaby. He felt content that, even if he did not own this lovely car and might well never own a Ferrari, at least he was travelling in one now. The power of 400 athletic horses gave wings to the great car as he dozed. He opened his eyes briefly as they surged round a sharp corner – and the shabby Morris Minor that had broken down halfway across the road rushed towards them with the speed of sound.

Carter would still wake in the night to the crunch of hot metal striking cold, the gusting roar of fire, the screams that died as flames soared up in a funeral pyre.

He and Akbar were both out of their seats within seconds, but still too late. Akbar seized the car's fire-extinguisher, but this was useless against the inferno. Trembling with horror and reaction, Carter crawled to the roadside and vomited on to the damp grass. It was there that the police found him when they arrived fifteen minutes later.

Next morning, the colonel commanding the course sent for him.

'I understand you were involved in a fatal accident last night, Carter,' he said shortly. He had no time for young officers with more money than sense; officers in the Golds were also not to his liking. He held a commission in an obscure regiment of foot, referred to by the Cavalry as the Grunts – Ground Reconnaissance Untrainables.

'Yes, sir. I was in a car that hit another car.'

'You were more than *in* a car, Carter. You were *driving* the damn car.'

'That is not so, sir.'

'No? You deny it? But three brother officers saw you leave here at the wheel of that car in the company of His Royal Highness Akbar Mohammed Khan, who has the honorary rank while here of lieutenant.'

'That is true, sir,' Carter agreed. 'He was showing me his Ferrari.'

'More than that. He let you drive it. You were seen to get in the driver's seat outside this house and drive the car away.'

'That is so, sir.'

'So why do you deny driving it?'

'I deny driving it when it hit the other car.'

'Who was?'

'I don't like to say, sir.'

'Don't give me this damned-fool public-school, *Fifth Form at St Dominic's* code of honour,' replied the colonel angrily.

'I'm not, sir. But I was not driving at the time of the accident.'

'Dammit, Carter, you were bloody-well *seen* driving the Ferrari by three witnesses. Minutes later it is involved in a fatal crash. You are found lying in your own vomit at the roadside, disgustingly drunk out of your mind, according to the blood-test reports. Do you deny it, man?'

'No, sir. But I do deny driving when the accident occurred.'

'You will find that hard to prove. You know what a drunken-driving charge means in any regiment, let alone the Golds?'

The colonel allowed his personal feelings to show in his voice.

'I am aware of that, sir. But I plead Not Guilty.'

'I have submitted a report to your commanding officer,' the colonel replied. 'If you are charged and found guilty, you may feel you have to resign your commission. That is not an absolute requirement, of course. But, in view of your refusal to accept unbiased eyewitness accounts, you might feel it wise and prudent to take that course. The gentleman's reaction, if I may be old-fashioned.'

'I have faith in the law, sir. And also in Akbar Khan. I stand by what I say. It is the truth.'

'I congratulate you on your faith in the legal constitution and also in human beings. But I must tell you that His Royal Highness is no longer here.'

'What's happened to him? Was he hurt, sir?'

'Not so far as I am aware. The Foreign and Commonwealth Office was, of course, immediately informed that he had been involved in an accident. And he has gone elsewhere.'

'What do you mean, sir – "gone elsewhere"?'

'I'm telling you all I know. He has returned to London to his High Commission. They are in Belgrave Square, if you are interested.'

'I am, sir,' said Carter. 'You mean, I am to take the rap for this accident – which was nothing to do with me?'

'I mean just what I say. Three witnesses saw you driving a car, after you had drunk several large brandies. I must say, I had expected better of an officer in the Golds. At least an admission of your guilt, an acceptance of your responsibilities as an officer – and a gentleman. I have nothing more to say. You can go back to your room.'

'There is a lecture this morning, sir. An appreciation of possible allies.'

'You will not attend that lecture. In all the circumstances, it would be most unseemly for you to do so. You will await the civil police, who wish to interview you.'

They did, within the hour. Carter's case came up quickly. He maintained his plea of innocence, but who would believe him? He had been seen driving the car. His fingerprints were on the leather-covered wheel and both door-handles; and a hippy in the back of the Morris Minor was dead. In life, the hippy might not have rated much in the scheme of things: he had a long police record; the car was stolen, unlicensed and uninsured; and he was stuffed with heroin, out cold on the back seat. In death, he assumed an altogether greater importance.

Carter was found guilty. Because his army record was good, with service in the Falklands and Northern Ireland, and even though the magistrate made it clear that the court could jail him, he was only fined £200. The real punishment came from his own commanding officer when he returned to the Golds.

'You know what this means?' he told Carter.

'Not entirely, sir.'

'I'm sorry to have to tell you that it could be in your best interests if you resign your commission. The fact that you deny responsibility for the accident in the light of all evidence has not shown you in a very good light.

'In fact, I'm disappointed by your attitude. Quite out of character, I would have said. When anything has gone wrong you have always accepted your share of responsibility – as I would expect from any officer. However, it's all water under the bridge now.'

He paused.

'As you know,' he went on. 'It's the Army Board view that any officer convicted of drunken driving where there has been a fatality *can* be asked to resign his commission. It is not an order, of course. But no doubt you will see the wisdom of it here. I am sorry, Carter, very sorry indeed. You have been a good officer, and I am extremely sad to lose you – especially like this. But there it is. I leave the decision to you, of course, but you know my views.'

'I wasn't driving, sir,' said Carter dully.

'So you maintain. But His Royal Highness could no doubt claim diplomatic immunity, even if he *had* been at the wheel. And, in any case, he is not here.'

'He can explain everything,' said Carter. 'Couldn't I get in touch with him?'

'That is up to you, but I think it unlikely. He has had a bereavement. His father has died of a heart-attack, and there is a family dispute as to who should succeed him as head of state of Abukali. He has an uncle who claims that right.'

'I've not seen anything about this in the papers, sir.'

'Very possibly because it hasn't been in the papers. Not yet. I have been informed of it privately.'

Carter did not say that he had written to Akbar Khan and telephoned repeatedly to the Abukali High Commission offices in London, but without any success. An official assured him that His Royal Highness was abroad on his country's business. Letters were awaiting his return. They had no forwarding address for him.

'It's tough on you, Carter. I accept that. Very tough. But at least you're not married.'

'Is Akbar Khan being shielded in some way? Is his father's death the real reason I can't contact him?'

The colonel shrugged.

'We're just soldiers,' he said wryly. 'There are possibly political motives. The Government's after concessions, so naturally the last thing they want is to antagonize one of the few pro-British black African states. You must remember, it is not simply a matter of drunken driving. Akbar Khan is a Muslim, and should never drink alcohol. It could be far more serious for him to admit drinking alcohol than if he had killed someone in a road accident. After all, it was only an infidel who died.'

'My career has been killed, too, sir.'

'That is a sombre assessment, Carter. It has harmed your *military* career, agreed. But you will find no doubt something in civilian life. You are very adaptable and, as I say, you have been a very good officer. I will give you a report to that effect.'

'If I resign my commission, is there any chance of getting it back later on – should Akbar Khan corroborate my account of events?'

'Possibly – if we went to war. But then, of course, you would probably be conscripted in any case.'

The colonel stood up.

'There it is, Carter. No point in prolonging the agony.'

They shook hands. Carter went into the mess. It was empty and, in any case, he did not feel like a drink. He glanced at the headlines in a newspaper with a soldier's eye. Bombings in Northern Ireland; reinforcements for the Middle East; army guards on nuclear waste to be disposed of out at sea. He would soon be one of the majority who only read about such matters or watched them on television news bulletins, no longer a member of the small elite directly involved. He felt immeasurably sad – and changed his mind about a drink.

After Carter resigned his commission, he took a room in a private hotel off the Cromwell Road in London. His parents were dead and his elder brother had emigrated to Toronto years before; he was on his own in the world. He had hoped to find a bedsitting-room so that he could be more independent while he searched for a job, but there was nothing.

The old-style 'digs' for students and newcomers to London were now described as 'flatlets' and offered for sale because, under the absurdities of the Rent Act, if a tenant rented a room, he could never be forced to leave, no matter what agreement he had signed. Prudent landlords and landladies therefore avoided this risk.

Carter's hotel room was the cheapest he could find, but was still too expensive for him. He put his name on various registers for employment, and was interviewed by men of his own age, who wore expensive suits and hand-made shirts, in agencies that described themselves as 'headhunters'. But nobody seemed eager to hunt his head. He was down to £75 in the bank – two weeks in his room if he ate one meal a day – when he ran into Tim Rowley in Shaftesbury Avenue.

They had known each other at Oxford. For their second year, they had had rooms on the same staircase; Akbar had been below them on the ground floor.

'What are you doing in London?' Rowley asked him after the initial questions about people they had once known.

'Damn all, to be honest. As I invariably am.'

'But I thought you were in the Army? Chief of the General Staff. In the making, at least.'

'That's all finished.'

'Why?'

Carter told him.

'*Were* you driving?' asked Rowley.

'No. I knew I'd had too much to drink. So I let Akbar drive.'

'I'm surprised at him. Not like old Akbar to take off like that. I always thought he fitted John Buchan's definition of a white man.'

'So did I. But there it is.'

'Bad luck,' said Rowley sympathetically.

'It's worse than that,' said Carter. In a sudden burst of frankness, he admitted: 'I'm down to my last few quid. Then it's the dole.'

He had to tell someone and, while Rowley would not have been his first choice as a confidant, he was a reminder of earlier, more carefree days.

'You serious? I always thought you were well heeled.'

'That's an impression some of us like to give.'

'I don't,' said Rowley primly.

'Perhaps you don't need to.'

'Well, that's true.'

'What line of country are you in exactly?'

'Property. Portugal. My mother is Portuguese.'

'I didn't know.'

'No reason why you should. She owns some vineyards up north around Oporto, and orchards of cork-trees to grow corks to plug the bottles. That's one branch of the family thing. I'm in the south, the Algarve. Holiday apartments, villas, beach-houses, timesharing. All that. Are you serious – you want a job?'

'Dead serious. Have you got one?'

'You don't speak Portuguese, do you?'

'Not a word, unfortunately. And it's not an easy language to learn, is it?'

'Not very. That makes things rather difficult – if you don't speak Portuguese at all, I mean. But there's something we could find for you, just for the summer, and speaking English. And it *might* lead to something – well, more permanent.'

'What is it?'

'Hardly property wheeling and dealing but, if you are *really* up against it, this might just give you time to think – and make some money while you're thinking. It will see you through the summer, anyhow.'

'What is it, man? Don't mess around.'

'We've just built a new complex outside Lagos, in the Algarve, place called São Sebastião. A lot of little houses around a clubhouse, and two pools. We rent them to weekly, fortnightly package tours. Popular end of the market. Not like the Golds. But it pays. Us, at least.'

'What is the job, though?'

'We'd a damned great swimming-pool there, but the architect designed it wrongly. Made it too big. People like a *small* pool. They're herd animals, especially those on package tours. So we've split it up into two. In one, we want to give swimming lessons, teach kids how to snorkel. All that. If we had a good man to teach 'em.'

'You've got one,' said Carter at once. 'Now, tell me. What do you pay, and when do I start?'

This was how he came to be in the Algarve. But what had at first seemed amusing, with some tourists rather pathetic through their need for homely reassurance in the form of tea and chips, soon became less enjoyable when Carter realized that the tourists were also smiling – not with him but at him, pitying him.

The fact that Carter's recent past was something of a mystery – for he never talked about it, and any rumours must have come from Rowley's office – gave him an added attraction in the eyes of young housewives, whose own dreary, penny-pinched lives were totally devoid of any depth.

They had married too young, often to the wrong man. They had read and believed too many stories in women's magazines, not realizing that the wedding ceremony which concluded so many of these sagas was not in fact the end of an association but only the beginning. Years of incompatibility and disappointment could lie ahead.

Carter found it easy to seduce women like this; they wanted it, half-expected it, not realizing that to Carter they were only a way of passing a dull afternoon. Their merit in his eyes – in the circumstances, 'virtue' seemed an inappropriate word – was that they provided a physical activity in which he could briefly forget his own unhappiness, his worry and concern about his future; and whether, indeed, he even had a future.

three

SOMEONE KNOCKED ON Carter's front door and his sombre thoughts scattered like confetti at a rich man's wedding. A messenger boy from the club was standing in the porch.

'Mr Rowley wishes to see you, senhor,' he said.

Carter followed him back to the house where Rowley had his office. To reach it, they had to pass the swimming-pools. For the time of day, a surprising number of people were lying around them on sunbeds and loungers. Their eyes followed Carter as he walked by with a wave to the women he knew. No one waved back, which struck him as unusual. He was still wondering about this as he faced Rowley across his greenwood desk. A sunblind shielded the window from the afternoon glare. From a calendar on the wall a nude smiled down at them.

'Glad I caught you in,' Rowley began awkwardly, not motioning Carter to a seat.

'I'm not too difficult to find. Usually in the pool or in my room.'

'Yes. I know. In somewhere.'

Rowley began to shuffle papers on his desk. This wasn't their old relationship, easy-going, bantering; this was something different. Rowley did not meet Carter's eyes. Carter felt like a boy up before his housemaster for some misdemeanour. Or was he up before an equivalent of his colonel, waiting to protest his innocence to a man who wouldn't believe him?

'Well, what's it about?' he asked as casually as he could, but his voice sounded strange. His mouth was suddenly dry. He felt fear grip his stomach. But what had he to be afraid of?

'I wanted to see you about winding things up,' replied Rowley. 'It *was* only a summer job, you know.'

'I know,' said Carter. 'But what's going in the winter? I thought this might have prospects. You told me so yourself. And you still rent houses here out of season.'

'Only a few. The weather's still pretty good, but people just don't come down in any numbers. We're geared around school holidays. We close the pools, cover them up.'

'So when do you plan to do that?'

'Next week,' said Rowley, looking at him for the first time. His eyes were neither friendly nor easy-going. 'A bit earlier than I'd planned.'

Something had happened. Somehow he had let Rowley down – or Rowley thought he had.

'But I've lessons for three kids next Monday,' Carter told him. 'I only fixed them up today.'

'You'd better cancel them, then. In all the circumstances.'

'In all what circumstances?'

'Look,' said Rowley, with the air of one whose hitherto infinite patience has finally reached the limit, like stretched elastic. 'Let's not beat about the bloody bush. I've had complaints.'

'From whom?'

'Oh, people.'

'Well, that's something. At least they're not from animals. About what?'

'I don't want to sound like Mrs Grundy, but about your behaviour with some of the mothers.'

'Meaning?'

'Meaning, in crude terms, you're screwing their arses off. And their husbands don't like it.'

'They've a remedy, haven't they? There's an old saying: "If the washing's not done at home, it goes out to be done." '

'Maybe, but we're not in the market for old sayings or old chat. It doesn't help our image here of a caring family resort – a happy place for children, where young mothers and fathers can relax and find new romance.'

'Maybe they *have* been finding new romance.'

'OK. Maybe, if I was handsome and single, I'd do the same –

if my family didn't own the company *and* I didn't realize what's at stake. It could be commercial survival, you know. You can't mess around with people who provide your bread and butter. One, never mix business with pleasure. Two, never screw the hired help. Two other old sayings for you.'

'They weren't the hired help, so far as I know. *I* was the hired help. You could say they screwed me.'

'Maybe they should have followed the maxim the other way round. Either way, it's bad for business. You must see you can't behave like this in a family resort?'

'Look, we're all adults,' said Carter. 'I've never gone after these women. They come pestering me.'

' "The woman tempted me, and I did eat," ' quoted Rowley sarcastically.

'So it was forbidden fruit. But has anyone complained about my behaviour at the pool? Or the standard of my teaching? Or said I molested the children?'

'Of course not. It's nothing like that. Just, well, one or two husbands have spoken to me. Privately. And I have to take action. They could make it hard for me if I didn't.'

'I'm sorry to hear it.'

'So am I. I was hoping you would come down here again next year.'

'And I was hoping you might have a job for me through the winter. I want more time to think out my future. I hoped I could have done that this summer, but there's been so much work I just couldn't get around to it.'

Carter did not want to admit that in any case the prospect was too painful, that it blocked his thoughts like a huge boulder. He had tried to avoid this problem of his future, assuring himself that something would – must – turn up; that someone would – must – want an ex-captain not yet thirty or, rather, *just* thirty. Surely some employer would value the qualities of discipline and organization? Carter was about to add 'and integrity', but decided against it. Could an adulterer have integrity? Possibly, but on different levels. That was a philosophical question he could have argued happily with his tutor over a glass of sherry, after he had read his weekly essay in those dear dead days not so long ago. What a bloody mess he had made of things!

'Well,' he said. 'Thanks for putting it on the line like that. At least I know where I am.'

'We'll give you an open air-ticket, for whenever you want to leave.'

'You want me to get out now? Run me out?'

'Well, not exactly run. Shall we say a fast walk?'

'Who the hell are these bloody husbands?'

'I would rather not say. But they could make trouble. We have to keep our nose clean in this business. All these critical television programmes investigating holidays, package tours. That stuff. Doesn't add to the image, if you take the wife and kids along – and the wife gets laid.'

'An unexpected bonus,' said Carter.

Rowley grinned. 'I've had no complaints from the wives.'

'That's something.'

'But not a lot, eh?' said Rowley.

'Not nearly enough. Well, thanks for giving me the job in the first place. Sorry I fouled it up – almost for you and totally for me. I'll see you before I go. Let's have a farewell drink together.'

'I'd like that,' said Rowley, much relieved, and picked up his papers.

Carter went out of the office, closed the door quietly behind him. He paused for a moment, wondering whether to go back to his house past the pools or to take another way. To hell with that, he thought, and walked with deliberate slowness past the sunbathers.

This time he did not wave to anyone but nodded and smiled to those he recognized. A few acknowledged his greeting, but awkwardly and with embarrassment. He wondered which husbands had complained, whether their wives had told other wives. It would make a topic for small-talk, better than the food or the news from home.

The heat of an Algarve afternoon felt like an open oven-door, and the brandy had begun to stir in his blood. He was foolish to drink so early in the day, of course; he knew that. It was always unwise to drink spirits before the sun went down. But then you rationalized by saying that the sun must be going down somewhere in the world, all the time. Sir Thomas Browne admitted that when he wrote in the seventeenth century, 'The huntsmen are up in America, and they are already past their first sleep in Persia.' When it was too early to drink in one country, it could be too late to drink in another. To hell with the rules. He reached his house, peeled off his clothes, had a cold shower, towelled himself dry, lit a Portuguese cheroot and poured another brandy. Ridiculous, of course, but it would steady the nerves, concentrate his mind.

What was he to do now? Carter had not saved anything during the summer. He had not been paid very much and what Carter had received had largely gone on food, paying the maid, hiring a Mini. He could return to England, traipse around the careers offices, type out a new *curriculum vitae*, adding to his accomplishments the fact that he had taught underwater swimming to under-sevens and under-tens, and had even issued them with certificates Rowley had printed.

You needed to have something printed on paper nowadays. Even lavatory-cleaners had degrees and diplomas. It was like India, as his father used to say, where people put 'Failed BA' after their names and unqualified quacks in the bazaar advertised the fact that they had 'nearly passed' their final examinations. Well, he had a degree, MA (Oxon), for what that was worth. Not a lot, really; it was more a dwindling social asset than a business qualification.

Carter poured himself another drink, then put away the bottle, closed the door of the cupboard. That would be the last. That must be the last – for that afternoon, at least. The evening was something else.

He sat in his chair while heat drained from the day, and the cries of volleyball-players on the beach gradually thinned and died. The pedalos had been brought up and chained together on the beach in case a freak wave set them loose. The windsurfers had gone home, and their surfboards were stacked neatly in a little hut set high on the beach near the rocks. Canvas sunshades were tightly folded around their poles. Only a diving-raft and a few privately owned speedboats remained at anchor. Within days, they would also be brought in, and then the only boats in the bay would be local fishing craft with their bright red and blue paintwork and painted eyes that dated from the time when the Algarve was occupied by Moors and called El Gharbe, 'the land beyond'. Summer was all but over. Soon, even the wooden beach-cafés would be dismantled before the high tides of autumn, and the season would be at an end.

Finally, Carter left his house and walked along the beach, relishing the ozone, hearing the familiar friendly roar and suck of the sea. He sat down on an upturned boat, noting that the Mercury outboard was prudently chained to a metal stake in the sand. There wasn't much trust around – but, then, why should there be? Rowley had trusted him, and he had let Rowley down. Before that, Carter had trusted Akbar Khan, and Akbar Khan had disappeared. He couldn't explain to Rowley that in seducing these silly women he was also trying to prove something to himself: that he wasn't finished, not entirely down and out; that he was still a man. Well, the equation had been proved – conclusively. Q.E.D.

He walked back along the hard firm sand, meaning to drive over to Lagos and sit in one of the fishermen's restaurants and ponder his future over a grilled linguada, or a split lobster and a bottle of vinho verde, but then he suddenly changed his mind; he was tired of his own thoughts, and of eating alone – and he wasn't hungry. He left the beach and walked up the narrow street, smooth with calcada on each side of the tarmac, placed there years before motor cars arrived to enable mules to find a firm footing. Hired cars raced past him, horns blaring, tyres squealing on these hot cobblestones, polished by generations of turning wheels.

Carter hated having to stand to one side to let each car go by, and turned into the nearest bar to avoid doing so. It was very dark inside, a long tunnel lined with leather-topped stools. Against a wall-mirror imitation candle-flames reflected bottles of blue curaçao, green crême de menthe, blood-red cassis. He sat down at the counter, accustomed his eyes to the gloom. At first, he had thought the bar was empty. Then he saw, at the far end, as though in the deep recesses of a cave, the tiny glow of a cigarette.

The barman knew Carter, mixed him a Brandy Alexander without being asked and expertly slid the glass, creamy head speckled with cinnamon, across the polished mahogany top.

Carter nodded in the direction of the bottles on their mirror-backed shelves. The barman turned down the taped music, prepared to mix a second. The first, Carter thought, would steady his nerves, soothe him, drown his irritation. The second would sharpen his mind, promote the consideration of future plans. Or was that all just make-believe? Alcohol was deceptively addictive – and these cocktails were deceptively strong. He sipped the cold, coffee-flavoured drink and glanced for a second time to see who was at the other end of the bar; a woman in a pale silk blouse and trousers, smoking a cigarette in a long holder, but not drinking.

'This is a bar,' he said by way of introduction. 'Have one on me and with me.'

'You've already ordered a second,' the woman replied. 'I'll have that.'

'How do you know what I ordered?' Carter asked her almost belligerently.

She turned around to look at him appraisingly, but did not reply. The barman poured the second Alexander and glanced enquiringly at Carter. He could either ask her to come and sit on a stool near him, as he would have done without question to any of the wives who visited him in his room, or he could say nothing. He sensed something different about this woman – an impression of latent authority. Instinctively he knew that she would find some simple, even amusing, but valid excuse for not coming to join him. He would then still be left at one end of the bar and she at the other.

Carter made his decision, picked up the two glasses, carried them the length of the bar, and sat down beside her. She smiled.

Their eyes met. He looked down at his drink, knowing that she had won a small victory – minute perhaps, possibly even infinitesimal, but still a score in the battle of the sexes. But why should he think of this incident as a skirmish in a battle? To win the first foray did not mean that you won the war. What war? His mind felt fuddled; he *must* cut down on this absurd drinking.

She did not toast him or say 'Bottoms up' or 'Down the hatch' or 'Here's to the next time', 'Happy days, happier nights', or any of the other tired third-hand clichés that young mothers liked, imagining they were smart because they had read them in a magazine on the plane to Faro from Gatwick or Luton.

She sipped the drink and wrinkled her nose.

'Too sweet,' she said critically.

'I like it like that,' he told her lamely, feeling as he spoke that he was reverting to a cliché he had so often abhorred in others.

'I can see you do.'

She glanced briefly at his figure. Carter drew in his stomach, held his breath.

'You drink too much,' she said. 'And you used to be so fit.'

'I am fit.'

'Everything is relative, of course. You *are* fit – compared to those soft, fat-tailed slobs I see on the beach masquerading as men.'

'I have been teaching their children how to swim. Perhaps they will be a fitter generation.'

'It could be,' she said. 'I have a theory.'

'About what?'

'The general sloppiness of men. It's because they never walk anywhere. There is always the company car. They take no exercise, except to raise their right arm in places like this. And they survive on convenience foods. Wives don't cook any more. They buy a packet of dust, as seen on television, add water, warm it and call it a meal. The chemicals we eat now will kill us all – if we go on eating them.'

'You may be right,' Carter agreed cautiously. He had not expected such vehemence.

49

'Of course I am. And another thing. When an animal loses interest in its appearance, it's sick, ready to die. The same is true of society. Look about you. Filthy jeans, dirty canvas sneakers, litter everywhere. Men unshaven, with long hair, women dressed in cast-offs and shabby hand-me-downs. All visible signs of a dying culture.'

'I suppose you have a point,' Carter said lamely. 'Two points, if you like.'

'Of course I have,' she replied, surprise in her voice that anyone could doubt the truth of what she said.

'I've seen you about here,' he said, slowly trying to change the conversation, but again painfully conscious of the unoriginality of his remark. It was on a par with the greeting in a dance-hall: 'Do you come here often?' Carter *had* seen her, but always at a distance. Once, in the local supermarket, the *supermercado;* then, in a car outside one of the smarter restaurants in São Sebastião and in Lagos, the nearest town, waiting at traffic lights near the market. He remembered cars, associated them with their drivers, their owners. She had been driving a green BMW, which meant that it was not a hired car but probably her own.

'What are you going to do now?' she asked him, pushing away her drink.

'What do you mean exactly, *now*? At this moment? After this drink? Or next month?'

'Next month. Next year.'

He noticed that the level of liquid in her glass had barely dropped at all. Was she, of all things, a teetotaller?

'The barman will give you more brandy,' he said. 'Or lemon juice, if it's too sweet.'

'No, thank you. You didn't answer my question.'

'Maybe because I can't answer your question. Pass.'

'Can't – or won't?'

She sounded concerned. Her eyes, very wide and dark, reminded him of wells, too deep to penetrate or understand. He felt vaguely uneasy. He had not met a woman like her before, or perhaps he had become too accustomed to easy conquests, to women who wanted him. He was not sure whether he wanted this woman sexually, but somehow he did want her approval, her approbation. Above all, and absurdly, since he did not even know her name, he wished to appear successful in her eyes.

'The first,' he said. 'Summer's over. I only had the job for the season.'

'You were in the Army before, weren't you?'

'Yes. For years.'

'Seven years, in fact.'

'You know a lot about me.'

'A little. You have a saying in the Army: "Time spent in reconnaissance is seldom wasted." '

'I think you wasted your time reconnoitring my military career,' said Carter, bitterness and alcohol sharpening his voice.

'We all have bad patches,' she said. For the second time he detected a hint of sympathy, small, but still there, like the trace of cinnamon in his drink.

'You are going back to England, then?' she asked him.

'I have a ticket. Undated. I can go when I like.'

'And your house here? You can stay on as long as you like?'

'No one has said anything about that,' Carter replied defensively. 'But why all the questions, why the interest?'

'Because I am, in a sense, headhunting for someone with qualities which you might possess. Which you certainly did possess once – if you haven't pickled them in brandy.'

'What the hell do you mean, "pickled them in brandy"?'

'Every time you drink a glass of alcoholic beverage you kill so many millions of your brain cells. Most people have so many millions more that they don't notice it. But, all the same, you're killing yourself quietly. You're like a multimillionaire with his fortune in stocks and shares. One stock goes down, but he doesn't feel it, it really doesn't matter. Then, another. That *is* a little annoying, but nothing more. Then a third, a fourth, a fifth. And suddenly he is only rich on paper. And paper isn't paper money. It's the same with drink.'

'I gather you don't like it. Don't approve.'

'I have seen too many people ruined by it.'

'Well, you'll not see me. Now, having disposed of that, exactly what sort of head are you hunting?'

'It could be yours.'

'Why mine?'

'I have seen you at the pool when you were teaching the kids. You got on with them, but you didn't let them fool around. You know what discipline is all about.'

'That's training,' he said.

'On a base of character.'

'What sort of job is your client offering?'

'One that could require those qualities.'

'Can you tell me any more?'

'No. Only my principal could do that. If he is interested.'

'So this could be a lucky meeting for me?'

'Maybe for him, too. It depends how you look at it.'

'But if I had not come into this bar I'd never have heard about it. In fact, I almost didn't. I was going into Lagos.'

'If I hadn't met you here tonight, then I could have come knocking at your door.'

'And then I might have driven a hard bargain?'

'To drive hard bargains you should be in a strong bargaining position,' she said.

'And I'm not?'

'I didn't say that.'

She pushed her glass away from her and stood up. She was tall, full-breasted. He could see the points of her nipples, like small thorns, through the soft silk of her blouse. He stood up, too. She was taller than he had imagined, sitting down.

'You're leaving?'

'I have an appointment.'

'I was going to ask you to have dinner with me.'

'You don't know me.'

'But you know my name?'

'Of course.'

'So you have one advantage over me. What's yours? How can I find you?'

'*I* will find *you*. My name is Celia Kent.'

He glanced at her hands. It was wise to check whether a woman was wearing a ring that could signify any attachment, engagement, even marriage, especially after his recent experiences. She wore gold rings on the third fingers of both hands, saw his glance, smiled.

'That's my married name,' she explained.

'And your husband?'

'I don't talk about him. That's in the past.'

'But you keep his name?'

'Why not? It's about all he ever gave me. Well, good night, Mr Carter. I will be in touch.'

'But I may not be here long.'

'None of us may be. It's an uncertain world. But if we both are here I will make contact with you. Thank you for the drink.'

She walked out of the bar and he stood, watching her. She did not pause at the door, as so many people did, as he guessed he might do himself that night because he had nowhere he particularly wanted to go, no vital direction to follow. She turned right, and a couple came in, middle-aged, holding hands. The husband was pot-bellied, like the men Celia Kent did not like; the woman, dumpy, already gone to fat. She wore a blue sun-top with beige bra-straps visible underneath. The man must have been quite good-looking once, well set up, a strong pair of shoulders. He climbed on to a bar-stool and sat, as though the effort had all but exhausted him, soft as a bag of sludge. When he got his breath back he ordered two long, sweet grenadines.

I could look like that myself soon, thought Carter with sudden alarm. He *had* to cut down on this drinking; trying to send his sorrows out on a floodtide of alcohol was madness. He would become like this fellow at the end of the bar, sitting side by side with a woman he didn't like, who didn't like him, drinking sweet drinks they didn't like, either. Unhappy people invariably ordered sugary concoctions; subconsciously they hoped to add some sweetness to lives already soured and bitter. Was that why he liked Brandy Alexander so much?

On impulse, Carter pushed away his own half-finished drink, put a note on the counter for the barman.

'Keep the change,' he told him.

'See you again soon, senhor?'

Carter nodded, but he wasn't so sure he would. Celia Kent had been speaking the truth; and truth was stronger than the strongest drink.

At the next morning's session in the pool, several mothers looked at Carter with calculating eyes. Shauna was not there; nor were her two children. Again, he wondered which of their husbands had complained. Not that it mattered, of course. With any luck, he could have a job through Celia Kent. This time, he must try to make sure that he was not just the equivalent of a day labourer, but had some continuity, some prospects.

He came back to the house at half-past one. The Portuguese maid had prepared a light lunch for him: slices of cold ham, a tomato salad. He was debating whether to pour himself a Sagres beer – even one beer could make him feel sleepy during a hot afternoon – when the maid, who had been hanging out the morning's washing in the little courtyard behind the house, came in with an envelope. He knew enough basic Portuguese to understand her statement that it had been delivered earlier in the morning. He ripped it open. On a small sheet of unheaded notepaper was a short typed note:

> Mr Carter, I have made an appointment for you to see my principal at half-past six this evening. I will pick you up at six o'clock.
>
> Yours, C. K.

He held the paper up to the light to examine the watermark. It looked expensive. He read the note again, then tore it into very small pieces and put them in the waste-bin under the sink. Its peremptory phrasing irritated him. There was no thought that he might not be available at six o'clock that evening, that he might have any other plans. If so, he could shelve them. This was the civilian female equivalent of the army command: Be there.

By five-thirty he had bathed, shaved, opened the drinks cupboard two or three times, closed it again and settled for a Sumol, an orange drink, from the refrigerator. He wore his best lightweight trousers, rope-soled yachting-shoes, dark-blue shirt and gold wristwatch, which had been a present from his parents on his twenty-first birthday. He felt acutely nervous, although he told himself there was no need. But deep down he knew there was every need. If this chance failed, if he blew the interview, how was he going to survive the winter? Or beyond the winter, into the spring and summer and all the summers ahead? He must not fail. He must impress this principal, whoever he was, whatever job he had to offer, requiring a candidate with discipline, that he was the right man, the only man.

At exactly six o'clock Carter heard a horn sound briefly and commandingly outside his front door. He looked through the window. A green BMW was waiting in the street; Mrs Kent was at the wheel.

Bloody woman, he thought. Hadn't even the courtesy to knock on the door, ring the bell, come in for a chat, a drink. She expected him to jump on command, and the terrible thing was that he was doing just that. It was worse than being a recruit in the awkward squad.

Carter opened his front door, closed it carefully on its double lock, climbed into the car. There was the welcome hum of air-conditioning. In the Algarve a small car could become a travelling oven, even in the autumn.

Mrs Kent drove fast and competently, as he had expected. They threaded their way through groups of holidaymakers out on the road between the two resorts of Luz and Burgau. Up the hill they went, past abandoned developments and half-finished high-rise buildings on which Portuguese labourers, wearing shorts and black felt hats, were still swarming up and down wooden scaffolding.

A trench had been dug in the main road to lay a new drain,

and a queue of cars had built-up, drivers sitting impatiently, in clouds of swirling dust. They moved forward slowly, and suddenly among the handful of tourists walking in single file against the traffic Carter saw a well-remembered face. Miranda. He swung around in his seat in surprise. What on earth was she doing out here?

She was holding the hand of a boy about eight or nine, who wore swimming-trunks and a wide-brimmed straw hat. That must be her son. He called out her name, but they were already past and accelerating away.

'Someone you know?' Mrs Kent asked him, not taking her eyes off the road ahead.

'Yes. At least, I did know her. Long ago. University. She's married now. They must be on holiday here. How odd. I haven't seen her for years.'

'Probably just arrived. Or maybe she's not staying in São Sebastião. There are lots of other places along the coast.'

'Of course,' he agreed quickly.

There were lots of other women, too, but none who could cause this strange, totally irrational feeling in him; this heady mixture of elation and nervousness. What would Miranda think of him now, after all his talk, his confidence that he could become a general at least, when he was in reality only an out-of-work swimming instructor? He drove these unhappy thoughts from his mind.

'Who is your principal?' he asked Mrs Kent.

'Someone very close to me.'

'You mean, your husband?'

'No,' she corrected him. 'I call him Father.'

'So what you say goes? You have influence with him?' Carter tried to keep the hopefulness out of his voice.

'A little, perhaps.'

'So what's the nature of this job, exactly? Can you tell me?'

'As I said last night, I'll leave that to him.'

They stopped outside a set of double metal gates in a whitewashed stone wall. A calcada drive stretched ahead, bordered with red and purple bougainvillaea and hibiscus.

Each bush had a small circular trough dug neatly around its roots in the red dry earth to hold water: all had been freshly watered. Carter could not see one weed, although he looked closely. Mrs Kent took an electronic gun from the glove-compartment, pointed it at the gates, pressed the trigger. The gates opened. She drove through. They closed behind the car and locked instantly.

'Does your father live out here all the time?' he asked.

'No,' she said. 'Just in the spring and autumn. When there aren't so many tourists.'

'He must be a rich man?'

'He wouldn't say so.'

'The rich never do. They always complain of their troubles. Their yacht's got barnacles on the hull. The second Rolls has a flat tyre. The pastry cook wants a rise.'

'Perhaps that is why they don't think they are rich,' she suggested, neither agreeing nor disagreeing. 'There are other riches than money.'

'Possibly. But all I want right now is the chance to prove that money won't make me happy.'

'I could show you many instances when it has only brought misery.'

The drive curved and ended outside a long, low, white house, with a high plantation-style porch. A Mercedes with Swiss registration-plates was parked outside, a speedboat strapped on a trailer behind it. Carter noted the two inboard/outboard Volvo engines, and the expensively tailored blue canvas cover, against sun and wind.

A middle-aged maid, wearing a dark-green uniform with the name of the house, Casa Serrafino, embroidered on it, came down a flight of marble steps to open the car door. Carter followed Mrs Kent to the front door.

Inside, the house was larger than he had imagined, far more luxurious than anything he had so far seen in Portugal. Carpets lay scattered like fallen white petals on floors of pink-grained marble. Huge plants trailed tendrils from pots large enough to hold the fattest of Ali Baba's forty thieves, and some more than one. A marble staircase with a black wrought-iron banister curved up to the second storey. Two big-bladed fans beat the air softly, and water trickled from a fountain into a square pool cut into the floor. Carter saw the slow, lazy flash of giant goldfish beneath the oily leaves of water-lilies.

Impressed by this outward evidence of wealth, he followed Mrs Kent through a room where books, bound in green, red and blue leather and stamped with gold, lined the walls. He wondered whether anyone ever read them; whether, indeed, they were real books, or simply an interior decorator's ploy to conceal a drinks cabinet or an unusually large hi-fi system.

Before he had time to reach a conclusion they were out on a terrace, no smaller than a tennis court. White wooden loungers with gaily coloured mattresses surrounded the pool. Carter wondered which was the deep end and which the shallow – and which of the two he was going into now.

A man detached himself from a deck chair in the shade. He was fat and small, with a pot belly and a head, burnished by sun, round as a cannonball and totally devoid of hair. He had neither eyebrows nor eyelashes and had narrowed his eyes against the evening sunshine reflected from the water. He wore expensively tailored trousers, a silk shirt, sambur-skin shoes. He could be a caricature of a rich man, Carter thought, but he wasn't. Yet one hard punch in that soft round gut and Carter could kill him.

But why should he suddenly think so violently and in such an instantly hostile way about someone he hoped would offer him a job? Something made him glance towards the arches of the patio – a reflex action after years of training. He had seen a slight, almost imperceptible movement. Someone was waiting behind one of the large pillars of the porch, someone not meant to be seen. So maybe, if anyone landed a punch in the fat man's gut, he would not land another. Carter felt flesh crawl on his back. Did every wealthy man need a bodyguard?

'Mr Serrafino,' said Mrs Kent, introducing the two men. 'Tony Carter. I told you about him.'

'Of course. I am delighted to meet you, Mr Carter.'

Mr Serrafino held out his hand. His grip was flabby and

damp, as Carter had expected. He felt the sharp indentation of Mr Serrafino's two large gold rings.

'Do sit down.'

Mr Serrafino indicated a chair.

'I'll organize some drinks,' said Mrs Kent. 'What will you have?'

'Brandy and American dry,' said Carter.

'I have a very good Portuguese brandy, not on general sale,' Mr Serrafino assured him conspiratorially. 'I own shares in the distillery. Controlling shares.'

'You get it at cut rates, then?'

'I like that,' said Mr Serrafino, smiling. 'That's very good. Yes, I suppose I do. But then I am losing on my profits. So I am cutting my own rates, my own throat, profit-wise! You can't win, Mr Carter.'

'From what I see here, Mr Serrafino, you don't seem to be on the losing side.'

'Here you see only one aspect of events, my friend. Life is like a diamond with many facets. You can only observe one at a time.'

'I'd say it was also like an iceberg, with six-sevenths out of sight.'

'You are a philosopher, Mr Carter?'

'I read philosophy once. I even have a degree to prove it.'

'You are very fortunate,' said Mr Serrafino, shaking his bald head in wonder at the good fortune of others. 'I lacked the benefit of a formal education. However, as they say, there is the University of Life.'

'And you have graduated with honours?'

Mr Serrafino allowed himself another smile. He did not agree or disagree. Why should he? thought Carter sourly. The evidence was all around him.

Celia Kent appeared carrying a tray of drinks: ice cubes the size of gold nuggets, crystal goblets as big as goldfish-bowls.

Mr Serrafino raised his glass in a silent toast, without saying who or what he was toasting.

'The first drink of the day,' he said appreciatively. Carter was about to reply that he wished he could say the same, but changed his mind. Of course he could say the same, but it would not be true, and Mrs Kent would know that, and this could go against him. She carried her drink into the house. The two men were alone.

Mr Serrafino swirled his drink thoughtfully. Ice cubes clinked comfortingly against each other. Somewhere, far away, a noisy two-stroke motorcycle tore the evening into shreds. Mr Serrafino watched Carter. The man seemed in fair physical condition, but a slight thickening around the jaw and the neck showed that he drank too much brandy, with perhaps too little ginger. In another two years he would put on weight and flesh, with no more muscle. But in another two years who cared what happened to him? It was here and now that mattered. Mr Serrafino made up his mind.

'Celia tells me you have been doing a good job teaching the kids – and some of their mothers, I understand,' he said.

'It was only a summer job,' said Carter easily. 'I was at Oxford with Tim Rowley. His family owns a development here. I'm a soldier by profession.'

'I was a soldier once, too,' said Mr Serrafino. 'A long time ago, of course. I am much older than you.'

He waited for Carter's denial. It didn't come.

'But all that belongs to the past – for both of us, I understand?'

Carter said nothing.

'What are your plans?' Mr Serrafino asked him. 'I mean, when you leave Portugal?'

'I'll return to London. There are a number of possibilities open to me. I have several contacts. I'll see what turns up.'

The words seemed stale and stilted, but what else could he say?

Mr Serrafino nodded, as though he totally understood Carter's situation.

'Like Mr Micawber, eh? I was brought up on Dickens. One thing I have remembered was Mr Micawber's personal philosophy. "Annual income twenty pounds, annual expenditure nineteen and six, result happiness. Annual income twenty pounds, annual expenditure twenty pounds and sixpence, result misery." I have followed his advice.'

'It's good if you can do that,' Carter agreed.

Mr Serrafino nodded.

'Yes. It *is* good.'

He was happiest speaking about himself, about his own success. To talk of it seemed to ensure that it must be permanent, something he could actually touch, that would constantly assure him that never again would he wake up hungry, as he had done so on so many cold, wretched mornings in his life, when there hadn't been this house in Portugal, the other house in Charles Street, Mayfair, the apartment overlooking Central Park. In those dark and bitter days he did not even have one bank account, and had never even heard of the Dutch Antilles or the Cayman Islands or Vaduz.

Sometimes, still, however, in the early hours when he could not sleep because age had weakened his bladder, he would look at his face in his bathroom mirror and fear that hardships might return as rain follows the sunniest day. Accountants, lawyers, experts in tax avoidance, all assured him that this was impossible; he was far too rich, too solid, in their description. Even if one country's banks collapsed, others would support him. But these men spoke from affluence and secure backgrounds; not one among them had made his money as Mr Serrafino had made his. In Mr Serrafino's opinion they were parasites on the profits of people like him who had willingly risked their freedom, even their lives, for wealth.

'I have a proposition to make, Mr Carter,' he said briskly. He could not afford to dwell for too long on the past; the most important deal must always be the next. 'It will not interfere with your long-term plans, and could, indeed, help you a great deal.

'I finance ventures that are not what you might call blue-chip investments. There is a bit of the gambler in me, Mr Carter.'

'I would only gamble if I owned all the machines, all the horses in the race *and* the bookmakers,' replied Carter. He had seen too many officers of his own age, desperate to keep up with richer colleagues, gradually sink into the harsh embrace of moneylenders when gambling certainties had inexplicably proved uncertain.

'You are wise. But this gamble is almost in that category. You have probably seen in the local *Algarve News* reports of diving expeditions off the Portuguese coast? One of Nelson's great naval battles against the French and Spanish fleets took place in 1797 off Cape St Vincent, less than twenty miles from here.'

'Nelson got the credit,' Carter interrupted, without really meaning to do so. He was nervous and wanted to impress his host. 'The real architect of his victory was Admiral Sir John Jervis.'

'I've not heard of him, Mr Carter.'

'Many haven't, but he was a hard man. As a midshipman, Jervis had been so poor he was forced to wash other midshipmen's laundry to make a few pounds. When he was promoted, he never forgot this – and, although always concerned about the well-being of his men, he insisted on the strictest discipline. He knew at Cape St Vincent he could take on twenty-six enemy ships with only fifteen of his own – and beat them. His men trusted him and he trusted them.'

'Is that so?' said Mr Serrafino slowly. 'I have the greatest sympathy for such a man.'

He remembered his own childhood. The half-caste father he so seldom saw; his mother, soft-fleshed and blowsy, helping her mother to run the rooming-house for sailors in Gravesend. He remembered the jeers and sneers of other boys at school because of his name, his plumpness, the fact that he had no proper father – or so they said. He couldn't beat them by force, but he could by guile and cunning – and, by God, he had. He sipped his drink to give him a moment to regroup his thoughts. Then he continued.

'If you visit the beaches at Burgau and Salema, two or three miles from here, you will see cannon these expeditions have recovered from several ships sunk in that battle. One was carrying twenty-four tons of gold bars, with boxes of silver coins. She was on her way from Montevideo to Seville with three other frigates when she went down. Her crew of 260 all perished with the treasure. A sad business.

'Now some Italian businessmen have formed a consortium, and they are in the process of raising the ship. Other teams farther up the coast are doing much the same thing. German, French, English. The Portuguese government rightly take its share of any treasure that is found. The divers take the risk.'

'And the backers take the profit, Mr Serrafino?'

'If there is one, yes, they have their share.'

'It's not a very big risk, surely, with all the sonar and electronic stuff around today?'

'Not so large as it was, Mr Carter, but it is still there. If it wasn't, people would have had all these ships up long ago. Gold is a very powerful attraction, Mr Carter. Do you know that for 6000 years people have fought for it, cheated for it, killed for it, died for it; yet the total amount of gold mined in all those years — only about 80,000 tons — would fit easily into the main room of this house?

'It is so valuable that gold refineries shut down every year simply to clean their chimneys — so that they can extract gold dust from the soot. Its qualities are such that a goldsmith can hammer one ounce of gold into a sheet ten feet by ten feet, thin as a sheet of paper, or draw it out into a single thread fifty miles long — or plate a copper or silver wire 1000 miles long. Gold never tarnishes, and it never fades. Gold is eternal. So you can see the fantastic attraction it has for gamblers. It's a fortune in a briefcase. Currency in any country.'

'And yet, as Dr Johnson said, "To have it is to live in fear, to want it is to be in sorrow." '

'How true, how very true. Like me, Mr Carter, I see you are interested in people and sayings of the past. But I would much rather live in fear than in sorrow — and so, I am sure, would you. Now, while others are seeking these long-lost treasures, I have mounted an expedition to search for one much more recent: the freighter *El Medina*, which was sunk during the Spanish Civil War, in 1938.

'That was a kind of dress rehearsal for the Second World War – a sparring match between two forms of dictatorship, fascist and communist.

'The Nazis in Germany and the Fascists in Italy backed the Nationalists under General Franco. Russia supported the Republicans. In Spain, neither side possessed many modern armaments of their own, so they had to rely on these backers to provide them. Which they did – at a price. There is always a price, Mr Carter. "Nothing for nothing" is the universal law.

'The Nazis took control of the Rif ore mines in Spanish Morocco in return for giving aircraft to Franco. The Italians established a so-called trading company to market Spanish olive oil, iron pyrites and woollen clothes to pay for their help.

'The Russians weren't interested in trade, but they were desperately short of international currency, as they are to this day. They only wanted one thing. *Gold.* By the end of 1937 – one year after the Civil War started – they had extracted half the gold reserves of the Bank of Spain and shipped them to Odessa in four Russian freighters. A cargo worth then $578,000,000. Think of its value today, Mr Carter!

'After 1937, gold still went to the Soviets, but smaller amounts – only a few million dollars' worth at a time – in freighters under all kinds of different flags: Argentina, Japan, Panama.

'*El Medina* was one of these ships. She sank with her cargo – literally a ship of gold – off the Portuguese coast about forty miles north of here.'

'What happened? Was she torpedoed?'

'It is possible but, I think, unlikely. *El Medina* left port in a hurry, according to all reports,' Mr Serrafino explained. 'She was not a very seaworthy vessel. She could have been sunk deliberately by someone hoping to seize the cargo, or maybe she ran into bad weather, which is what I personally think happened. All that matters now is that, on her way to rendezvous with a larger Russian ship off West Africa, she went down with all hands – and the gold.'

'So what is your proposition, Mr Serrafino?'

'Simply this. I have asked you to my home to make you an offer. You are a military man, Mr Carter. You are used to discipline, and to instilling strict discipline in others. I want you to take over this side of my enterprise. I look after all the administration, and I have employed others who do the diving. But divers are individualists by the very nature of their calling. They do not all like taking orders. Sometimes they get drunk. They have fights. Then they cannot dive. And I cannot afford any more delays. Autumn is already here. Winter is just around the corner. Already the sea gets cloudy. Winds are strong in the Atlantic, and growing stronger. Soon diving will have to stop.'

'What nationality are the divers?' Carter asked.

'East German. They have the attitude of surfers in California, and hippies all over the world. They like sun, sea, drink, women – and as little work as possible.'

'They are not alone in their tastes or their order of priorities,' Carter pointed out.

'Agreed. But I want you to emulate the excellent Admiral Jervis you have just mentioned. Discipline them ruthlessly before they become a rabble.'

'How many divers are involved?'

'Six. Two are always in reserve in case of illness or accidents.'

'How long would the assignment last?'

'A month at the most. After that, the weather will become unpredictable, and operations have to stop.'

'Whether you find gold or not?'

'Yes. Conditions will be too bad for diving.'

'My duties would not involve diving?'

'In no circumstances. Your job would be to look after the divers, see they keep to their agreed work-schedules. Minimize disturbances and displays of temperament.'

'I see. Now, how exactly is the gold stacked? As loose bars? In wooden crates?'

'If it had been stacked loose, the crew of *El Medina* would have known instantly what it was – with the risk of mutiny or piracy. There wasn't time to build crates – after all, the

Republicans were losing their war, and wooden boxes would have had to be very strong.

'The gold was concealed in liquid concrete, packed into old boilers and metal drums.'

'Do your divers know what they are diving for?'

'Only that there is a possibility of gold, but they don't know how much is in the ship. It is better that way. Makes your job easier, too. If they knew they were looking for millions of pounds' worth of bullion, they might get dangerous ideas.'

'Understandably. Now to ask the ultimate question Mr Serrafino. What is in this for me – apart from physical damage – if I come to blows with any of these individualists you employ?'

'I can offer you your living expenses and accommodation, with the use of a BMW car for the period of your assignment and the equivalent of one thousand pounds sterling per week, with an extra thousand pounds as a bonus, if we finish the operation within three weeks. In any currency you like and tax-free, of course.

'What do you say, Mr Carter?'

'I say, no, Mr Serrafino.'

'Really? I am surprised at such a prompt and unequivocal refusal. May I ask why you decline this offer?'

'You may, Mr Serrafino. And I will tell you. Because it isn't good enough.'

'I thought that, in all the circumstances, it was generous.'

'You say that the gold is worth millions to you. With a crew of mutinous or reluctant divers you will not lift it out this month. That means, by your own calculation, you will have to leave the whole enterprise until next spring.

'I would also say, from my slight experience of local regulations regarding foreigners working out here, that your permission to dive will probably expire at the end of the year, and you will have to renegotiate it for next year. And by that time others may have come in as competitors. Who is to say what bribes may not change hands so that you do not receive a second chance?

'In my view, you have to get that gold up pronto or forget it altogether. And whether you get it up quickly depends entirely on the divers. If you are having problems already, it will be up to me to keep them on their toes, to use an army phrase. Not an easy task, Mr Serrafino. One new boy against six old hands.'

'You are entitled to your thoughts, Mr Carter, and I accept some of your points. However, I have made my offer. Now come back with yours.'

'Twenty thousand American dollars. Half on signature of our agreement, and half to be paid after four weeks.'

'That is a large sum of money. I would not think you are in a position to strike too hard a bargain.'

'For every task, every man, every woman in all the world, there is a price. That is mine.'

Carter sat back in his chair. His mouth felt dry and yet his back was damp with perspiration. Had he blown his chance? Should he have accepted the offer – because he had nothing else? He sipped his drink and did not meet the reproachful gaze of Mr Serrafino's heavy-lidded eyes.

Behind them, the sun had fallen into the sea and evening was staining the sky a deeper blue. Tiny birds fluttered like parentheses above the swimming-pool. Some dipped their beaks nervously into the water and sipped and flew on with a great flapping of wings. For the first time since early morning, the air felt cool. Carter put down his empty goblet on the marble-topped table and stood up.

'Thank you for the brandy, Mr Serrafino,' he said, trying to keep disappointment out of his voice. He had hoped that his host would come back with an offer, probably not all he asked for, but maybe half – something. But, no. He had blown it. He looked towards the house under the huge curved arches of the terrace. Lights began to glow in polished brass lanterns, a Bratby sunflower flamed on a far wall. Celia Kent put a cassette into the largest stereo machine he had ever seen, and the Pasadena Roof Orchestra poured music across the terrace in great billowing waves of quadrophonic sound.

'Good night, Mr Serrafino. I am sorry we could not agree.'

Carter turned, began to walk up the steps to the house. He

had reached the vast room with its polished red tiles the colour of blood spilled in the sun, its white rugs scattered in extravagant profusion, when Mr Serrafino called to him.

'Why are you running off so quickly, Mr Carter?' he asked. 'I have something to give you. To be exact, ten thousand American dollars. You have a deal.'

Carter was back in his own house by eight o'clock. He went into the kitchen, pulled the curtains carefully in case anyone could look through the window and see him, and then he opened the envelope and examined the notes Mr Serrafino had given him.

He had never handled so much money in cash; just to hear the rustle of the dollar bills was comforting. He replaced them in the envelope, and had just sealed the back with a strip of Sellotape when the doorbell rang. It was a timid ring, the single ting of someone reluctant to press the button too hard in case the wrong person might hear it.

Carter put the envelope in a drawer under some folded tea-towels, for he felt vulnerable with so much money in his pocket; then he opened the door. A shadowy, forlorn figure stood in the doorway. It took him a moment to recognize Shauna.

'An unexpected pleasure,' he said, meaning it for the first time. The difference some money made! She took a step forward.

'Let me come in,' she said. 'But don't put on the light. Please.'

He closed the door behind her and led the way into the kitchen.

'Is something the matter?' he asked her.

'Everything,' she said. Despite the fact that the sun was down, she still wore dark glasses. He put out one hand and removed them gently. As he had half-expected, her left eye had been blackened. She grabbed the spectacles from him and replaced them quickly. She had been crying. Both eyes were puffy, and her face was still streaked with tears.

'I'll get you a drink,' he said.

She shook her head nervously.

'I don't want it to smell on my breath,' she explained.

'Vodka,' he replied, and poured out four fingers, added ginger ale, two cubes of ice.

'You're not having one?'

'No. I've drunk enough today. Who gave you that?' He nodded towards her black eye.

'My husband. Didn't you hear?'

'What about?'

'He's complained to the villa manager, Mr Rowley, that you'd made a pass at me. Several other husbands suspected you had seen too much of their wives, too. They also went to the management. I came to tell you. To warn you.'

'Thank you,' he said. 'But it's too late. I'm going.'

'You've got the sack?'

He smiled at the use of the old expression. 'Getting the sack' originally meant that the employer handed to the dismissed workman the sack in which he kept the tools of his trade so that he was free to look for work elsewhere.

'Yes,' he said. 'Mine was only a summer contract. Now summer's over.'

'*Were* there other women?' Shauna asked miserably.

He looked at her: a lonely, unhappy woman, beginning to climb the long slope to middle-age, due within hours to fly home to a life she didn't like with a man she didn't love.

'No one like you,' Carter assured her gently.

She put out a hand, stroked his arm.

'I'm glad,' she said. 'I didn't expect to be the only one.'

'You were unique,' he told her.

She began to cry.

'I like you very much,' she said. 'I think – I think – I love you.'

'You mustn't talk like that,' Carter told her. 'Look on our meeting as a summer thing. In the old days, it would have been a shipboard romance, or like *Cinderella*. It all ends at midnight. And you're on the early-morning flight.'

'Would you like my address?' Shauna asked him.

Carter shook his head.

'If I had your address, then I might call on you and everything would be different.'

'I suppose you're right.'

'Not always – not even often – but about this, yes.'

She sipped her vodka and then began to gulp it down hurriedly.

'I'd better be going,' she said suddenly.

'Where does your husband think you are?'

'At the supermarket, getting some last-minute soft drinks for the children for the journey to the airport.'

Carter opened the fridge, took out four bottles of Sumol, slipped them into a plastic supermarket-bag.

'Here they are. Cheer up, now. Maybe I'll be back here next year. Maybe we both will.'

Carter kissed her, not passionately, but like a friend, as a mark of understanding. Then he switched off the light, let Shauna out into the street, and stood for a moment watching her walk away.

He went back into his house, changed into a pair of old dark trousers and a dark-blue rollneck shirt and a pair of blue canvas shoes.

He put the envelope with Mr Serrafino's money under his shirt, against his skin where it would be safer than in a pocket, and set off up the road. Ten thousand dollars in notes was a lot of money to be carrying around loose in a holiday town at the end of the season.

He walked into the Nautilus bar he used when he wanted to be on his own. It was run by a young Portuguese named Manuel and decorated with huge plaster seashells. The walls were white and the lights dim and blue, giving a vague impression of life under the surface of the sea.

Manuel was reading a newspaper behind his bar. On a leather-topped stool in front of the bar sat Manuel's Border terrier, Gamba, the Portuguese name for shrimp. Gamba thumped his stumpy tail enthusiastically when he saw Carter;

he approved of Carter, who sat down on the nearest stool and stroked him.

Gamba had two tricks. He could leap from the ground up to the top of the stool, a distance of about a yard – no mean achievement, in Carter's view, as the dog stood less than a foot high. He also possessed a remarkable homing instinct. At the height of the tourist season Manuel would lay bets with customers that they could take the dog away for one, two or even three miles in their car, let it free, and it would run back as fast as its game little legs could carry it.

'Has he had many walks lately?' Carter asked.

'Not too many,' replied Manuel. 'Not so many customers.' He waved a hand to embrace the banquettes around the room, each surmounted by a gigantic scallop-shell, and all empty.

'You've got one now,' said Carter. 'The usual. Brandy Alexander. Treble.'

The barman measured out the brandy, the chocolate liqueur, the cream, poured them into a shaker, added ice, shook vigorously, then strained off the strong, frothy, syrupy liquid, dusted on the cinnamon.

'Seven hundred escudos,' he said, pushing the glass across the counter, almost reluctantly, as though he did not wish to relinquish his creation.

'A lot of money,' said Carter.

'A lot of drink, senhor. A drink for three men, not one.'

Carter placed a thousand-escudos note on the counter.

'Keep the change, if you will do me a favour.'

Manuel's face remained as impassive as the bottles on the shelves behind him.

Carter took the envelope from his pocket.

'Will you keep this in your deep-freeze until I collect it in the morning?'

'What's in it?'

'Nothing that would interest you or me. A friend of mine has these dirty photographs he doesn't want his wife to see. He's leaving on the morning plane, but his wife does the packing.'

'You seen them?' asked Manuel.

'Yes, they're all bent. Masks, chains, animals. Hang on to them for me. Don't let anyone, but *anyone*, have them if they ask for them. Not matter who they say they are. Only me. Understood?'

'Understood.'

Carter left the bar, holding open the door for a middle-aged Portuguese to enter. He wore a crumpled linen suit, and nodded his thanks. Carter walked on up the Burgau road, stepping into the shadows whenever a car came up behind him, lights bright, spinning wheels raising dust.

He reached the gates of Casa Serrafino and passed them without pausing or stopping. Ten yards beyond them he climbed the low wall on the other side of the road and walked back cautiously so that he could examine the gates through a break where lime had crumbled and the stones of the wall had fallen away.

The gates to Mr Serrafino's house were firmly shut. The lens of a surveillance camera poked its snout between the hanging fronds of a eucalyptus-tree. Carter's training told him that this was the camera he was meant to see. There would be others, better hidden, but how to discover them? He could not see any tell-tale reflection, so he walked up the hill again, keeping behind the wall. After fifty yards, he crossed the road, climbed the wall on Mr Serrafino's side and dropped down into his garden.

The earth felt soft and well dug, with a cloying honey-sweet smell from a red-and-orange-flowered bush which only poured out its scent after dark. Crickets wound up their ratchets and began to whirr. Carter could see lights burning in the house and, carefully keeping in the shadows, he circled the building. All the windows had shutters, and he could not see inside the rooms without approaching too closely. He moved back towards the road, having discovered nothing. But was there anything to discover, or was Mr Serrafino simply as he appeared, a rich man who wanted to become richer?

Mr Serrafino was at that moment sitting in an inner room,

glass in hand, facing three closed-circuit-television monitor screens. One covered the area of the gates; the second was fed by a camera behind the wall; the third showed pictures from a camera that continually turned, like a slow weather-cock, on the roof.

The first screen stayed blank. The other two had been activated when Carter climbed the wall, and Mr Serrafino had followed his progress around the grounds and his approach to the house. Surely the man realized he would be watched? Yet he had not made the cardinal error that thieves, or attempted thieves, so often did, and climbed the main gate. Why not? Was he a fool – or a knave?

A broad-shouldered man wearing a short-sleeved sweatshirt, with initials on the breast pocket, stood by Mr Serrafino, slightly behind his chair, chewing gum.

'Shall I get him?' he asked.

Mr Serrafino shook his head.

'No,' he said. 'Let him go, Franz. We need him. And what good would it do to beat him up?'

'I wouldn't necessarily beat him up. Not at first. I would just ask him what he wanted, prowling about your garden in the dark.'

'Which would make him even more alert and suspicious. That's the last thing we want. Let him go.'

Mr Serrafino held out his glass for his companion to refill.

Carter walked into the Nautilus bar. To hell with Mrs Kent's advice; another drink was what he needed. Tomorrow, he would be sober. Tomorrow and tomorrow, all his tomorrows. Then, as the door swung shut behind him, he changed his mind – to prove to himself that he could control the craving. He had to start sometime; this seemed as good a time as any.

Manuel looked up from his newspaper. The Portuguese in the linen suit was still the only other customer. He sat on a banquette, sipping a blue curaçao.

'The same again?' Manuel asked Carter hopefully.

'I think not. Something soft. *Agua mineral*.'

'Maybe the pictures have got to you?'

Carter had never ordered a spa water from him.

'Maybe it's the bondage, eh?'

Carter shook his head, amazed that the barman could be so indiscreet. The Portuguese drinker looked up at them. He had cross-eyes; one regarded Carter, the other was fixed on the far wall.

'Bondage,' he repeated slowly. ' "Disguise our bondage as we will, 'Tis woman, woman, rules us still." '

'You read Thomas Moore,' said Carter. 'Can't be too many in the Algarve who do.'

'Numbers do not concern me,' the man replied lugubriously. 'I go my own way. Let others take their routes as they wish.'

He came up to the bar, ordered another curaçao, sat down on the stool next to Gamba, fondled the dog's head. Gamba's tail thumped appreciatively.

'You know this dog?' he asked.

'Very well,' said Carter.

'I often take him for a walk, don't I, Manuel?' asked the man.

Manuel nodded.

'Fine animal. Leave him anywhere and back he comes. You should have called him Pigeon. Like the English homing pigeon, eh?'

He sipped his drink.

'I like the English,' he said. 'I read a lot in English. Poets, mostly. Auden, Isherwood, Spender, Betjeman. Germans, too. Goethe and Schiller.'

'I've just been speaking to someone else who reads a lot of unlikely books for bits and pieces of wisdom. Name of Serrafino. Know him?'

'The name does sound familiar, but it is fairly common here. Like Smith in your country.'

'It's a pity we have few native poets here in Portugal,' said the barman.

'But you're not short of equally valuable attributes of civilization,' Carter replied. 'Like brandy, port, sunshine, sea and seafood.'

'I'm glad to hear my country spoken of so highly,' said the Portuguese customer warmly. 'I in turn hold the highest regard for the literature and traditions of your country.'

'Let's shake on that.'

They did so.

'You live here?' Carter asked him.

'Some miles inland. I avoid the coast in the season. It becomes so crowded. I usually come here each autumn for the increasingly rare pleasure of solitude. But sadly not on this occasion. Allow me to introduce myself. I am José de Silva.'

'Carter is the name.'

'He teaches underwater swimming at the pool,' Manuel explained.

'Did,' said Carter. 'The contract's over.'

'So's the season,' said Manuel sadly.

'I wish my present job was,' said de Silva. He grimaced.

'What's so unpleasant about it?'

'Usually, nothing. I work on a part-time basis for the British consulate in Portimão. There may be the odd drunk to bail out. Someone who's lost their air-ticket home or their wife, or even both. But tonight I have to tell a young woman that her husband has met with an accident.'

'Will that disturb her?'

'It is possible.'

'What happened? Car accident?'

'No. The man seems to have been walking over the moors near the west coast, and somehow lost his footing and fell down a ravine. It can be very windy out there, of course.'

'I've heard of people losing their balance and falling off pavements,' said Manuel.

'Perhaps a car hit him if he was walking along the road, and he lost his sense of direction,' Carter suggested.

'It is possible, but not probable, I think. He was in a lonely part of the coast, and might not have been found for weeks. Fortunately, a shepherd looking for a lost ewe came across him.

Went through his pockets to see if there was anything valuable, found a British passport, and contacted us.'

'Where was the wife, then?'

'I have no idea.'

'Couldn't have been too close, surely, if he was out there and she was elsewhere?'

'Not necessarily. She might not have been in Portugal at the time of the accident. He could have been out here working, while she was on her way out from England to see him. All kinds of explanations. Anyhow, she is now in São Sebastião.'

'Been in the papers yet?'

'Not yet. Managed to keep it quiet.'

The remark reminded Carter of the colonel telling him that the death of Akbar Khan's father had not been in the newspapers. Had someone also managed to keep that a secret from the public? A telephone rang in the back room behind the bar. Manuel moved away to answer it.

'As a matter of fact,' de Silva said softly, 'we have been requested to play it down.'

'Why is that, do you think?'

'No idea. Ours not to reason why, as your poet Tennyson so wisely said.'

Mr de Silva took a plastic folder from his inner jacket pocket, pulled out a British passport, opened it. The pages were stuck together and the photograph so blotched by water it was difficult to make out the features.

Carter read the name in the peculiar turquoise ink favoured by the Foreign Office, now blurred and misty. Then he looked more closely at other details: occupation, place and date of birth.

'What's the matter?' asked Mr de Silva. 'Do you feel ill?'

'I've had a shock. I know this man. He's married to an old friend of mine.' He remembered seeing Miranda and the little boy – could it really have been only a few hours ago? 'I must see if I can help him.'

'That, my friend, is unlikely.'

'Why? Where is he?'

Mr de Silva looked at his watch.

'At this precise moment he is lying on a slab in the deep-freeze at the police mortuary in Lagos.'

four

EMPEROR ODONGO SAT on a three-legged stool, his Homburg hat pushed to the back of his head, a revolver in his hand. He was watching a vervet monkey climb a strangely formed tree with roots that grew down into the earth from overhanging branches, known locally as a strangling fig-tree.

This began as an apparently harmless creeper, too weak to stand on its own. Then it entwined around the trunk of any larger tree, and as it grew stronger the fig steadily strangled the life out of this tree that had originally supported it, and finally emerged as a tree independent of all others. But, because its trunk was still slender, its branches became subsidiary roots, sprouting down to hold the tree upright, as guy ropes support a tent. Eventually it spread, and grew up and down and outwards to such an extent that what appeared to be a whole grove of fig-trees was actually still only one.

Odongo admired the strangling fig, and had ordered a likeness of it to be incorporated in the coat of arms the Englishman had insisted he should have designed for the country he called Menaka. The tree was now held sacred by his decree, so any bird or beast that settled in its branches was committing a sacrilege against him. The skin tightened with concentration on his huge forehead as he waited for the monkey to pause and present a sitting target. Finally it did so, pulling at a leaf, then covering its black face with both hands. Odongo fired twice. A cluster of green-feathered bee-eaters and shrikes fled from the sheltering branches as the shots echoed through the forest.

For a moment, the monkey did not move. Then, with hands still pressed into its eyes as though it could not bear to see what had happened, it slowly rolled off the branch and dropped. Odongo grunted with satisfaction.

He crossed the dusty track and stood looking down at the monkey. Grotesque with its white whiskers, green back and silver-haired stomach, like a manikin made up for a fancy-dress party, it moaned and twitched in the agony of death. He pointed his revolver at the animal's head and fired a third shot. Blood and brains splattered the tree-trunks. Odongo wiped sweat from his own forehead with the back of his other hand, and set off up the track to his house.

He felt satisfied. He had maintained the honour of the tree whose life he felt so closely paralleled his own. At first, like the young fig-tendril, he had been harmless, an army corporal. Then he had been hurriedly commissioned when his country became independent and had been given more power. Next, he had seized complete control of his country and, like the strangling fig, had squeezed influence and life from those who once had been his superiors. Thus he would deal with his enemies, and soon, very soon. He would prise them from their perches of power as swiftly as this insolent monkey. The thought cheered him, and on impulse he emptied his revolver at a mass of black ants, each an inch long, crawling in the dust at his feet. When the dust blew away, thousands were still alive, and the sight infuriated him. How could creatures as small as these dare to stand against him?

Odongo reloaded and fired until he had no more cartridges. He was sweating now with a mixture of fear and loathing. He hated ants; they always seemed so busy, so independent – and there were so many of them. Most of all, Odongo hated the giant ant-hills that the white ants, the termites, constructed. These were not the small plum-pudding-shaped nests harmless ants would build, but pyramids or cone-shaped mounds fifteen or twenty feet high, like the pictures of fairy-tale castles the Englishman had shown him in children's storybooks. They were made of dry, powdery earth, sometimes camouflaged with dead leaves and pocked with ventilation-holes several inches across. Snakes and rats lurked in these cavities and spiders built webs outside, five feet wide, to catch flies foolish enough to seek sanctuary within them.

On several occasions Odongo had forced a prisoner to stand with his bare arm thrust into one of these holes up to the elbow as a test of innocence or guilt. If the ants ignored him, he was judged innocent; if they bit him, he must be guilty. Odongo liked to watch the prisoner's face, to see how desperately he sought to conceal the pain as a myriad ants began to feed on his flesh, his sinews and muscles, in the vain hope that if he did not cry out he would be set free. But finally the agony would become too much for any man to bear and he would tear out his arm alive with ants that had bitten down to the bones, and by so doing would admit his guilt and deserve to die.

Odongo had once staked out a man, accused of treachery, with arms and legs apart, tied by the wrists and ankles to bamboo poles driven into the earth near one of these ant-hills. Then Odongo's personal guard had poked long sticks into the heart of the hill until the infuriated ants swarmed out like a moving carpet and, sensing the prisoner's terror, had completely covered his body. Odongo enjoyed the memory of this shining scaly-backed heaving mass in the vague shape of a man, choking and screaming and dying. Then the ants had moved away, leaving the prisoner's bones stripped of flesh, pink and smooth and shining in the sun. So would it be with all foolish enough to rise up against him, Lord of the Central Hills, Liberator of the People.

The track led up a hill where he had built himself a house or, rather, a fortress for any eventuality that could call for seclusion, and what the Englishman had referred to tactfully as a regrouping of his forces, or a time to adopt a new tactical approach. In a cruder word, revolution.

The hill was only about a hundred metres high, but it commanded a wide view across the shimmering green expanse of thick mangrove swamp. The mangroves grew to a height of sixty feet in places, with roots that turned from the soil and came up like groping, searching, blind fingers. Mission-school teachers had told Odongo as a boy that mangroves did this because, when God first created them, they had not liked the swamps where He had decreed that they should live. This had angered the Almighty, so that from henceforth it was decreed that mangrove roots would grow up as well as down. The Englishman had laughed at this story, but Odongo did not laugh. He knew what the white man would never accept, that old and evil gods lived in the sweating darkness of the forests, not the God worshipped by the missionaries. These other gods could take the shape of reptiles and serpents, and their power was absolute. In this last attribute, of course, they resembled him, as he resembled them.

The earth in these swamps was the colour of soft coal. Where mangroves had rotted or been burned, or died of some disease, patches of soaking black earth, with dead roots sticking out of them, appeared like huge scabs, ringed with inky water of unknown depth. Odongo felt secure surrounded by such swamps. Nothing could move in them. Only serpents could slip through, and then with difficulty.

A few birds turned and wheeled above him now as he walked; they scented the death of some animal that had foolishly attempted to cross these treacherous marshes – or could it be the monkey he had killed? Let them feed. They would have a feast when he overcame his enemies.

Odongo's fortress was built like a house in the old colonial style, but with some important unseen differences. It stood on stilts about ten feet high, made of timber from the kembo-tree, known locally as ironwood, the hardest wood in Africa. Around the outside was a veranda with a kembo balustrade, and above this a fine metal mosquito-mesh. The roof was of corrugated iron and, like the wooden walls, was painted dark green. Here and there narrow horizontal slots had been cut into the walls which were all reinforced by thick plates of steel seized (in the interests of the State) from a building project being funded by a naïve but generous charity in the middle west of the United States. Odongo had personally fired thousands of rounds at these walls, from all directions and angles, and at distances from ten metres to a hundred. No cartridge currently in his country could pierce them. Similar shields of metal lay beneath the floorboards of the veranda, and the Englishman had sited the slots so that defenders within could aim machine-guns at attackers outside.

Unusually for Africa, the house possessed a deep basement lined with reinforced concrete. In this were two huge deep-freezes, a refrigerator of gigantic size and an electric charging plant, which now hummed and put-putted away, a faint frond from its exhaust shimmering over the rear of the building. The basement was divided into bedroom, bathroom, kitchen. A pipe had been laid to one of the few fresh-water springs in the area, and in addition to the electric pump a propeller above the roof powered a standby pump. The Englishman had assured Odongo that under siege he could survive here indefinitely.

The last room in the basement contained the radio set, a powerful transmitter and receiver. Aerials had been cleverly concealed in the roof of the house, and a secondary aerial was stapled to one of the larger palms on the edge of the forest, where no one was likely to see it.

The mangroves had been cut back to an area of two hundred metres all around the house to prevent any intruder arriving unseen. Only one hard-surfaced track led into Odongo's last redoubt, and this was guarded in several places by armed troops. They kept metal barricades concealed in the bush to drag across it, and grilles of high tensile steel wire could quickly be unravelled and stretched across the road from one giant baobab-tree to another to make a deep net able to stop any vehicle.

Odongo also had another and secret path leading away from the clearing, and concealed by a clump of bamboos. Although unsurfaced, the path was wide enough for a car during the dry season and led out to the main road, some miles away, following the bed of a dried-up river. He had walked along it earlier that morning, and was infuriated to see that the accursed ants had built several of their gigantic castles across it. He must remove them, but he did not care to do this work himself, and yet was unwilling to order others to carry it out in case they realized the use to which he might put this hidden escape-route.

So far as he knew, no one suspected its existence and so could not imagine that he might ever contemplate a retreat along it, abandoning everyone else, if that was the only way he could personally survive. It would be madness to allow his followers to realize that their emperor should ever consider flight. He would order one soldier to destroy the ant-hills and then shoot him with a silenced gun when he had finished. The ants would eat the flesh from his bones within minutes. Then Odongo would conceal the skeleton. That would be the best and easiest solution.

Odongo's aircraft had brought him from his captured capital to a specially built strip of hard gravel ten miles away and concealed by palm-trees. No one knew of its existence except his pilot and engineer and the Englishman. Odongo had originally brought the construction workers who built it from the south of Menaka, through miles of savannah. He had given them more food than they had ever seen before, and housed them in wattle bashas, with women provided, and as much palm toddy as they could drink at the end of each baking, toiling day. They were helped in their labours by earth-moving equipment, shipped in by another benevolent relief organization as part of a generous aid programme to help the Third World. When at last the airstrip stretched like a white scar against the green, Emperor Odongo had addressed his workers in a speech the Englishman had written for him, full of the flowery words he liked.

'We are a great nation, a great country,' he told them. 'And we have accomplished in a matter of weeks what colonial powers did not attempt in generations. And while they would have forced our ancestors to toil like slaves, with wooden implements and home-made axes, we have harnessed science and all the technology of the West to work for us.

'Let us never forget, even momentarily, that, above all else, we are Africans, proud of our Africa, and of the heritage of all things, animate and inanimate. Let us therefore dig a trench with this new equipment and put into it all the rubbish from these bashas. Tear them down, so that once more green will grow where they have stood, and give forth fruit in abundance. Then you shall eat and drink, and drive in triumph back to our villages, money in your pockets, pride in your hearts and hope in a new tomorrow.'

The men had cheered him deliriously. Odongo, always with the aid of the Englishman, could clothe their secret dreams with words, so that they became realities. Great and glorious was his name.

Immediately, one group smashed the bashas with axes. Others drove the bulldozers and mechanical shovels into the mangrove swamps, crashing through splintering raw branches, raising a foul, fetid stench from the roots. As soon as the trench was dug, water appeared in it, black and oily, like tar. Strange snakes, unknown reptiles, slithered or crawled away to escape the onslaught of the diggers.

Drums of food and kegs of toddy were unloaded from the trucks that had arrived to carry the men home, and the workers ate and drank and a few fought among themselves from sheer animal exultation.

'Throw all rubbish into the pits so that the earth receives back the gifts it has given to us,' Odongo commanded them after this celebration meal.

The men, exhausted after their work in the burning sun, heavy with food and tipsy with drink, but still buoyed up by the thought that soon they would be back in their homes and with their families, filled the trench with the debris of their camp.

'Now,' said Odongo gravely, addressing them from the bonnet of one of the trucks, movie camera slung around his shoulder, 'let me photograph you as you stand, having given back to the earth our mother that which is hers to own.'

They lined up in a row along the edge of the trench, grinning sheepishly. Men in loincloths and underpants, shabby trousers, tea-cosy hats, ebony bodies varnished with the sweat of twelve hours' effort, but content with what they had achieved. At that moment, the soldiers, hitherto hidden in the swamps, opened fire.

The labourers staggered and fell into the trench. The soldiers came out of the swamps and smashed the skulls of the wounded with rifle butts. The smell of death was terrible in the evening sun, and the sky grew dark with the flapping of vultures' wings.

When all the dead and dying were finally in the trench, the soldiers walked along its edge, emptying jerry-cans of petrol on the bodies. A few who were still alive screamed in agony as the spirit seared their wounds. Then the officer struck a match, lit a long taper of dried reed, and applied it to one end of the trench. Flames swept through the chasm with the roar of an express train.

Odongo waited until the flames had died, and then walked the length of the trench, aiming his camera at the charred remains of his workers. He did not do this solely out of ghoulish curiosity, but because he wished to run the film in slow motion and examine every frame. He wanted to be quite certain there were no survivors.

'Get the men into the truck,' Odongo ordered the officer as he reached the end of the trench. When they were all inside, the officer rolled down the canvas back and buttoned it tightly, then jumped into the cab beside the driver.

'Follow me,' Odongo told them. 'Keep about a hundred yards behind. No farther, but no closer. Be alert. We may yet meet enemies on the way.'

He climbed into his Mercedes, switched on the air-conditioning. His body was damp with sweat from nervous effort and the strange, half-religious, half-sexual exultation he always experienced after the murder of other men. It was as though he drew new life from their death. He set off, yellow beams from the headlights cutting a tunnel of light through the brilliant green walls of mangroves. Huge night moths and bats fluttered and then sped away from the unaccustomed light and noise.

Five miles along the track, Odongo took from the dash-board

locker a little black box, about two inches square with a bell push on one side, that he later took with him into his aircraft. He pressed the button. The truck behind him exploded in a roar of flame and fire.

Odongo stopped his car, climbed down, and stood by the driver's door, hearing the shouts of the trapped men. Within seconds their screams drowned in the roar of hungry flames as the truck's petrol-tank took fire.

Odongo stood watching the blaze subside, leaving a skeleton of the truck, with ribs that had supported the canvas roof. The steering-wheel seemed thin now without its plastic rim, and tyres flickered with flame. Wind blew away the odour of burning oil and paint and flesh in a cloud of powdery, fiery ash.

Odongo approached the truck cautiously, revolver drawn, in case, incredibly, anyone had survived the inferno. The Englishman had once read to him a story about the ancient pharaohs. On their death, slaves who had built the pyramids which would be their tomb were buried with them so that no one would know exactly where they lay. It was a story that moved him: all rulers had to guard against treachery, and the dead were silent witnesses.

He walked around the truck. The bodies were slumped in grotesque attitudes crowded towards the rear of the truck where they had tried to fight their way out. Here and there a skull still wore a steel helmet, all paint blistered. He knew what he would say. Enemies of the people, of the State, had done this. If anyone doubted his word, he could also die. He had already in his rule killed men – hundreds, thousands – who might bear false witness against him: some on his own initiative; others, like these, on the wise advice of the Englishman. Odongo, Ruler of Middle Africa, Liberator of the People, would never be vanquished, so the Englishman had assured him, and he had not failed him yet.

The thought cheered him now as he walked up to his house. No one not close to him by bond of blood even knew he was here. The Englishman, the aircraft pilot and engineer, his personal servants were all members of his family now, for they had sworn allegiance to him, slashed wrist against slashed wrist, so that blood mingled, theirs and his. He felt beyond treachery, for treachery against him would be to act against themselves – and what man would ever betray himself to his enemies? Such a creature would surely burn for ever in fiery torment, about which he had read in the English Bible.

He liked those Old Testament passages: they had obviously been written by men who knew right from wrong, who allowed no compromise, no half-measure, no mercy. Scorpions stung the evil-doers; plagues, pestilence afflicted them; mountains fell into the sea and the earth departed like a scroll that is rolled together. This was Odongo's language, spoken with the tongues of men and of angels. This was his world, and he would once again be its ruler, for the Englishman was planning a coup that would reverse all earlier setbacks, all minor defeats. It seemed such a simple idea; but, as the Englishman had explained, all the great ideas in the world had been simple.

'Think of the safety pin,' he said. 'Only a piece of metal bent over, turned and twisted, and yet its uses are immense. I commend to you the jet engine. In the days of ancient Greeks, a man named Hero heated water in a pan enclosed like a kettle, with a tube to take away the steam. He directed this jet of steam to the blades of a fan – and invented the turbine. Think of the wheel, the lever. Think of everything that has changed mankind and history and brought greatness to those who deserved it – like you.

'What I tell you now is simple, but it is also without precedent. To be the first with an idea or a feat of skill or arms is always the most important thing. Who remembers the name of the *second* man who flew the Atlantic or who travelled to the moon?

'My scheme will make you the most powerful man in all Africa, a ruler to be feared and wooed by West and East alike. You will speak, not just with the voice of a man, but with the authority and strength of a god. Beyond all men, above all rulers, Odongo will not only be emperor, but king. King-

Emperor, as in the days of the British Empire we once served together.'

'You speak well, my friend,' Odongo had replied, much moved by the sentiments the Englishman expressed. 'I will reward you to the utmost of my power.'

He did not add that he had decided he would never let the Englishman leave after he returned. In truth, he missed him sorely. Sometimes he had been not only at a loss for words, but even without thoughts to put into words. He had the muscle, but the Englishman had the mind. They had exchanged their blood; they were as brothers – one black, one white – but after his return they would be like those twins of Siam, about whom the Englishman had also told him, men joined by an invisible umbilical cord.

Odongo had served with him on those frontiers of Burma and Siam long ago. He had not been an emperor then, only a corporal. Together, when he returned, they would build a capital city here on this hill, as beautiful as Paris, imperial as Rome, modern as anything in Brazil or North America. Truly, he would be King-Emperor.

'O King, live for ever,' his guard would call as the Englishman had promised him they would.

When Odongo had heard this prophecy of fame and power to come, which reflected all his dreams, he had taken the Englishman's hand and clasped it to his own broad chest, so that his blood brother could feel the beating of his heart.

Odongo did not particularly like the man's hand, for the nails were small and bitten and the fingers flabby, as though they had been immersed in hot water for too long, like a woman's hands when she washes clothes. But it was not the man's hands that attracted Odongo; it was his brain, his mind, his vision. Together, they would be invincible. All that remained now was for the Englishman to arrive with the rare gift of which he spoke. And this arrival should surely not be long delayed. He consulted the gold calendar watch that Cartier had fashioned especially for him, encrusted with diamonds, hours marked by rubies instead of by figures. Within a week, at the latest, he would have the power to change not only his life but also his whole world.

A buzzer bleeped in his pocket; he was wanted on his secret radio. He walked back slowly into his house. He never hurried. The Englishman had told him that in the days before British policemen carried guns they had learned to control immense crowds by never appearing to hurry. Their walk was always a slow and measured step, and like a stately metronome this instantly reduced haste and hysteria in others.

Odongo acknowledged the salutes of his armed guards, went downstairs into the basement to the radio room. The air-conditioning machine hummed, and the air had the strange metallic smell and taste that comes from being piped through many filters in galvanized metal ducts. He shut and locked the metal door behind him. The room was padded, completely soundproof. A light flickered above the big Decca set. He picked up the headphones, adjusted the dials, and a voice said: 'Baobab-tree calling Sunflower. Baobab-tree calling Sunflower. Over.'

An endless tape played on the transmitter. Needles on hair-springs trembled nervously against their dials as Odongo pressed a button.

'Sunflower speaking. Sunflower speaking,' he said and released the button.

The Englishman's voice spoke in the padded silent room.

'Flower in four days. Over.'

'Message received, my friend, and understood. Over and out.'

Odongo sat for a moment, looking at the quivering needles on the dials and the flickering lights. He liked those words he had learned nearly forty years ago in the service of a king-emperor now long dead. *Over and out*. He had been proud of his rank then, with the sleeve of his uniform ironed every day at the apex of his two stripes. There had been a quality about those days missing in these present times. Perhaps he now had too much responsibility for any one man, for a strange gloom sometimes gripped him, quite inexplicably. At such times he would seek refuge from his depression in an orgy of violence, pain, death. He might fire a thousand rounds into the bush, hopefully for the squeal of animals he had wounded. Then he might send out men after the animals to find them, and fire again, and hear their shouts of pain and pitiful cries for help. Even this could not always extract him from the gloom.

He felt sometimes as a man might feel out in those mangrove swamps on a starless night, alone and sinking into a bottomless sump of black and clogging silt. With every struggling desperate movement he made with hands and feet and elbows and knees, he only sank a little farther down, until finally nothing could save him. Like such a wanderer, far from the known way, he felt he was being drawn into a morass of darkness from which there was no escape but death.

Odongo shook these gloomy thoughts from him, switched the set over to Receive, went out of the room and up the metal stairs into the air-conditioned main room of the house. At one end, on a dais, stood his golden throne, constructed by craftsmen in the rue St-Honoré in Paris, then dismantled and brought in separate small pieces by the diplomatic bag to be assembled again. He had arranged its position – with the Englishman's help – so that when he sat on it he could command a view of the road that led to the palace through the slits in the wall.

In the last extremity, should all his guards be overcome by an enemy force, he could sit and watch enemies come down this road, not realizing that it was mined in several places, that machine-guns under bamboo and rattan screens on either side of the forest were laid on fixed lines for him to fire by remote control. Then he could escape by his most secret route.

Odongo sat now on the throne and looked along the white road. By some illusion of evening, it seemed to stretch to infinity, and by another evil trick of eyesight the swamps on either side appeared to be moving together imperceptibly. When they met, the road would be completely covered, and become as though it had never been, like lost kingdoms and vanished empires.

Then he realized the true significance of what he saw or thought he saw. The road was the enemy, the swamps on either side represented the Englishman's guile and his own strength. Together they would drive out the usurpers. It would be as though *they* had never existed.

To show his rise in spirits, Odongo seized the machine-gun he kept hidden beneath the throne and fired a burst along the empty road.

The explosions rang bells in his ears, and he went on firing until the room was filled with the smell of cordite and his mind with the chattering music of the gun.

Behind the house, in the guardroom, off-duty soldiers looked at each other uneasily. They feared these wild outbursts, this random firing at any target and at none; again men could be killed, as they had been in the past when this fitful madness coursed through their emperor's blood.

The police mortuary in Lagos lay half-hidden behind a Roman wall and the ancient fortress that overlooked the harbour. Near it, in the centre of a large square dotted by trees hung with coloured lights that trembled in the autumn wind, Henry the Navigator, whose caravels had been built in Lagos for their voyages of discovery to Africa and the East, stared in stone across this square to the Lagos river and the sea. In times past, the fleets of Rome and Carthage had lain at anchor at Lagos and, later, ships carrying crusaders to the Holy Land had paused here on their long slow voyages.

Later still, the square had been crowded by slaves from Africa, marched in manacles to be auctioned under the arches of the Customs House where Mr de Silva was now parking his car. A few stray dogs prowled hopefully in the gutters, and from a bar the sad notes of a *fado* stroked the night with the music of lament.

The duty police sergeant sat at a desk behind a thick glass window. Mr de Silva spoke softly to him, and showed a pass like a plastic credit card. The sergeant nodded to a constable, who detached himself from a wooden bench, picked up a bunch of keys and led the way along a stone corridor. The smell of formaldehyde and ether grew stronger with each step. The policeman unlocked a door into a white-walled, high-ceilinged room.

The atmosphere here was so cold that their breath hung in the air like fog. Fluorescent tubes trembled on the cracked ceiling. Part of the room was taken up with a grey-painted metal structure like a giant filing-cabinet. Each drawer had a plastic-covered handle, now white with frost, and above each handle was a small nameplate. The constable rubbed one clear with the elbow of his jacket until Carter saw the name: *Senhor Jack Bridges, Ingles*. The constable pulled the handle. Rollers squealed as the drawer opened slowly, and a puff of frozen air rose like steam.

Carter looked down at the body lying on its back, hands stiffly by its sides in the position of attention. Only the face was visible. A green canvas sheet covered the trunk and legs. Carter could see blue-green bruises on the frozen flesh, dark blood still on the cheekbones. Some animal had eaten out the eyes and nibbled at an ear. Carter glanced down at the third finger of Bridges' right hand, where he usually wore the ring Miranda had given him. He was not wearing it now.

'Know him?' de Silva asked, watching Carter closely.

'I knew him,' Carter replied.

'A very sad case.'

'What about his clothes?'

De Silva repeated the question, and the constable opened a metal cupboard. Inside were several cardboard boxes. He lifted the lid from the nearest. Neatly folded and stiff with frozen dampness lay a pair of jeans, shoes, underpants, a blue T-shirt, a pocket handkerchief.

'Had he been in the water?' Carter asked de Silva.

'Yes. His clothes were immersed in sea-water. They also found traces of sand in his hair and under his fingernails.'

'How could he have been in the sea if he was found inland?'

De Silva attempted to focus both eyes on Carter and failed.

'If we knew the answers to every question, we would all be wiser and richer men, senhor,' he said solemnly. 'Perhaps he had been for a bathe and then took a walk and fell?'

'He would hardly bathe fully clothed.'

'I have known it happen.'

'But only at parties,' said Carter. 'Had he been drinking?'

'I understand a pump was applied and the contents of the stomach examined, but no trace of alcohol was found.'

'Had he been robbed?'

'Not so far as I know.'

He spoke to the constable, who opened a small metal drawer with a key on a chain.

'Here's his wallet. Two thousand escudos in notes, some small change in coins. A National Westminster Bank chequebook and two unstamped envelopes and a fifty-escudos note clipped to each.'

The paper-clips were already rusting from the sea-water. Carter picked up the chequebook. Its grey cover felt cold and soggy. Three cheques had been drawn and the back cover was torn off. He replaced the book in the drawer.

'A watch?' Carter asked.

'There wasn't one,' said de Silva. 'If you look at his wrist, you will see his skin is tanned. There is no white mark to show that he usually wore one.'

'You're right,' said Carter. 'He never wore a watch. He used to say there was electricity in his body which interfered with them. He always wore a signet ring, though. It had an unusual crest, a grasshopper with a crown.'

'He wasn't wearing one when he came in.'

'You think the shepherd took it?'

'I doubt it. He seemed an honest man. He didn't even ask for his expenses. That is unusual.'

'I believe you,' said Carter. 'What do you do now?'

'I visit the widow, Mr Carter, and ascertain her wishes.'

'She knows nothing of this so far?'

'Nothing at all.'

'Look, I know her. At least, I *did* know her quite well. We were friends when we were students. I could break this to her, if you want. It might come easier from me.'

'I think it would, senhor. But there are certain forms she will still have to sign. Then, does she wish the body to be returned to England? Interment can be arranged here quite easily, if that is what she wants. Are you in contact with this lady?'

'No. But I saw her for the first time in years in the street in São Sebastião earlier this evening. I've no idea where she is staying, though. I didn't have a chance to speak to her. I was in a car.'

'I have her address.'

Mr de Silva took a visiting-card from his pocket, scribbled the number of a house and its road on the back, handed the card to Carter.

'Perhaps she or you will get in touch with me, care of the consulate, as soon as possible?'

'How long can the body stay here?' asked Carter.

'Indefinitely. But there is a charge, you know.'

'There is always a charge. Nothing is for free in this world.'

'Or, if we are to believe some religions, in the next either, Mr Carter. The prospect of life after death is good – but the chance of a happier life before death appeals to me even more. Let us have a brandy in the bar across the square to warm our blood.'

Rowley was on the telephone to Lisbon about a consignment of bed linen that had somehow gone astray in Albufiera when Carter came into his office. He motioned him to a seat, raising his eyebrows in mute surprise that Carter should still be in São Sebastião.

'Come to say goodbye,' Carter explained, when Rowley finished his call. 'I'm going to Arrifana. Been hired by a man called Serrafino who's trying to raise gold bullion from a sunken ship up near there.'

'I heard about that,' said Rowley. 'Quite a few people in that line of business around the coast.'

'So he told me. Know anything about him? Anything at all?'

'Not really. Our company has a contract to look after his pool and garden when he's not living there. He always pays on time, which is a point in his favour, believe me. He's some business in Africa, I think.'

'I see. There was something else, too.'

'About your house? You can stay there as long as you like, of course. We won't be letting it during the winter.'

'No. It's about Jack Bridges.'

'Old Jolly Jack. What's happening to him?'

'What happens to us all sooner or later. But to him rather sooner. He's dead.'

'*Dead*? What do you mean? An accident?'

'Of a sort.'

'When did you hear this?'

'Last night.'

'But what happened? A car-crash? Heart-attack?'

'Maybe an attack of a different kind. He was found at the bottom of a cliff near Castelejo. I ran into a fellow from the consulate last night who told me. He took me into the morgue in Lagos to see the body.'

'And I thought I had news for *you*,' said Rowley, shaking his head sadly. Bridges was too young to die; death should stay a long way off; it was something that only happened to old people. 'You know Miranda's here?'

'Yes. I saw her in the street last evening. But I haven't spoken to her yet.'

'She popped in to see me after breakfast. She's renting one of our houses, and had some problem. Said she was expecting Jack down from Lisbon. Has she any idea of this?'

'Not so far. I'm on my way to tell her. Thought I'd tell you first.'

'Thanks. Well, if there's anything I can do. . . . Be sure to tell her that. She's in 12 Rua Vasco da Gama. One of our smaller villas. Not on the phone. She's booked it for a fortnight.'

Rowley looked for a moment through the horizontal sunshades that shielded the window. A young mother was smacking the bottom of a child, who started to cry and stamp his feet.

Surely that boy was a long way from death, at that age? Surely they all were? Rowley turned to Carter.

'I would like to see his body.'

'Why? Don't you believe me?'

'It's not that,' he said. 'I just want to be sure. I feel I owe it to him. Jack Bridges was my cousin.'

'You've never told me before.'

'Why should I? You never asked. His father married my mother's sister.'

'So he's half-Portuguese, too?'

'He was, if what you tell me is true.'

'It's true, all right.'

'Poor old Jack. I was never really close to him. I suppose in a sense we were rivals. He did much better at school than me. But I won a scholarship to Oxford. He didn't. But he could have done. He was clever enough. He branched off to the Foreign Office, then joined some exporting company. I came out here to run fortnightly holidays for dental mechanics and building society clerks.'

'Probably pays better.'

'Money isn't the only thing in this world.'

'So people keep telling me. But only those who have enough. If Jack was your cousin, do you want to break the news to Miranda?'

'No,' said Rowley. 'She never liked me much.'

Carter nodded. She had never shown much interest in him, either. Yet he had always felt that sudden irrational blip of the heart when he would see her cross the High, or in the soft light of a cream-shaded reading-lamp at the next table in the Radcliffe Camera. But she was always reserved; or could she just have been shy, like him, in those days?

Carter turned over these thoughts in his mind as he walked along the Rua Vasco da Gama, hating the prospect ahead of him. He had met Bridges for the first time at Miranda's wedding, when he had admired the signet ring with her family crest that she had given him. They had run into each other in the Strand once shortly afterwards and exchanged good wishes, asked about a number of mutual friends, and then gone their separate ways.

He remembered Miranda from afternoons in a punt on the river, playing cassettes of Gershwin or Cole Porter; at the Trout Inn at Godstow, with the roar of the weir as a background to imperious shrieks from the peacocks strutting the lawns. Now she had borne Bridges' son, and Bridges was dead and he was the bearer of bad news outside number 12, a small two-storeyed building designed in the Moorish style with round windows and curved arches.

Carter walked past without slowing his pace. He had not yet made up his mind what to say, how much he should tell her. There was no need, surely, to go into details about how her husband had apparently been in the sea *and* suffered blows to the head? He could not explain this, so it would be kinder for her to think he had met with one accident, not two. Nobody had two accidents like that.

Carter retraced his steps and pressed the bell on Miranda's front door. A red and blue bathing-towel was draped like a flag over a patio wall. A little boy opened the door and looked up at him questioningly.

'You want my mummy?' he asked.

'If she's in, yes.'

The little boy nodded gravely, held open the door. Carter went inside. Miranda appeared from the kitchen door. She was drying a plate.

'Good *Lord*,' she said in pleased amazement. 'Where the devil did you spring from?'

'Actually, Tim Rowley's office. I spotted you and your son on the road last night. But I was in a car and couldn't stop.'

'How *nice* to see you. What a wonderful surprise!'

Miranda came into the little hall, flung her arms around his neck and kissed him warmly.

'Have a drink?' she asked him.

'It's a bit early,' he said cautiously, mindful of his new job, his new resolution.

'Coffee?'

'If you are making it.'

Carter sat down on a stool in the kitchen. Miranda flicked the switch on the electric kettle.

'What are you doing here, then? Holiday?'

'I have been working here for this summer.'

'On a course or something? I always said you would end up Chief of the General Staff. Or maybe that's what you told me?'

'I thought I would, or at least *could*. Once. But I've left the Army, Miranda.'

'Why?'

'A difference of opinion, shall we say?'

'You always were a bit high-minded. Not like me. Are you working out here, then?'

'I was. But that's finished, too. I was teaching children to swim in the pool. Tim Rowley suggested it.'

'Good old Tim. He's Jack's cousin, you know.'

'I only discovered that today.'

'Jack's due here this afternoon. He's been in Lisbon on business. When I heard the bell, I thought he must have arrived early. So I sent Tom Jim to open it. He's a real father's boy.'

'Yes.'

The kettle switched itself off. Miranda put two teaspoons of instant coffee into two cups, added hot water, milk.

'You didn't take sugar?'

'I still don't.'

He looked down at the little boy.

'We haven't been introduced formally.'

'I'm Tom Jim.'

'Of course. I'm Tony,' said Carter.

'Then I'll call you Uncle Tony. You know my dad?'

'I've met him.'

'He's going to teach me to swim this holiday.'

'I've been teaching children like you to swim here all this summer.'

'Is it difficult?'

'Not really.'

'My dad's a good swimmer.'

Carter nodded, suddenly recalling Bridges' sodden clothes. If he had been swimming, was it from the beach – or from a boat? If he had swum in from a boat, he must have been a very strong swimmer to survive the currents off Castelejo – and who would want to swim from such a dangerous rocky beach?

'Why don't we all go out for dinner tonight, when Jack arrives?' said Miranda brightly.

She turned to her son.

'You could stay up, Tom Jim. As a special treat.'

Carter looked at her sharply and Miranda looked at him. Something in his eyes made her suddenly feel uneasy. Carter gave an almost imperceptible nod towards her son.

'I promised you a Sumol if you helped me in the supermarket today, and you did,' she told him brightly.

'I'd rather have a Coke,' Tom Jim replied.

'You shall have both,' said Carter. He put his hand in his pocket and pulled out a fifty-escudos note.

'Is that all for me?' Tom Jim asked, awed by the sight of so much money.

'You only.'

'Now, drink them slowly,' said his mother, 'or you'll get tummy ache.'

The boy ran off.

Carter waited until the front door was shut, then he turned to Miranda.

'This isn't just a social call,' he said awkwardly. 'I wish it was.'

'What is it, then?' she asked him warily.

'It's about Jack.'

'Why? Has he been delayed? Given you a message to deliver, or something?'

'Not exactly. I don't know quite how to say this, so I'd better come to the point quickly. Your son will be back soon. Jack's had an accident.'

'Where? How do you know?'

'I met someone from the British consulate. He told me.'

'Is it serious? Where is he? In hospital in Lisbon?'

'No.'

'You mean he's down here?'

'Yes.'

'Well, where? I must go and see him.'

'I wouldn't.'

'What do you mean, you wouldn't?'

She looked at him in amazement and saw his set face, his unhappy eyes not meeting her gaze.

'You don't mean . . .?'

She could not bring herself to speak the words.

Carter nodded.

'It was a fatal accident. He's dead.'

'But how? What happened? Was it a car accident or something?'

'No. He was out walking and fell. He was found at the bottom of a ravine off the west coast about forty miles from here.'

'But he was coming straight down from Lisbon. What on earth was he doing out there?'

'No one seems to know.'

'Was he alone?'

'Yes. He hadn't been robbed, either. Still had his passport.'

He was about to mention the absence of the signet ring but changed his mind; he had no wish to hurt her further.

'You're certain it is Jack?'

'Yes. I've been to the mortuary.'

'I just can't understand it. Perhaps he lost his footing?'

'He must have done.'

'But why was he there at all? What clothes had he on?'

'A blue shirt and jeans, canvas shoes. They were soaking wet with sea-water.'

'Sea-water? Where exactly was he found?'

'About two miles in from Castelejo.'

'Oh, my God!'

She sat down, hands trembling. Her face was suddenly very pale.

'Tom Jim was so looking forward to seeing him again. He was away such a lot.'

'What was his job, exactly?'

'Oh, import/export. He left the Foreign Office. Promotion too slow. He worked for a company in Winchester. On the contracts side. Flew all over the world. He'd come home for a weekend, then be away for three weeks. I never knew where he was half the time.'

'He was good at his job?'

She shrugged. 'I don't know. We were sort of drifting apart, you know. Only Tom Jim kept us together.'

'I had no idea.'

'No reason why you should. But we saw so little of each other, and really we hadn't all that much in common, I suppose. When he was home, he seemed tired and worried and irritable.'

'I always thought you must both be very happy,' said Carter.

'Everyone always thinks other people are happy – especially if they are not happy themselves,' said Miranda sadly. 'But happiness isn't a state of life, it's a state of mind. Well, what do I do now? I have a friend whose husband died abroad. She had the most awful job getting his body back. Airlines don't like to carry dead bodies, apparently. Passengers think it's unlucky. Her husband travelled home in a box labelled "Tropical Fruit: This Way Up". Imagine!'

'It would be easiest if he was buried here.'

'He liked Portugal. His mother was Portuguese, you know.'

'I only heard that today, too.'

'He'd be as much at home here as anywhere. Probably more so.'

'What about young Tom Jim?'

'I'll tell him,' Miranda said firmly.

They heard footsteps outside, an imperious ring on the bell.

'He's back already,' said Carter. 'I'd better be going.'

'How can I contact you?'

'I'm in the next road, but I'm moving on Monday. Going to Arrifana up the coast. Got a job with a commercial diving company.'

He gave her his telephone number.

'You will stay for the funeral?'

'Of course. I'll arrange it for you, if you like.'

'Dear Tony,' said Miranda. 'You were always good at organizing things.'

'I haven't made much of a go at organizing myself,' he replied wryly, and kissed her gently as he said goodbye.

five

FROM WHERE THE corporal stood, thin, slight and suddenly very alone, behind a broken window in the kitchen of the burned-out Burmese bungalow, he could see ten men coming across the paddy field towards him.

They walked slowly, spread out in extended order, as he had learned to cross open country at the infantry depot. They were small men, with dark-green uniforms and puttees and yellow leather boots. They wore linen caps with strangely long peaks and a red dot instead of any regimental badge. They moved silently, and he stood transfixed, as though watching actors in a film, not something that could conceivably involve him in any way. And yet he was most desperately involved, for No. 6300414 Corporal Serrafino, J. C., at the age of nineteen, was in charge of a patrol of eight West Africans on that May Saturday afternoon in 1944. These ten men approaching were the enemy, a Japanese advance patrol.

He had taken his men into the bungalow because it seemed an ideal place to brew up some tea, have a cigarette and a brief rest. He had been warned that Japanese were in the area, of course, but it was one thing to be told this and altogether another to see them, only yards away and coming nearer with all the terrible inevitability of death.

He had examined coloured pictures of men like these in posters headed 'Know Your Enemy' at the jungle school in Comilla, but true life added a horrifying dimension to printed illustrations. They were much closer now; he could see sweat shine on their faces. The leader had a blood-soaked bandage around his right wrist. They must have no idea that the bungalow was occupied or they would not be walking so openly.

Words that Corporal Serrafino had repeated parrot-fashion so many times in training now came back to him.

'Enemy ahead. Hundred yards,' he whispered hoarsely. 'In your own time, fire.'

The West African soldier next to him fired first. The noise of the shot echoed like a cannon blast from the bare walls of the tiny room. Then the others fired hastily and the room was suddenly filled with blue smoke and the smell of cordite.

They all missed. Serrafino fired at the Japanese soldier leading the patrol – and missed him. Why the hell didn't the bastards drop? By the rules, they should have totally wiped out all ten of them – and instead they hadn't even winged one. The men were in their sights, just as his instructor had told him the perfect target should be: blade of the foresight right between the shoulders of his backsight. The range was nothing – so why, oh, why, had they missed them all?

Then one Japanese dropped down on his hands and knees, throwing away his rifle as he fell. A gout of blood gorged from his mouth, and he sank forwards on the parched brown stubble. The others fell flat and began to fire systematically at the windows of the bungalow.

The man next to Serrafino suddenly started to scream in a high-pitched, blubbering way. Serrafino turned, surprised at the noise he was making. Then he saw with horror that half the man's face had been shot away. His upper jaw and teeth looked like the jaws of cows and pigs he had seen at the butcher's shop in New Cross where he had worked briefly before he joined the Army. The man had no tongue and made a horrible moaning sound as he crouched in a foetal position on the floor.

The other West Africans also saw and heard him – and ran away through the back door.

'Wait! For Christ's sake!' shouted Serrafino, but they were already out of the bungalow, screaming incoherently in their terror. He could hear the drum of their heavy boots diminish on the stubble, and took aim again at the nearest Japanese and squeezed the trigger. Nothing happened. In his panic, he must have fired the entire magazine.

Corporal Serrafino's mind seemed frozen. He knew he had another clip of cartridges somewhere; he was certain of it, and he began to grope in his ammunition-pouch, in his pockets. But his fingers seemed numb and without direction, out of his control. By the time he found the cartridges, the Japanese were in the bungalow. He thought they would kill him at once and he threw away his rifle, and stood facing them, sweating at the approach of death. He said hoarsely and appealingly, 'Sorry about that,' as though they would obviously understand his situation, and accept his apology, man to man, nothing personal intended, an unfortunate misunderstanding.

For answer, the nearest Japanese jabbed the butt of his rifle into his face. Serrafino twisted and missed the main force of the blow, but the butt caught him on the shoulder and forced him down on his knees. The Japanese soldier stood staring down at him, perplexed.

Why did this wretched creature not take his own life? How could any man call himself a warrior and so demean himself as to be captured – and then further humiliate himself by begging for mercy on his knees?

The soldier kicked Serrafino to his feet. Serrafino staggered across the room. The wounded West African was beginning to scream now and the Japanese soldiers noticed him, as though for the first time. One took a long sliver of bamboo from his pocket and picked his teeth with it reflectively. Serrafino saw that his teeth were yellow, like his skin, even his eyes. Then he prodded the man with the bamboo, first in the neck, up his nose, in an eye. Finally, he drove the bamboo spike like a lance deep into the raw quivering mass of bloodied flesh that had been the West African's jaw.

The wounded man shrieked in agony.

Serrafino thought: I have a phial of morphia somewhere, but it's all too late now. And I've got to think of myself, not of him. I may need it. He turned away so that he did not have to meet the man's beseeching eyes.

The Japanese who had kicked Serrafino now spoke to him. Serrafino could make out a few English words like 'what' and 'unit', and he opened his mouth to reply, ready to tell them anything they wanted to know. Then suddenly the Japanese spun like a top and dropped dead at his feet.

The soldier next to him lurched back against a wall, arms outstretched as though crucified, and sank down on the floor. The others fled out into the paddy field. A hail of bullets sprayed around them, ripping through empty windows, raising puffs of plaster. As suddenly as the firing had started, it ceased. In the silence, Serrafino could hear a man running towards him across the paddy. Serrafino picked up his rifle, slammed in the cartridges. Feeling had returned to his hands, his mind unlocked.

Corporal Odongo came charging through the door. One of the Japanese was not quite dead, and Odongo raised his rifle and brought the butt down like a jungle club on the man's face.

'You got trouble, then?' he asked Serrafino casually, as though the events of the previous few moments were an everyday affair.

Serrafino nodded; he could not find words to explain his feelings.

Odongo looked down at the wounded West African on the floor.

'He'll never make it, that man,' he said with finality. Pointing his rifle at him, he squeezed the trigger. The wounded soldier jerked like a marionette and died.

'It is best,' said Odongo simply.

'Where have you been?' Serrafino asked him. Odongo should have been up with the section. He was annoyed that in his own terror he had not even noticed his absence.

'Having crap,' Odongo explained simply. 'I didn't like the look of this house. I felt safer outside. My ju-ju saved me.'

He fingered an amulet tied to a leather bootlace around his left arm.

'Then the others came running out, and told me what had happened. I thought I had better rejoin.'

'Thank God you did,' said Serrafino. 'But why shoot this poor devil? He could have recovered.'

'No,' said Odongo. 'How could he have done? We would have had to put him on a mule, take him fifty miles. How could he stand that journey with half his head shot off? It is better he die quickly. It is I who say so. Odongo. *Odongo*. . . .'

Serrafino always woke from this dream – or was it a nightmare? – at these last words. They summoned him back into the present world where he was no longer only a corporal, no longer thin, no longer afraid. He struggled into wakefulness, rubbed his hand across his eyes to drive away the memory of the recurring vision.

He was sitting in the back seat of his Mercedes, parked in a lay-by off the main road north from Lagos to Lisbon. This lay-by had several stone seats grouped around stone tables; Portuguese motorists would picnic on longer journeys, but unlike the French they did not carry chairs and tables with them. Air-conditioning made the car feel as cool as a bodega. How different from the salty, sweaty heat of the Arakan so long ago!

Odongo. . . .

Serrafino had been posted after this episode and so had not seen him again for six months, when he was on leave in Calcutta, staying with several hundred others in a local museum which had been hastily turned into a leave-centre for British soldiers. With a month's pay securely in the breast pocket of his bush-jacket, Serrafino had taken a rickshaw to Coraya Road, in the red-light area.

This was out of bounds, of course, but after dark the road was none the less jammed with taxis, rickshaws and gharries, all disgorging soldiers, airmen, sailors, British, American, Polish. The knowledgeable knocked on certain doors. Newcomers, like Serrafino, walked up and down the road until touts emerged from the shadows.

'All clean girl, sahib. All matriculate. All pink inside – just like Queen Victoria.'

Intense and furtive bargaining sessions took place: how much for how little, how little for how long? An Indian boy put out a hand and touched Serrafino on the wrist. His fingers felt hot and dry as though with fever; his eyes glowed appealingly in the dark.

'I got sister, sahib. Very fine jig-jig. Five rupees. Last price.'

Serrafino allowed himself to be led down an alleyway, through an open door and behind a curtain, into a living-room. The air felt sweet with the smell of burning joss-sticks. A servant stood pouring tea into a cracked cup for an enormous black man who looked up, frowning, as Serrafino entered.

'*Odongo*,' said Serrafino in amazement, feeling that he had somehow lost face for a second time by meeting him in such a place. Odongo smiled as though he understood how Serrafino felt, but there was something strange about his face; his eyes did not smile.

'You seeing this woman?' he asked Serrafino shortly.

'I suppose so.'

'You not to.'

'Why?'

Odongo leaned towards him. Tea slopped into the saucer. The little boy looked at them both nervously, not understanding a word, but sensing danger.

'She's unclean. She's given me a dose.'

'You sure?'

'I know.'

'You want to see the MO, then. Didn't you remember your early-treatment packet?'

'I don't bother with such things. But she will not infect anyone else. I, Odongo, will stop that.'

'How?'

'I will kill her.'

'*Kill* her? You must be mad. That won't cure you. And you'll be done for murder. Topped.'

'Who will prove it?'

'It's obvious.'

'Nothing is obvious, my friend. Only to a fool is everything obvious. I will go into her room and leave by the window. These Indians will only know a West African was here. But so were dozens of others.'

Odongo's face was shining with sweat and an elation that frightened Serrafino: the prospect of violence, the promise of murder. Serrafino remembered him firing at his wounded comrade, clubbing the Japanese soldier. He could imagine Odongo's huge bunch-of-banana fingers gripping the girl's windpipe. He shuddered.

'You *want* to kill her?' he asked.

'Of course. Wouldn't you?'

'No,' said Serrafino. 'I'm getting out of here.'

'Wait, sahib,' said the little boy. 'Other man only short time. Very best jig-jig.'

'Not for me,' said Serrafino, and went out thankfully into the hot damp night, sweet with the smell of rotting mangoes. He ran rather than walked back to the leave-centre, ignoring the entreating cries, offers, suggestions, even threats from hoarse-voiced touts in the warm dangerous shadows.

Two days later, in Chowringhee, the main street of Calcutta, he bumped into another British corporal also on leave from the West African division. They had a beer together, exchanged items of gossip. The adjutant had stepped on a mine and lost a leg; a colour sergeant's wife had written from England to say she was pregnant by a Yank; the civvy police in Calcutta were looking for some West African who had killed a tart.

'Where?'

'Knocking shop in Coraya Road.'

'What happened?'

'Bloke went berserk, throttled her and then pissed off.'

'Left no clues?'

'No. Except that he was big and black.'

'Why did he do it?'

'Perhaps he couldn't get it in.'

'Or perhaps she'd given him a dose,' replied Serrafino thoughtfully, remembering Odongo. 'Well, that's how it is, then. I'll be on my way. Got a cousin out in Alipore. Going to look him up.'

Serrafino walked back slowly to the room in the natural history section he shared with twenty other soldiers and several prehistoric skeletons. He had no cousins anywhere, but he wanted to be on his own. This must be the woman Odongo had murdered. He could not prove Odongo had killed her, of course, but he sensed that he had. Odongo was a bloody madman. And as dangerous and unpredictable as a rig, a half-cut stallion.

He still thought so, years later, when he recognized Odongo's face on his television screen. There had been a coup in one of those new African countries with funny names. The Marxist president had been overthrown and shot against a wall with all his family, even his pet dog. Hundreds of his supporters had been arrested. Captain Odongo was now in command. Under him, the army would run the country for six months to ensure stability. Then he would hold free elections. He, Odongo, had spoken.

The British Foreign and Commonwealth Office cautiously welcomed the news. Anything seemed better than a Marxist government with Cuban and Russian advisers and an increasing financial indebtedness to the West. But Odongo? Was a psychopath so much of an improvement? Serrafino wondered, but nevertheless he had written to Odongo; he sensed there could be pickings from him – if he was quick enough and smart enough.

'Remember that time in the paddy fields in the Arakan when you cleared out the Japanese, and then in Calcutta? I am glad to see you have prospered. I am sorry I cannot say the same for myself.'

This was not strictly true; Serrafino had enjoyed his share of many small-time rackets, but nothing on Odongo's scale. Why, the man had taken over an entire country.

Two weeks later, Serrafino received a telephone call from the High Commission of Menaka. An air-ticket was waiting for him in their office in Belgravia on the personal instructions of President Odongo. When Serrafino collected the ticket he saw that it was for a single outward journey, not a return. By the time he reached the capital, Odongo had promoted himself to Emperor.

Serrafino had felt rather nervous as he waited in the anteroom of Odongo's house in Menaka. This had previously been the home of the Chief Justice when Menaka, under another anglicized name, had been a colony. The judge had unfortunately been killed in an earlier revolution a few years after independence, but oil paintings of former judges, wearing robes incongruous in the heat, stared down disapprovingly at Serrafino.

He was conscious of the fact that he was Odongo's subordinate and inferior, physically and – even worse from his point of view – financially, and when the Emperor arrived in a beautifully cut tropical uniform he was also surprised to see that Odongo now wore ribbons of the Victoria Cross, the George Medal, the Distinguished Service Order with medal ribbons awarded for Second World War service as far apart as the Pacific, Italy and the North Atlantic.

'How good of you to call,' said Odongo.

His handclasp was firm, but the flesh felt unusually dry and warm as though he had a fever. Serrafino recalled the touch of the Indian boy in Calcutta, and instinctively recoiled. Odongo's eyes were more deeply sunk in his head than Serrafino remembered, and the man's voice boomed like a provincial actor declaiming a part. As he spoke, flecks of foam gathered at the corners of his mouth. Serrafino felt frightened of him; incidents of violence were still vivid in his mind. This man, once a corporal with him, had risen to rule his country, not by ability or worth, but by treachery, cruelty and murder. Worst of all, he had obviously relished every violent step of his journey.

'I wish you to stay here with me,' Odongo told him now. 'I need an adviser I can trust. White people in your country and in the United States are cunning and devious. They think I am a fool just because I am black. But I have strength of mind as well as strength of muscle. With you to guide me, there is nothing we cannot achieve.'

'That's very kind of you,' said Serrafino cautiously and then, incongruously and tactlessly and simply because it was the question uppermost in his mind, he asked: 'What happened about that little trouble you had in Calcutta?'

'Trouble, my friend? I recall no trouble of any consequence in Calcutta or anywhere else.'

'Medical business,' said Serrafino, now awkward, not wishing to remind his host directly that the last time they had met he had complained of having contracted pox.

'Ah, that.' Odongo smiled. 'It was nothing. I was cured within days. Almost instantly. Because I had faith.'

'You saw the MO?'

'I did not. I consulted a local Indian practitioner in the bazaar. He gave me a draught of medicine. Then sent me on my way.'

'And you were cured?'

'Completely. For a day or two, I had some minor irritation, then – nothing. If I had gone to the MO, the facts might have been entered in my paybook, a mark against me. I might have even lost my stripes. How odd to think what two stripes meant to me then! Last week I was elected Emperor of my country. A great honour.'

'Of course. Who elected you?'

'Who else but the one man best suited to know the path along which his country should tread to peace, power and prosperity? I, *I*, Odongo. I elected myself emperor, and you will stand at my right hand. That is my wish, my order.'

Serrafino soon discovered that his new status, as undefined as it was unexpected, offered hitherto unimaginable opportunities for enriching himself. Companies in France, Germany, Britain and the United States, whose governments had cautiously recognized Odongo's regime, largely because since it existed they could do little else, now pressed for commercial concessions.

One firm wished to export cars; another sought to supply arms; a third to overhaul water and electricity supply systems that had been badly damaged during the revolution. Odongo was secretly impressed by these polite emissaries but he turned over the actual business of decision to Serrafino, who selected the successful applicants on the offers they could make to him. Soon he had bank accounts in Switzerland, the Dutch Antilles, the Cayman Islands.

Fearing Odongo as much as he distrusted him, Serrafino felt it prudent to reveal his interest in these matters, and offered to share his commissions, as he called them, with the Emperor.

'I make my own arrangements,' Odongo replied, but was obviously moved by this gesture. 'On one thing I now insist. You are my friend. Better than my brother, closer than my own family. I ask nothing more of you than you become the second citizen of my state after me.'

'You mean, give up my British passport?'

'Of course. All that is past. The empire which we both served has gone. I remain. I, Odongo, will go forward. You will march with me, as we marched years ago, side by side, under the Burmese sun.'

It was impossible to have any conversation with Odongo in a normal tone of voice. Every discussion ended with Odongo standing up, waving a fist and shouting, the whites of his eyes darkened by blood and rhetoric, flecks of spittle foaming at his mouth. The man's mad, thought Serrafino. I'll make my pile, and get out as fast as I can.

Then something happened that made him realize how difficult this could be. Another European in Odongo's employ, an East German doctor, had the same idea: make a fortune and leave as soon as possible. He and Serrafino got on well together, for both wanted wealth and yet were not competing against each other for this prize. The doctor had been one of a team of advisers from various communist countries, and had decided to stay on when his colleagues went home. He liked the warm climate, the abundance of free whisky which the Emperor provided for his favourites, and the opportunities for personal enrichment.

'He is mad, of course,' the doctor told Serrafino once after they had shared a bottle of Glenfiddich. 'Tertiary syphilis. I've seen the symptoms time and again. They often go like this.'

'He told me he had been cured in Calcutta. With some special medicine.'

'Impossible. The symptoms can disappear early on and then the patients imagine they are cured. But it's all an illusion. For centuries, quacks have used this medical fact to their advantage. But syphilis doesn't give up so easily. It's eating away inside his body and brain all the time – and one sign is all this shouting and cruelty.'

Next day, Serrafino called on the doctor professionally; he had cut himself opening a bottle of whisky when the neck had snapped. Surprisingly, the doctor was not at home, and no one seemed to know where he was. He had simply disappeared. Serrafino mentioned this to Odongo.

'He has left,' the Emperor replied shortly.

'But I saw him last night. He didn't say anything about leaving then.'

'He did not know he was leaving – then,' Odongo explained. '*I* decided he would go.'

'*You?* But why? He's a very good doctor.'

'Was. He had the wrong ideas. He talked about his patients.'

The Emperor paused and looked at Serrafino through narrowed eyes.

'He talked about me.'

'So?'

Serrafino could not bring himself to finish the sentence.

'So he has gone. He will not be coming back.'

'You mean, you've got rid of him permanently?'

'Permanently. Or, rather, by his loose talk he has got rid of himself. As you say. Permanently.'

Serrafino realized that Odongo was growing increasingly suspicious of all his colleagues. Everyone was watched and reported on, and others watched the watchers. He was involved with a homicidal lunatic, and he must tread warily or he would also simply disappear.

With this alternative in mind, Serrafino reluctantly became a citizen of Menaka, but he kept his British passport buried in an empty cocoa-tin beneath a flagstone behind his house. It seemed safe there from termites and mildew; it was not safe from the Emperor's spies.

Odongo summoned Serrafino to his office one day, took the passport out of his desk and waved it in his face.

'I asked you to surrender this,' he began, his voice thick with anger. 'You gave me your word you would, and you had. But now I find that it still remains. I trusted you.'

'It is a mistake,' stammered Serrafino. 'I only kept it for sentimental reasons, memories, the old days.'

'They are past,' said Odongo shortly, tearing the passport into pieces. 'Finished. *Now* is our hour. I, Odongo, decree it.'

He threw the fragments on the ground. As Serrafino slunk away, he remembered he had not even made a note of the passport number, or of when it was issued. He did not dare to visit the British High Commission to ask for a new passport. He would do so in good time, he assured himself, but he knew that the buildings were under constant surveillance, and details of everyone who entered or left the gates were daily reported to Odongo. He would wait until Odongo was on a visit out of the country to Idi Amin or Bokassa, and then he would try to arrange a social meeting with one of the High Commission staff so that he could casually raise the question of another passport without going to the office. Otherwise, he could be trapped in Africa for ever; a man without a proper country, without any real identity.

This had happened to Bob Astles, who had followed Idi Amin, grown rich from Amin's patronage – and then been arrested when Amin was overthrown, and flung into jail. And, because Astles had relinquished his British passport, there he had stayed.

This was a horrifying prospect that haunted Serrafino, but he found some comfort in totting up the holdings in his various bank accounts, for they grew with surprising speed. The only depressing aspect of his wealth was that he had so little opportunity to enjoy it.

Millions of pounds and dollars in foreign aid, in the form of grants and loans that Odongo accepted, were divided between

Odongo's accounts and those of his cronies. An aircraft arrived every week from Britain, crammed with cases of whisky, brandy, rum and gin for distribution to the corporals of his army. This was the most senior army rank that Odongo had achieved by his own ability, and as his disease bit more deeply into his brain, so his sentimental attachment to corporals grew. They were the salt of the earth, he would say. The real communicators – the only link – between the men and their officers. Napoleon had been a corporal. So had Hitler.

Mr Serrafino found it surprising how quickly millions of money could disappear, and how, with equal speed, the country crumbled. Building programmes were announced for roads, hospitals, schools, but work never actually commenced. Foundation stones were laid to fanfares by military bands, Tapes were cut, salutes given and taken, and then everyone went home, for that was the end of the matter. Odongo and Serrafino and ten or twelve other of Odongo's appointees enjoyed the luxury of air-conditioned cars and palaces; the poor existed in shacks with walls of old oil-drums hammered flat, roofed with palm-fronds. These hutches, burning like ovens by day, thick with mosquitoes by night and lit only by rush-lamps, were without sanitation or running water. If the poor were lucky, they shared a standpipe between half a dozen hovels. If they were not, they carried buckets and cans to the nearest well, perhaps half a mile away.

In these conditions revolution had been inevitable; but, even so, the shock of waking to gunfire and screams and the rattle of tank tracks outside his windows had frightened Serrafino. The sounds uncovered other half-buried, half-forgotten nightmares; especially the recollection of ten Japanese advancing towards him across a paddy field.

Odongo had at first attempted to crush the revolt, as he had strangled all other earlier opposition, with the bullet, the bludgeon, the knife. But all the jails in Menaka were already full; worse, the warders had not been sufficiently bribed. Private soldiers and sergeants also resented the perks for the corporals, and many officers feared that they would join colleagues who had faced firing squads on ridiculous charges and unsubstantiated accusations. Fear and resentment drew the people together; if they did not move now, before Odongo by wild and extravagant promises could rally his supporters against them, they might never have a second chance. So the Army acted, and the tanks came out on the streets.

Odongo raced to the radio station, but the revolutionaries had already reached it before him. A hail of bullets met his car, and he drove back to his palace at even greater speed. Here, he discovered that half of his personal guards had already deserted him. Their wish to survive had overcome tribal loyalty and a reliance on his bribes. Everyone wanted to be on the winning side, and the word was that Odongo's number had finally come up.

Even so, the early gains of the revolutionaries seemed limited to the capital and the more remote parts of Menaka. The provincial towns reserved judgement, for news travelled slowly, and Odongo's name was still held in respect among people who had no first-hand knowledge of him or his rule of fear.

But Mr Serrafino sensed that the tide was running strongly against Odongo; against corruption and coercion, against murder, and fear and favouritism; against everything on which Odongo had built his empire.

Mr Serrafino usually waited for Odongo to send for him to seek his advice in drafting a speech, or framing a reply to a Western diplomat's question about human rights, or even a letter to *The Times*. But now was not the moment for delay. He drove directly to the palace, and was surprised and alarmed to see that the guards no longer stood at attention at the gates, but were lolling around smoking cigarettes, uniforms unbuttoned, rifles dirty. They did not even challenge him as he drove past.

Odongo was in what he called his throne room. On a dais at the far end, he had a huge throne copied from a picture of one he had seen in the *Illustrated London News*. It was made of dry zone mahogany, covered with thin sheets of gold leaf. He had chosen wood from this tree because it was so rare. Years previously, this particular mahogany, and ivory, had been among his country's main exports. But since independence the elephants had been shot out, and the trees cut down for firewood, although Odongo's predecessor had protected the mahogany and forbidden any of its wood to be used. Odongo immediately cancelled these orders to show his own power and importance. Now he sat on the throne, smoking a cigar and drinking brandy from an enamelled army-issue mug. His black Homburg lay on a carved stool. Now and then he glanced at it as though half-expecting that the hat would have some message for him, some comfort. The air-conditioning had broken down because of a power cut – the revolutionaries had shelled the generating station – and Odongo was sweating. His face shone like waxed ebony, and he looked at Serrafino without any comprehension: they might have been total strangers to each other.

Serrafino saw the vacuity in Odongo's eyes, the tell-tale white rim of salt around his thick blubber lips. In this mood Odongo could denounce him, have him shot as a traitor, an imperialist spy – or just as easily give him half a million dollars as a reward for loyalty.

'Emperor,' Serrafino began. 'I have a plan.'

'Plan?' replied Odongo dully. Drink and disease slurred his speech. Saliva dribbled out of his mouth.

'I have always given you good advice, you know that.'

'I know that,' repeated Odongo, almost as a question rather than an answer.

'Well. Listen to me now. Your enemies are advancing on the palace. The radio station is putting out propaganda against you – who gave everyone there his or her job. Think of the ingratitude. The guards outside the palace don't give a damn for their duties. But what I say can save you and restore you to power which has been so wrongfully seized from you.'

'I don't understand you,' said Odongo, trying to focus his eyes on Serrafino. He gulped his drink. The brandy slopped down his chin, staining his khaki drill-jacket. He reached out to touch his hat.

'You are like a great lion,' shouted Serrafino, desperate to get his message across before brandy finally stupefied his listener. 'A lion of the forest brought down by the poisoned arrows and blunted knives of evil hunters. You can destroy them all with one blow of your paw, but they are severing your arteries, your lifeblood is gushing out. I can staunch the flow. I can make strength return. Then you will push them to one side, as in the ancient days the giants of yesterday destroyed their enemies. Now, *this* is my plan. . . .'

He drew near to Odongo to whisper in his ear, afraid others might be listening. The room could be bugged, and he needed Odongo's permission to leave. When he returned, he would hold all the cards in the pack, for he would be in the position of a man who owned not only the racecourse and every horse running, but the bookmakers as well. He would make a financial killing that would place him in a league alongside such legendary figures as the Rothschilds and the Rockefellers. There could be a Serrafino high-rise building, a Serrafino Foundation. If a man could make his fortune manufacturing weapons and then give a prize for peace, as Nobel had done, nothing Serrafino could do or give could ever seem in any way incongruous.

Serrafino explained his plan as simply as he could, repeating its main points, banging his left hand into the palm of his right to force a dazed Odongo to assimilate the basic essentials.

'So, I have your permission to leave?' he said at last.

'Of course,' said Odongo. 'Of course.'

Serrafino had already typed out a letter giving him this permission, and now he handed it to Odongo with a pen. Odongo wrote his name in a huge childish hand.

'I like your pen,' he said. 'I served under an officer once with a pen like that. A Lieutenant Carmody.'

'I give it to you. It is a link with the past. With Mr Carmody and all those who have gone before,' Serrafino said, presenting him with the pen.

'You are a very good friend,' said Odongo, beginning to weep. 'My only friend.'

'All you have to do is to hold the rebels at bay for a few weeks

– if they even find where you are, which is unlikely. Then I'll be back, and together we will advance and crush them all.'

Mr Serrafino then left the palace and drove straight to the airfield. The Cessna he had ordered was ready, engine running. He flew over the rainforest and the frontiers, west towards Banjul. Within a day, he was in Lisbon putting his plan into operation.

Lisbon. . . .

Again, Serrafino struggled awake. He was on the Lisbon road and must have dozed off for the second time. Perhaps he had drunk too much too early in the day? The chauffeur was looking in his rear-view mirror and pressed the intercom button.

'He has arrived.'

A small Renault had pulled in behind them. A man climbed out, locked the door carefully, smoothed back his thinning hair. He wore a short-sleeved shirt, polyester trousers of unfashionable colour and transparent plastic sandals over grey nylon socks. He walked on tiptoe, partly out of deference to the man he was about to meet, partly because he was a person who disliked noise. He approached the Mercedes and stood for a moment by the car, unwilling to disturb anyone.

Mr Serrafino opened his door. His visitor climbed inside. Mr Serrafino did not offer him greetings or a handshake.

'What have you got for me?' he asked bluntly.

'I kept watch as instructed,' the man replied nervously. His sallow face shone with sweat, even in the chill of the air-conditioning. Mr Serrafino regarded him with distaste.

'I found that the Englishman, Carter, attended the funeral of his fellow-countryman Bridges. He appeared to know Mrs Bridges well. He held the hand of her child by the side of the grave. He returned with them to their house.'

'Did he stay long?'

'About half an hour.'

'Did he get across her?' Mr Serrafino asked crudely.

'No. I was able to observe them from the window of an empty house opposite. They appeared to sit on the settee, had a drink, two drinks actually. The boy had a Coca-Cola. There was a lot of discussion.'

'Did you bug the house?'

'It was impossible, senhor, otherwise it would have been done. However, I have a friend who has an interesting party trick. He is a lip-reader.'

'So what were they saying?'

'They were discussing the manner of Bridges' death. Mrs Bridges had no idea why her husband should have been walking on a hilltop on the coast. She believed he was in Lisbon.'

'He was in Lisbon,' agreed Mr Serrafino, as though that ended the matter. 'What else?'

'She wanted to go home to England with her son, but air passages are all booked at this time of year, and as she has a seat on the charter flight she has decided to stay on until then.'

'And Carter?'

'He assured her he would do anything he could to help her and the boy.'

'I suppose he advised her to have Bridges buried here rather than endure all the business of having the body flown home in a special coffin in case it bursts in mid-air and so on?'

'I do not know for certain, senhor, but it is likely.'

'And Carter? Is he still with her?'

'He should now be on his way to Arrifana.'

Mr Serrafino nodded briefly to show that their conversation was at an end, and opened the door for his visitor. The Mercedes drove off, leaving the man standing in the lay-by under the eucalyptus-trees. He did not return to his car until the Mercedes was out of sight. Then he walked slowly to the Renault, sat for a moment behind the wheel, mopping perspiration from his face. Christ on a plastic crucifix looked down at him from the driving-mirror. Mr de Silva made the sign of the cross. He felt he had been saved from great danger.

six

CARTER SAW THE sign to the left of the road – *Arrifana: 8 km* – and for a moment he slackened speed. Then he made up his mind and drove on for another three kilometres into the next town of Aljezur. Once he reached Arrifana he expected to start work immediately, and then, as he had found at Tim Rowley's swimming-pool, there might be very little spare time in which he could plan ahead. He felt that he needed a few moments on his own to try to analyze his mixed feelings about Mr Serrafino's offer.

He drove slowly into Aljezur, past vineyards and flat fields, brown now after the long summer. On the left a conical hill towered like a huge sandcastle above the town. Little houses perched on its sides, below a ruined castle. Shops in the main street had windows edged in blue, the colour recalling the Moorish occupation centuries earlier. Blue was their good-luck colour. I could use some good luck, Carter thought wryly as he parked on the shady side of the main street, outside a café.

He went inside, ordered a black coffee. He was the only customer, and every other shop, even the banks, seemed to be closed. It was the middle of the day; they would open again late in the afternoon.

As he sipped his coffee, he tried to find a reason for his doubts about his new assignment. He was being paid a lot of money for a month's work which surely was well within his capabilities. In the army, he had accepted without a second thought many dangerous or tedious duties. But then he had been backed by a regiment, and behind the regiment was a brigade, and behind this a corps. Now he was on his own in a strange world he did not quite understand. His uncertainties really boiled down to one question. Could he trust Mr Serrafino? He thought that, in the last analysis, he couldn't or, at least, he shouldn't. But, then, he wouldn't have to trust him for long, just for a month at the most. And even if Mr Serrafino welched on his contract, and did not pay him the second $10,000 he owed, Carter had already received $10,000. He could not lose financially, so what else could he lose?

He suddenly thought of Bridges, dead in the mortuary. He could lose his life. But surely this was being too dramatic? There was probably a very simple explanation how Bridges had lost his footing and fallen, and no evidence whatever to link Mr Serrafino with his death.

Carter paid his bill, walked back to his car, pausing for a moment to savour the sunshine. Farther along the street, half a dozen orange and white Route Nacionale buses were parked in a line, waiting for the afternoon trade. A man walked across the bridge by the side of a donkey carrying bales of hay. Three old men sat on a bench, black wide-rimmed hats over their eyes, watching him. Carter could see no other sign of life in the town and yet he had the curious feeling that other eyes were watching him from behind the carefully drawn white curtains at upper windows above the shops. But who – and why?

Perhaps they regarded all foreigners as suspect if they appeared out of the tourist season. Or maybe, because he was in a German car, they assumed he must have something to do with the diving expedition. This in turn might mean that there had been some friction between the divers and the locals. Perhaps that would be one of his first tasks to sort out?

He drove back along the road, came to the sign for Arrifana and followed the side-road up into the hills. The air soon sweetened with the smell of sage and thyme, and he could look down on Aljezur, with its castle and white houses and farms and vineyards and a long winding ribbon of river. As the road climbed, the grass grew more thinly, and yellow flowering shrubs sprouted from dry cracking earth. The heat of summer had killed other vegetation; grey leafless branches and dry fronds trembled in the wind, cactus plants sprouted on parched patches of the landscape.

The road branched left to Mount Clerico, right to Arrifana. He turned left; time spent . . ., etc. It was always wise to sound out the area around a target. Mount Clerico. Could that be translated as the Clerical Mountain, the Hill of God? If so, what did that leave for the other road – the way to hell? The idea was as absurd as the translation; but it was somehow a part of his general unease.

There was no shade now, for trees had been cut down on either side of the road. The sun beat on the roof of his car like the pounding of a drum. Several shacks of unpainted wood stood by the roadside, like huge packing-cases; a few abandoned cars without wheels; chicken-coops had stones placed against crude front doors to keep the chickens inside. Then the gradient eased and he was out of this shanty area and driving on a half-finished tarmac road, past concrete lamp-posts into a huge new housing development. Smaller roads branched off neatly on either side, leading to partly built houses of red terracotta bricks, amid wooden scaffold-poles. Clearings had been hacked out of the forest and gardens created around a few completed houses with sun-awnings and green-tiled roofs. Several were shuttered for the winter. One had a sprinkler playing on a verbena lawn, and a hundred yards farther on he saw Mr Serrafino's black Mercedes outside a newly painted front door.

He came through what would one day be the town centre, with a handful of nearly completed shops, and then he was rolling down the hill to Arrifana. This village crouched in an elbow of hills overlooking a vast sandy bay. Breakers came in slowly, almost hesitantly, as though tired after their long journey across the Atlantic and not quite certain of their reception. Small houses crouched on the hillside, grey-roofed, red-roofed with vivid blue and green walls, all facing the beach. They were shuttered and empty, the holiday homes of Lisbon families.

Summer wind had blown sand from the beach across the road

and the hillside; green shrubs poked through the sandy wastes. A few children still played among rock pools near the sea. Two young men wearing trackshoes and shorts and floppy canvas hats were buying melons and bread rolls from an old woman with a motor-tricycle in a square at the centre of the village. Behind them, next to a single-storey beach-café, were parked four caravans. The shuttered houses looked down emptily, like the faces of the dead.

Carter parked his car in the square. The men, big and blond with wispy beards, watched him warily. They had pale hostile eyes, and wore heavy leather belts, one with a fisherman's knife in a black rubber scabbard. Carter locked his car and strolled towards the nearest caravan. Mr Serrafino opened the door.

'How nice to see you,' he said warmly. 'On time, as I expected. Let me show you your quarters. This is just the office.'

'Where's the ship you're diving from?'

'*Quendon*'s just gone up the coast. We were running low on fuel oil, and needed some provisions. You can buy basic things here, but not much more.'

Mr Serrafino led the way across the square, to a house with yellow shutters. He took out a key, opened the front door, handed the key to Carter. They went inside. The house smelled damp and uninviting. Silverfish scuttled across the kitchen draining-board.

'It will look better when you get your kit in,' Mr Serrafino assured him.

'I haven't got much kit,' said Carter. 'I prefer to travel light.'

'The best way, if you can. A local woman will come in and look after you, clean the place. We bear the cost, of course.'

He was opening drawers and doors as he spoke.

'There are sheets in this cupboard. Towels here. Eating-irons.'

'That's an army expression,' said Carter.

'You should know it, as an army man,' agreed Mr Serrafino. 'I was also a soldier, years ago, in Burma. In the Second World War.'

'That's where my regiment got its name. The Golds.'

'A bit before my time,' said Serrafino. 'But I had luck there, I must admit. Made my first money.'

'Unusual, surely, in such a place – at such a time?'

'Not if you kept your wits about you. I'll tell you how it was,' he began expansively, and sat down on a cane chair. Carter opened the shutters and windows to dispel the smell of dampness.

'Actually, the war was just over, and I was in Moulmein. You remember Kipling's old Moulmein pagoda looking eastward to the sea? In fact, it looks west. Kipling got it wrong. But that is by the by. I like to be accurate, though. But where were we? Oh, yes. I was stationed in a rubber plantation. All the trees were dripping with latex like condensed milk, and the Japs had been ordered to drive in every car and truck they had seized when they invaded the country in 1942. There these cars were, lined up in rows – Buicks, Chevs, Austins, the lot. Then the officer in charge was posted home for demob. I was left. Things were running down, you see. Nobody cared much. The war was over.

'One day, a local Burmese came to see me and asked me very civilly who owned these vehicles. I said: "I don't know", he said. "They could help to rehabilitate my country." I said: "Possibly. But what's in it for me?" He said, quick as you like: "A hundred thousand rupees." '

'A lot of money,' said Carter.

'The equivalent then of nearly £8000. Not much today, agreed, but I tell you it was a fortune then.'

'So what did you do?'

'Took it, of course. What would you have done, eh? The man brought in other people every night and they drove the trucks away, several at a time.'

'But they weren't yours to sell?'

'A very good point, Mr Carter, and one that does you credit. But, if *I* hadn't sold them, someone else would. And what are a few trucks anyway? Today people are selling whole countries that are not theirs to sell. So maybe I helped Burma after all.'

'You certainly helped yourself.'

'Of course. As an educated man, Mr Carter, you are no doubt acquainted with Aesop's fables?'

'Not for a long time.'

'Then let me refresh your memory. They are full of good sense. One tells how a wagoner got his wheels bogged down to the axles in mud. So he went down on his knees and prayed to Hercules, the God of Strength, to pull his wagon out for him. And do you know what Hercules replied? No? Then I will tell you.

' "Put your *own* shoulder to the wheel," he told the wagoner. "The gods help those who help themselves." If ever I decide on a coat of arms and a motto, I will choose that, Mr Carter.'

'A most appropriate choice, too, I am sure,' replied Carter.

Next afternoon *Quendon* returned, and Mr Serrafino took him out in his speedboat to meet the divers. As the boat put-putted up against the hull, Carter was surprised to see how old and shabby *Quendon* appeared. Great blisters of raw red rust wept sea-water. They climbed up a frayed rope-ladder. The divers towered above Mr Serrafino, blond, broad-shouldered, bearded, narrow-hipped, in jeans or shorts. Several had knives in their heavy leather belts.

'You all speak English?' said Mr Serrafino, more as a question than as a statement.

'A little,' corrected one of the East Germans. He had a broken nose and a cut above his right eye, so that the lid never quite closed. His thumbs rested in the top of his belt.

'Then I will speak slowly,' Mr Serrafino replied. 'I am introducing Mr Carter. Tony Carter. He will be in charge of day-to-day routine. When I am not here, you will take orders from him.'

'Is he a diver?' asked someone.

'*You* are the divers,' corrected Mr Serrafino. '*You* know the rules, what time each shift starts, what time it finishes. But, if you are sick, Carter will arrange a doctor. If you have queries about pay, conditions, weather reports, he has the answers. I will communicate with you through him when I am not here.

He knows exactly what we're fighting against. Time, winds, tides. Especially time. Any questions?'

No one spoke. Carter thought that this definition of his duties differed considerably from Mr Serrafino's original brief to him, but this did not seem the time to mention it. Or perhaps this was simply a diplomatic way of introducing him?

Carter followed Mr Serrafino along the line of men. Carter could smell sweat overlaid with hair oil and aftershave lotion.

'This is Jan. Hans. Kurt. Franz. Ruskie.'

Carter put out his hand. No one moved. Jan put his hands deliberately in his trouser pockets. Franz looked outwards to the horizon, eyes narrow against the sun's glare reflected from the sea. His jaw moved steadily as he chewed gum. Mr Serrafino appeared not to notice their attitude. He turned to Carter and handed him a folder he had been carrying.

'Here are the times of the diving sessions. Now, I'll leave you to it.'

He signalled to a crew member to hold the rope-ladder steady while he climbed down. The speedboat headed for the shore in an arrowhead of foam. All the divers began to drift away, except for Franz.

'Have you a percentage share?' Franz asked Carter.

'In what?'

'In what we're diving for.'

'That's my business,' said Carter, not wishing to admit he was on a set fee. He should have followed his employer's example and been smarter and asked for a cut. But he had been so grateful to be offered the job that the thought had never entered his mind.

'That probably means you are, then,' said Franz grimly, misinterpreting his reply. 'My friends won't like that. I don't myself. We are doing the work. You are getting money by standing around. It's wasteful to employ people who are not needed. I hate waste. It would be healthier if you gave up your job.'

'For whom?'

'For you.'

'Maybe,' said Carter easily. 'Or it could be healthier for you and better for both of us if you shut your mouth over things that don't concern you.'

Franz smiled, put one hand in his jeans pocket, took out a metal whisky-flask, flipped it open, gulped down the spirit.

'You know Mr Serrafino's rules,' said Carter. 'No drinking at work. And in the list here you're on the next shift.'

'I make my own rules.'

'Not here, you don't.'

'Want to prove it?'

Franz slowly tightened the silver cap on the flask as though deep in thought. He removed a gobbet of chewing-gum from his mouth, pressed it carefully on to the cap, and then, with a speed surprising in such a large man, he smashed Carter in the face with the edge of the metal.

Carter had been watching Franz's eyes, not his hands. He had seen their infinitesimal narrowing prior to the blow, and was ready for it. He ducked to one side as Franz's arm shot past his head so closely that the flask scored his left ear.

For a split second, Carter was not on the deck of a shabby ship; he was back in the gym, with an army PTI shouting instructions. In a totally reflex action, he pivoted on his heels, gripped Franz's arm above the elbow and bore down on it with all his weight. Franz, not anticipating this reaction, soared over Carter's head and crashed on the deck. The flask slid from his hand. Carter kicked it away, crossed the deck and stood looking down at him. No one else moved.

'Does that answer your question?' Carter asked him gently.

Franz lay for a moment as though pole-axed, and then slowly he stood up. Other members of the crew waited, watching the two men. Suddenly, Franz jumped to his feet and butted Carter in the stomach with his head.

Carter gasped for breath with the force and unexpectedness of the attack, and brought up his knee against Franz's nose. The cartilage cracked like a pretzel stick. Franz collapsed, clawing at his nose with both hands. Carter stepped back, partly in case Franz kicked him, partly to prevent anyone from jumping on him from behind. He stood with his back against the warm white wall of the main cabin. No one moved. They waited in silence, watching Franz.

Carter nodded to Hans.

'Pick up the flask,' he told him. Hans paused for a moment, saw Carter take a half-pace towards him, bent down and picked it up. The piece of chewing-gum had become detached.

'And that,' said Carter. 'Waste not, want not.'

He turned to the other men.

'Everyone back to work,' he told them, and looked at his watch as casually as he could. 'Next shift is due on right now. Ruskie, you take Franz's place.'

The men drifted away – except for Hans, who helped Franz to his feet. Blood was still streaming from his nose, down between his fingers.

'You may be tough, Englishman,' Franz said slowly. 'But you have made a bad start.'

'I didn't start the fight,' Carter pointed out.

'Maybe you won't end it, either,' Hans replied, as he led Franz to the companionway.

Carter walked around the decks to familiarize himself with the layout of the ship. The more he saw, the more he was shocked at the slipshod appearance of everything. Empty cigarette-packets and beer-cans littered the scuppers. Davits for the lifeboats were rusty, their pulleys seized solid through the action of sun and salt without lubrication. And where, for a serious expedition in search of gold ingots, was the sophisticated diving equipment he would have thought essential for such a specialized search?

Quendon had two derricks aft that could be swung out on either side and which would presumably lift up whatever was found, but he could see no sign of diving bells, decompression chambers, air-pumps and lines that he had read modern divers used. Nor were there any underwater television cameras or monitoring screens on which controllers could see exactly where the divers were working – and warn them of any obstructions and dangers they might not be able to see for themselves.

Perhaps this equipment was too valuable and too delicate to keep on deck and was kept locked away somewhere; but, although Carter tried to accept this explanation, he was not entirely convinced. The feeling of uneasiness he had brushed aside in Aljezur returned, twice as strongly.

The speedboat that had taken Mr Serrafino back to shore now bobbed invitingly at the bottom of the rope-ladder. A man Carter had not seen before waited behind the wheel. The engine was running; a faint blue mist from the exhaust lay on the surface of the sea. Carter climbed down the ladder. The boat ducked and rocked under his weight as he jumped aboard. The man looked at Carter enquiringly.

'To the shore?' he asked him.

'Yes. You didn't bring the boat out?'

'No. We take it in turns.'

'What's your name? Mine's Carter.'

'I know. Irwin. Carl Irwin. I'm the radio operator.'

They shook hands.

'Got a pretty tough bunch here,' said Carter conversationally.

'Very much so. I would watch myself with Franz.'

'I tried to.'

'He's the head diver, sort of spokesman for the others.'

'He's done a lot of this sort of work, then?'

'I don't know about that. But he's well qualified in marine biology, ecology of the sea. Even nuclear physics.'

'So why is he a diver here and not a professor somewhere?'

'Maybe he likes the life, the contrast to academic work. Or maybe he's killing time. Like me. When my contract's up at the end of the month, I'm going to university. Heidelberg. Going to read electronics.'

He paused.

'You on a share of the profits?' he asked suddenly.

Carter smiled.

'That's what Franz wanted to know,' he replied blandly.

They approached the shore. Irwin cut the engine, swung the boat around expertly in a wide arc against the current.

'Come up and have a drink?' suggested Carter.

'You know Mr Serrafino ordered no alcohol?'

'That's for the divers. We're not diving.'

'Only one, then.'

Irwin moored the boat, followed Carter up the track into the house. Carter took two bottles of Sagres beer from the refrigerator.

'Have they found any gold so far?'

'No. Trouble is, the bottom of the sea is very sandy. But someone brought up a china plate with the name on it and a crest. *El Medina*. The divers say her holds are packed with thousands of tons of sand. I can't see how they can shift it.'

'There was that British ship, HMS *Edinburgh*, off Russia. Divers recovered millions of pounds' worth of gold from that,' Carter pointed out.

'She wasn't lying on a sandy base, though. And they weren't using the gear they've got here. It's primitive.'

'Reckon they'll find anything before the weather breaks?'

Irwin shrugged.

'I don't know,' he said, paused as though he meant to say something else, then thought better of it.

'I must be off,' he said, finishing his beer. 'We've a minibus that goes to Aljezur or Sagres most nights. Tonight it's Sagres. A good restaurant there run by Germans. Not much on here at night.'

'I can imagine,' said Carter.

He watched Irwin walk away. He could quite like the man. Only one thing disturbed him and made him cautious with any confidences. On the little finger of his right hand Irwin wore a signet ring with an unusual crest.

The last time Carter had seen that ring Jack Bridges had been wearing it.

Carter stood at the door of his house, watching the sun go down, questions chasing answers in his mind and never quite catching them. Had Irwin known Bridges so well that Bridges had given the ring to him as a present? This seemed unlikely when it had been his wife's first gift after they became engaged. Or had

Irwin simply found the ring and kept it? Was it not more likely that Irwin had some involvement with Bridges' death, or at least the discovery of his body?

The sea slowly changed colour from amber to red and then to blue-black ink. Lights flickered in a few of the houses where divers were billeted. Still damp from the ebbing tide, the shore shone like glass. By a trick of light, or perhaps because his eyes were tired, each time he looked at the cliffs and the rim of white and now distant waves it seemed as though they all moved in closer together. He had the uneasy feeling that events were also somehow closing in on him.

He shut the front door to block out these disturbing fantasies, drew the curtains and, instead of turning on the main light, lit a reading-lamp. Why am I behaving like this? he asked himself. Who could possibly be outside wanting to do me harm?

He needed a drink, and to hell with what Mrs Kent said. And he missed the company of friends. Being on his own gave him too much time to think, and thoughts soon centred on regrets, a regurgitation of what he should have done about the dangerous-driving charge. He had been a fool to resign his commission so quickly; he should have stuck things out. And this job had no more real prospects than teaching children to swim in Tim Rowley's club. Rowley. Miranda.

He wondered where she was, whether she would know if her husband had given away the signet ring – or whether he had lost it. He reached for the telephone to call her, and then remembered she was not on the phone; he would speak to Rowley instead. He felt a curious sadness at the thought that he would not be able to hear Miranda's voice. The fact was, he wanted to see her, to talk to her, to ask her advice over this and the problem of his career. In helping him she might also help herself to forget her husband's death, for what lay ahead for her now? A job? A second marriage? He dialled Rowley's number, waited impatiently until Rowley answered.

'Tony here,' he said. 'Just thought I would ring,' he added rather feebly.

'Good to hear from you,' replied Rowley with the forced

heartiness of a man who wishes he had not been disturbed but does not want to appear unfriendly. 'How's the job going?'

'Too early to say. Could be interesting. But I was really wondering about Miranda.'

'I'm having dinner with her tonight.'

'How's she bearing up?'

'Pretty well, considering. Worst part is all the paperwork. You'd never believe the trouble you cause when you die abroad.'

'I'll bear it in mind. Well, give her my best wishes. Tell her. . . .'

Carter paused.

'Hello?' said Rowley irritably. 'Hello? Are you still there?'

'Yes. If you get the chance, will you ask her about that signet ring she gave Jack? Did he lose it – or give it away? Does she know if there are any others like it? Or is it unique?'

'Well, all right. But why this sudden interest?'

'Can't say now. But it could be important.'

'Will do. Must dash. I'm late already.'

Carter put down the receiver, went into the kitchen, put three eggs in a pan with water, boiled them, made a slice of toast, opened another bottle of Sagres beer. He turned on the television set and ate this bachelor-style meal watching a Japanese film with Portuguese subtitles. Everyone spoke in high-pitched voices, men wore kohl eye-shadow. He couldn't understand what was happening, and he didn't greatly care. He must have dozed, for suddenly he was awake. The Japanese film had been replaced by an American serial. Car tyres squealed along neon-lit highways; dark-skinned men wearing sharkskin suits regarded each other malevolently from the corners of their eyes; policemen with revolvers chewed gum and telephones rang off-screen. Something had wakened him, but not this. Then he heard the noise again above the raucous nasal voices and a crescendo of music: a tiny tap on a window-pane. It might be the beak of a bird or a twig blown by the wind – except that he had never seen any nocturnal birds in Portugal, and the nearest tree was several hundred yards away. This noise seemed unnatural – and therefore dangerous. He switched off the set and the lights and stood listening. The sound continued.

'Who is it?' he called out. 'What do you want?'

'Open the door,' a voice replied in an urgent whisper, muted by the glass, but still full of entreaty; a woman's voice.

He opened the front door and stood to one side. Someone came inside quickly, closed the door behind her.

He was face to face with Celia Kent.

'What's the matter?' he asked her, greatly relieved. 'Why didn't you ring the bell? Why all this drama?'

'I don't want anyone to know I'm here.'

'There's no one out there surely?'

She did not reply and moved into the main room. He made to switch on the lights.

'Don't,' she said urgently. Her voice sounded unfamiliar, tight with emotion. Foreign. That was the word: foreign. Mrs Kent didn't sound cool and English and in control of herself and all events that could concern her, as she had appeared at their previous meetings. She was frightened, and fear had scratched the veneer of her county accent.

'But why not?' he asked her. 'What's the trouble?'

'You just rang a certain number,' she said.

'Yes. But how do you know?'

'Because, you fool, the line goes through Mr Serrafino's house. Every call in or out is monitored.'

'Bloody nosey bastard.'

'He doesn't care what happens personally. It's his scheme he is worried about.'

'What scheme?'

'I can't tell you now. It's too long.'

'Why are you here, then?'

'That ring. Why are you so interested? Who the devil are you?'

'You know damn well. You told me when we met in the bar that I'd done seven years in the Army. Then resigned my commission. I hadn't told you.'

'But what's your real job?'

'You know that, too. You got it for me. This.'

'Don't mince words. Why were you asking those questions?'

'Why shouldn't I?' he replied angrily. 'I knew Miranda Bridges long ago. Before she ever met Jack. Then I saw that the radio operator, Irwin, was wearing a ring she'd given to her husband, who was found dead the other day.'

'Did you know him?'

'Not well. Now let me ask you a few questions for a change. Did *you* know him?'

'Not well,' she replied evasively.

'So we are evens. Why the fuss?'

She looked around her nervously.

'You alone here?' she asked.

'Of course I am. Unfortunately.'

'Have you checked the house out?'

'What the hell do you mean – checked it out?'

She took a piece of paper from the pocket of her jeans and a stub of pencil and wrote: *Is it bugged?*

He shrugged his shoulders.

'There are a few things I would like to tell you about the job. They could help you,' she said, speaking slowly as though for the benefit of any hidden microphone.

'Thank you very much,' Carter replied in the same stilted tone.

She scribbled on the paper: *Bring car to back door without lights.*

He nodded.

'Shall we have a drink?' he asked her.

She shook her head, but he clinked two glasses together on a brass tray in case someone was listening. Then he went out of the front door, crossed the square, unlocked his car, aware all the while that he was tensing his back muscles in an unconscious reflex action to help him deflect a blow or a bullet. Carter had done this many times in Northern Ireland, but had hoped that such feelings were far behind him. Wrongly, it seemed.

He opened the car door a little way, felt inside to switch off the interior light before it could light up. Then he jumped in behind the wheel, drove around as quietly as he could to the back of the house. Here, a white wall surrounded a small tiled courtyard behind the kitchen door, which was used for hanging out clothes to dry and for storing gas-cylinders for the cooker. He sat, engine running, waiting for Celia Kent. She did not appear. He switched off the engine, wound down the window. He could hear nothing except the distant roar and murmur of the sea, uneasy as a great beast in slumber. Why was she so long?

Carter climbed out of the car, walked into the courtyard. Perhaps she was trying to come through the kitchen in the dark and had missed her way? On a washing-line, three white tea-towels flapped like flags of surrender. A bundle of clothes lay on the tiles. What the devil were they doing there at this time of night? He crossed to them, and then knelt down by the crumpled body of Celia Kent.

'Are you all right?' he asked her softly. Perhaps she had fainted or tripped and hit her head. She did not reply. He rolled her over gently, feeling for her pulse. There was no beat. Under the moonlight he saw a tiny hole like a third eye above the bridge of her nose. A .20 bullet, he thought professionally; anything larger would have splintered the skull.

Carter had seen no one else and heard nothing, but someone must have been waiting in the courtyard. Probably someone else had been waiting in front, and if he had come out with her they might have picked him off as well. He opened the back door, pulled her body into the kitchen, drew the curtains, turned on the light.

What had she wanted to tell him? Had she been trying to warn him, or help him – or both? He opened her handbag. It contained lipstick, a folded handkerchief, a pearl-handled pistol, cocked, with the safety-catch on.

He uncocked it, slipped it into his back pocket, shut the handbag. Then he went into the drawing-room. By the telephone lay a typed list of numbers he might need: a local doctor, the post office at Aljezur, the coastguard station, Mr Serrafino.

He would ring the doctor first. He picked up the telephone, but the line was dead.

He jiggled the telephone rest up and down. He recognized from past experience the symptoms of a cut wire. He had no idea where the doctor lived, so he would have to report personally to Mr Serrafino. After all, he was the employer, he was in charge.

Carter turned out the light, lifted one side of the curtain and looked out across the moonlit square. It appeared deserted, empty as a dead man's eyes. But, then, he had seen no one before, and somewhere a killer had been hiding. He had not heard anyone move away, so he – or she – could still be out there watching, waiting.

He walked across the room, opened a small casement window on the far side of the house, climbed out as quietly as he could. Bent double, he raced across the patch of moonlight to the safety of the shadows. Then he paused and looked back. The window was open, kitchen light still burning behind its curtains. Beyond the house the sea lay unexpectedly calm. Two or three lights moved slowly across the water as the local fishing fleet headed south towards Sagres. The café was closed, windows shuttered. The moon threw long shadows from parked cars on the sandy forecourt. Up in the hills, lights shone in uncurtained windows of the houses where the divers lived. Somewhere music was playing, and Carter heard a sudden rise and fall of frenetic studio applause. Two stray dogs, standing on their hind legs to reach the rubbish in a dustbin, paused and looked towards Carter suspiciously. The moon shone yellow in their eyes.

He did not want to risk going round the house to his car, and so he kept in the shadows, pausing always before he crossed any open space from house to house as he climbed the steep rocky road to the top of the hill. Here, he looked back at the bay. *Quendon* lay silhouetted against the moonlight on the silvery sea. A few lights glowed from portholes. The village square appeared empty. He turned and walked on.

By each side of the deserted stretch of road ahead, weeds

trembled in the breeze. He paused now and then to look back, listening, in case he was being followed, but the only sounds were the diminishing roar of the surf and the castanet rattle of dried thistles in the waste patches of land.

A Spanish-style lantern was burning in the porch of Mr Serrafino's house. Carter knocked at the front door. A dog barked, then Mr Serrafino's harsh voice silenced the animal. A man Carter had never seen before opened the door and looked at him enquiringly.

'Mr Serrafino. Most urgent.'

Mr Serrafino peered over the man's shoulder.

'Goodness, Mr Carter! What's the matter? You look as white as a sheet. Has something happened?'

'Yes.'

'Come in and tell me about it. And have a drink to perk you up.'

'Thank you. I will. A brandy.'

The man who had opened the door produced a bottle of brandy and a glass on a tray. Carter poured himself four fingers, drank them thankfully. Mr Serrafino looked at him disapprovingly, like a father regarding an erring but pampered son.

'Now, what brings you here in such a state?'

'I have some grave news, Mr Serrafino. About your daughter, Mrs Kent.'

'Really? What about her? What's happened?'

Mr Serrafino's smooth face creased with concern.

'I'm sorry to have to tell you – more sorry than I can put into words – she's dead.'

'*Dead?* Has there been an accident? Where? How?'

Mr Serrafino crossed the room, and stood looking at him in astonishment.

'She called on me a few moments ago to see if everything was all right, had I settled in and so on. She was only in the house for about five minutes, and I was going to run her back in the car. I went out, started it up. But she didn't appear. So I went to see if anything was wrong and there she was – shot. She was lying in the back courtyard. Dead.'

'*Dead? Shot?* No one's shooting partridge at this hour of night.

'I don't think they were after partridge, Mr Serrafino. Whoever shot her wanted to hit her – or me.'

'I can't believe it. I hear that in the officers' mess they frequently indulge in what I call a schoolboy type of humour. But, please, we are adults. Tell me, is this a joke?'

'I wish it were. But unfortunately it's the truth. You had better come down and see for yourself.'

'Have you telephoned the police? The doctor? She may have just had a fit or something. Fainted.'

'The line is cut. I couldn't get through. That's why I came up here to see you.'

He watched Mr Serrafino as he spoke, feeling sorrow for a father who had lost his daughter. But he did not appear greatly grieved. Concerned; yes. Worried; a little. Surely, while a father might not weep openly, his face would at least show sadness at the death of his daughter?

Carter said: 'I am especially sorry because she was your daughter.'

'How kind of you to be so sympathetic. But I must tell you, she was not *really* my daughter. Only in the broadest sense did I regard her as such. And she did me the great honour of thinking of me in a fatherly light.'

He paused.

'You walked here, Mr Carter?'

Carter nodded. Mr Serrafino turned to the man who had opened the door.

'Bring the car around,' he told him.

They sat in the back in silence on the drive down the hill. The driver switched off his engine, they all climbed out. Carter opened the front door with his key.

'She's in here,' he said, and crossed the hall into the main room. Then he stood in the doorway, staring in astonishment at the carpet.

Celia Kent's body had gone. It might never have been there. Perhaps it never had been? Carter felt the same almost overwhelming sense of disbelief that he had experienced when the colonel had accused him of driving Akbar Khan's Ferrari: he had been, but not at the time of the accident. Mrs Kent's body had been here, but it wasn't here now.

Mr Serrafino looked at him quizzically.

'Well, where is the corpse you speak of?'

'I have no idea. But it was here. Right where I'm standing.'

'It can't have been. Or, if she *was* lying here, Celia most certainly wasn't dead. As I said, she must have fainted.'

'She *was* dead,' retorted Carter stubbornly. 'I've seen enough dead people not to make a mistake. I felt her pulse. She had a bullet-hole between her eyes.'

Carter knelt down, looked across the red polished tiles towards the kitchen door. The surface showed two faint streaks where heels could have dragged. He pointed out these marks to Mr Serrafino.

'Anyone moving a chair or a side-table could have made them,' he replied irritably. 'I find all this quite extraordinary, Mr Carter. How did you leave the house?'

'Through the window.'

'The window? What was wrong with the door?'

'I thought someone might be waiting outside it to shoot me.'

'Have you been drinking, Mr Carter?'

'Only your brandy.'

'Any before?'

'Well, a small drink of beer.'

'I see. So after what you call a small drink – a beer, apparently – you jump out of a window rather than use your own front door. Then you run up to me, to tell me that the dear lady I regard as my daughter has been shot, murdered, and bring me down here. And now there is no sign of her, and the room is empty. You're *sure* you feel all right, Mr Carter?'

'I'm all right. Of course I am.'

'I find that difficult to accept. Now. let us understand each other. We have a business arrangement, remember. I have hired you for a large fee to keep my divers up to scratch – and what do you do?

'Your first day here you are involved in a fight with one of my best men. Not simply a diver, but a graduate of Leipzig University with various first-class degrees. Not a rough man, but a man of great culture and learning, whose judgement I regard highly and whose experience is vital to our whole operation. You hit him so hard for no reason that I can discover that only by the greatest good fortune is his nose not broken. Had that happened, of course, I could have been forced to abandon the whole expedition.

'As if that is not enough, this happens. I must say, I find your behaviour very unsatisfactory. You have had two chances, Mr Carter. I will not give you a third.'

He nodded towards the driver, who went out to start the car. Carter shut the front door behind him, before Serrafino could leave, and slammed home the bolt.

'Now, look here, Mr Serrafino,' he said. 'Let's talk as in Germany, *unter vier Augen* – eye to eye – while your strong man is away. I *know* Mrs Kent was shot because I was here. *I* didn't pick a fight with Franz. He picked one with me. You are accusing me of odd behaviour, but let me tell you something. I don't like men who eavesdrop when I use the telephone.'

Mr Serrafino's eyes narrowed. He glanced uneasily towards the door. The servant shouted through the wood.

'Are you all right, Mr Serrafino? Shall I come in?'

'He's all right,' Carter told him. 'Stay where you are.'

'I don't take orders from you, Englishman.'

'I'm not giving you orders, just advice.'

'Everything is under control, Juan,' called Mr Serrafino nervously.

'So why do you listen in?;

'Calls from all the houses and caravans happen to go through a private exchange in my house.'

'Then, you happen to know I made a call to São Sebastião? Mrs Kent knew that. So presumably you did.'

'I know nothing about it.'

'In that case, I will return your compliment and give *you* some advice, Mr Serrafino. If you won't give me any more chances, I will extend the same to you. I just want to do my job, be paid, and then get the hell out of here as soon as possible.'

'I can assure you, Mr Carter, I will do everything in my power not to delay your departure.'

Carter waited in the doorway, watching the tail-lights of the Mercedes climb the hill and disappear. Then he shut the door and paused for a moment, wondering what he should do. In the distance, faintly, he heard the put-put of a small engine starting. He opened the door, puzzled by the sound of an outboard motor after dark. The moon was briefly obscured by drifting clouds, and he could only make out the position of *Quendon* from her riding-lights. The noise of the little engine diminished and died.

It must be a small fishing boat, he told himself, but questions still nagged at his mind. Had the engine stopped because whoever was aboard had put out a line, or because the motor-boat had tied up at her buoy? Either was unlikely because the sound had been growing fainter as he listened. So perhaps someone was ferrying a crewman out to *Quendon*? He shrugged his shoulders, shut the door again, locked it and went into his bedroom, switched on the light.

The room looked as though it had been the centre of an explosion. All the drawers were ripped out of the dressing-table and their contents tipped up on the floor. His trousers and jackets had been torn from the cupboard and sleeves and pockets hastily turned inside out. The mattress was upside down by the side of the bed, slit by a knife, horsehair stuffing bulging from it. The pillows had been cut into strips, and piles of white feathers on the bed resembled the down of some gigantic bird.

His portable alarm radio was still by the side of the bed, his underwater watch on the bedside table, a fountain pen, even his passport on the floor. So whoever had done this had not been casual thieves. They must have been after something specific: something they thought was in his possession. Perhaps Mrs Kent had also found out too much about it – or too little. *But what could it be?*

Carter looked at his face in the dressing-table mirror. He was grey and tired, his skin tight above his cheekbones. He felt the salty taste of fear in his mouth. He switched off the light, shut the door, went into the kitchen.

A man was sitting in the rocking-chair, head back, feet outstretched. He turned and looked up at Carter with languid eyes.

'*Akbar*,' said Carter, his voice taut with astonishment.

'You know what that name means in my language?' said Akbar Khan. 'It means *news*. Judging from your conversation out there, you have much to tell me.'

'And you owe me an explanation, too. How the hell did you get here?'

'My usual form of locomotion. Two feet, half a dozen credit cards – and my father's money. And when your front door was shut I came in through that window.'

'Did you see anyone here? Or hear anyone?'

'No. Nothing.'

'How did you know *I* was here, then?'

When Carter had needed Akbar after the accident, there had been neither sight nor sound of him. Now, far too late to help him, here he was, smiling and pleasant as ever, as though nothing whatever had happened. And, of course, nothing unpleasant had happened to Akbar. In his position, Carter could also have been smiling and urbane.

'You don't seem very pleased to see me,' said Akbar, frowning. 'Aren't you even going to offer me a drink? We had a few last time we met, as I recall.'

'Too many,' said Carter.

'Didn't notice it. You seemed pretty sober to me.'

Carter went into the other room, took a bottle of Borges from the cupboard, filled two glasses.

'Here you are, then.'

'You seem a bit grudging about it,' said Akbar Khan. 'What the hell's the matter?'

'You know damn well what's the matter. You ruin my career, and when you could have saved it with one word you go to ground. I couldn't find you. No one could. Even your own High Commission said they didn't know where you were. Now, when all that's over, you turn up here large as life and, to be quite honest, Akbar Khan, twice as bloody nauseating.'

Akbar stared at him in amazement.

'I don't understand you. What are you getting at? *I* have ruined *your* career?'

'I'll put it in more simple words, then. We were out in your Ferrari in Dorset. You were driving. Right?'

'Right.'

'So there's an accident. Someone's killed. I am knocked out. You disappear. OK so far?'

'Go on.'

'Various characters in the mess said they saw me driving your car – which was quite true. I *was* driving as far as the road, then you took over. So where was Moses when the light went out?'

'How's that ruined your career?'

'Because the Golds are stuffy and rather old-fashioned. They like honour, integrity, and so on. I insisted I wasn't driving, but three impartial witnesses said otherwise. They were right. I was right, too, but it was three to one. It looked as though I was lying to save my skin. I didn't have to resign my commission, but not to do so could have been more unpleasant.'

'Well, let me tell you something,' said Akbar, serious now. 'I had no idea of any of this. I didn't realize you had become involved in any way. Obviously, I would have admitted to anyone I was driving – if only I'd been asked. I'd no idea it was a fatal accident.'

'No? Well, it's too late to admit it now. You should have done so then.'

'I couldn't.'

'Or wouldn't?'

'Let me tell you what happened.'

'I know what happened.'

'On my side. Your country thinks mine is pretty important, because of its minerals, uranium deposits and so on. So do lots of others. The Eastern Bloc. Syrians. Libyans. Cubans. You name them. There is always the risk of trouble from one quarter or another, so in England, where my name unfortunately appears in too many gossip columns, I have a bodyguard.'

'Where the hell were they in the Ferrari? Hanging underneath by their thumbs?'

'Hardly. They were actually two hundred yards behind us, all the way. When I crashed, they thought it was an ambush. They had me out of that car and away within seconds.'

'And what then?'

'They reported to the Foreign and Commonwealth Office that there had been an accident, and I went back to the High Commission. Then I heard about my father.'

'What about him?'

'He had died suddenly. He'd had a bad heart for years.'

'So you are now head of state of Abukali?'

'Technically, yes. But my uncle, my father's brother, is disputing the succession. He'd like to be number one man. And he's not too fussy about how he presses his claim.'

'I see.'

This did put a rather different complexion on things. At last Carter could understand why he had been unable to contact Akbar Khan, how a wall of silence had separated them.

'I'm sorry,' he said awkwardly. 'I didn't realize any of this.'

'You couldn't be expected to. I'm more sorry than I can say about your commission. I had no idea whatever that you were so deeply involved. Perhaps I could put a word in for you there, ask whoever deals with these things to think again?'

'It's too late,' said Carter. 'You can't backtrack in the Army. But to come back to my first question. How did you know I was here?'

'Quite simple. I was out of the country, I had to go to Africa. On my return to England I tried to contact you, but no one seemed to know where you were. Except the Army. You are still on the reserve, you know. Will be called up in time of war, they say. So I found out you were down in São Sebastião with Tim Rowley. He wasn't there, but someone in his office gave me this address. So here I am.'

'On your own, or with a bodyguard?'

'Travelling light this time. On my own.'

'Well, while you seem to have gone up in the world, Akbar Khan, I've come down. I'm in charge of a group of East German divers here, searching for sunken gold, of all things. And all I did for Tim Rowley was to be a glorified swimming-pool attendant. But it was damn good of him to give me a job at all. No one else did.'

'What's that fellow who brought you back got to do with sunken gold?'

'Everything. He's my boss. Mr Serrafino. He hired me. You saw him?'

'Yes. But he didn't see me. I didn't want him to see me.'

'Why not?'

'Because he might jump to the wrong conclusions, and when that man jumps to any conclusions it can mean trouble. He's bad news, Mr Serrafino. A greedy little man who wants desperately to become a greedy big man. Rather like the frog in Aesop's fable.'

'Don't you start. He's already quoted Aesop to me. Surprising for a man of his sort, I thought.'

'Nothing's surprising about him — except his wealth and how he made it.'

'But at least he has given me a job.'

'And himself a huge bonus at the same time, I've no doubt. How did you meet him?'

'Through a woman. A Mrs Kent.'

'Who's she?'

'Who *was* she. She's dead.'

'Recently?'

'Under half an hour ago. Shot.'

'Shot? An accident?'

'If you consider being shot right between the eyes outside my back door here an accident, yes.'

'What the devil do you mean?' asked Akbar.

Carter told him.

'Know anything about her background?' Akbar enquired.

'Nothing. She was said to be Mr Serrafino's daughter.'

'That's a lie for a start.'

'I know. Serrafino told me he only regarded her as his daughter.'

'Interesting. Mr Serrafino has – shall we say? – a certain reputation in Africa. For years he has been behind that vile murderous character who called himself Emperor Odongo. His country shares a frontier with mine, so I know a lot about him.

'These new dictators like Odongo usually have men of Serrafino's type behind them, to write their speeches, tell them what to do, how to react. That other lunatic Bokassa, who thought he was the reincarnation of Napoleon, who had a suit sewn with 2000 diamonds and ruled from a golden throne, surrounded by an imperial guard of women in kinky uniforms, he had a Frenchman in the background.

'Idi Amin in Uganda had Bob Astles. When Amin promoted himself President, Astles wormed his way in and ended up with all the usual perks of office. Amin could hardly write his own name, let alone a speech, but Astles had the gift of words. Serrafino is in the same tradition, but cleverer – and richer.

'He has a rag-bag mind for proverbs and aphorisms which he passes off as the wisdom of the ages. That greatly impresses Odongo. So friend Serrafino cuts himself a large slice of the financial cake. When Odongo bought himself a jet for $2½ million, Serrafino took a ten-per-cent commission. Then Serrafino suggested Odongo should start his own bank using all the handouts that woolly liberals and do-gooders in the West gave him. Why bother to rob people when you can have your own bank?

'He's used people and then had them killed, either in fake accidents or after equally suspect trials for capital offences. I think that he – or Odongo, or both – could be trying to do himself some good through my uncle's aspirations. That's why I'm not keen for him to know I'm here.'

'Serrafino doesn't seem interested in crossing any borders here, surely?'

'For him, there are no borders. He'll have passports in half a dozen names and nationalities, probably most of them diplomatic passports. He goes where he can make money. He must be worth millions and millions, but money is an addictive drug. You either have none or you never have enough.'

'I'm in the first category,' said Carter. 'But hoping for promotion.'

'Maybe, if you find gold, you'll get it. What sort of equipment have you got out there in *Quendon*?'

'Not too much. I saw wetsuits, but no oxygen-cylinders or underwater television cameras.'

'They can't be going down very deeply, then. They'd need a diving bell and all kinds of tubes to supply helium and oxygen if they were. Even piped hot water to keep divers warm, because at any real depth divers lose body heat so quickly they can flake out. Sounds a pretty amateur operation to me.'

'Not necessarily,' said Carter. 'There's a lot of diving at this level done all around the Portuguese coast every summer. It isn't particularly sophisticated, but it doesn't need to be. The water is clear and at the right time of year there are no currents. It's cheaper to hire several men to dive in relays than to hire a huge ship like *Stephaniturm* the team used that brought up millions of pounds of Russian gold from the cruiser *Edinburgh* off Murmansk. This is totally different. You just don't need to go to that expense. Anyway, there it is. So far as I'm concerned, Serrafino's paying me well. Now, I take it you've eaten? There's not much here except eggs, if you haven't.'

'We stopped on the way.'

'*We?* What do you mean? Who's with you?'

'Miranda and her son, Tom Jim.'

'You mean you've brought them up here, too? Where are they?'

'I've just put Tom Jim to bed, and waited until he fell asleep. He doesn't like it in a strange house and he's been moved about a lot recently,' said Miranda from the doorway.

'This is *wonderful*,' said Carter, cheering up at the sight of her.

'She's had a letter from her husband,' said Akbar. 'I thought you should see it. She was going out to dinner with Tim but I suggested she cancelled that and delivered it here in person.'

'A letter?' said Carter, disappointed. This didn't sound as though she had come to Arrifana to see him. 'Was it delayed? How has it just arrived?'

'You know what the postal system can be like out here. According to the postmark it's taken ten days to reach me.'

'Where was it posted?'

'Aljezur,' said Akbar.

'That's only about three miles away. I stopped there on my way here,' said Carter. 'What did he say?'

'Read it.'

She took an envelope out of her pocket, handed it to Carter. Inside was a grey cover torn off a National Westminster Bank chequebook. He remembered seeing a chequebook with its back cover missing in the Lagos police mortuary. A message was scribbled on one side in pencil: 'Miranda, Ring 0820653142. Give my name. Tell him Fortissimo. In greatest haste. Jack.'

'Mean anything to you?' Carter asked her.

Miranda shook her head.

'It's a Lagos telephone number,' Carter said. 'I know the code well enough after living here all the summer. Have you rung it?'

'My house doesn't have a phone. Can we use yours?'

'No,' said Carter. 'All lines go through my employer's house. He listens in.'

'Is there a public box around here?'

'I'm not going to find one tonight. I'll go to Aljezur tomorrow morning, and ring from the post office.'

The postmistress in Aljezur wore a black bombazine dress and was cranking the handle of a primitive telephone exchange when Carter arrived. She looked up at him enquiringly as she pushed home the two plugs and threw the main switch.

'You speak English?' he asked her.

'A little.'

'Thank you. I would like to make a call to 0820653142.'

She dialled the number, pointed to one of three booths at the back of the entrance-hall.

'Number One,' she said. He went into it, shut the sliding concertina door, picked up the receiver.

A voice said: ' 'Allo, 'allo.'

'Hello,' said Carter. 'You speak English?'

'I do.'

'I have a message. Fortissimo.'

The man at the other end of the wire did not reply.

'Are you there?' Carter asked him, fearing he had been cut off.

'I am. I seem to recognize your voice.'

'I recognize yours, too, Mr de Silva. We met in the Nautilus bar the other night.'

'Of course. So we did. But, despite the message, I did not know Mr Bridges.'

'No one has mentioned him,' said Carter. 'Even so, I think it important that we meet very soon.'

'Where?'

Carter thought for a moment. He wanted somewhere in the open air to minimize the chance of being overheard or, worse still, being rushed and attacked. But who the devil would want to attack him? As he asked himself that question, he asked another: who had wanted Bridges dead – or Mrs Kent?

'Carrapateira,' he said, giving the name of one of the longest beaches in the Algarve, about twenty miles to the south, near Sagres.

'Whereabouts?'

'The cliff overlooking the beach. A track goes right to the top. I'll see you up there. My car is a green BMW.'

'When?'

'An hour.'

'It is very difficult,' said Mr de Silva uneasily. 'I have an appointment in an hour.'

'I know. With me.'

Carter rang off.

'That will be fifty escudos,' said the woman. He gave her the money and walked to the door, and then, as though on an impulse, turned back.

'I wonder if you could help me.'

He took out the envelope of Bridges' letter.

'It's a private bet,' he said. 'You understand "bet"?'

'A wager?'

'Yes. Can you remember anyone bringing this envelope into your office here to post it?'

She turned it over, shook her head.

'Most are posted in the box outside. Was there anything special about this?'

'There might have been. It could have had a banknote clipped to it. Fifty escudos.'

'Ah, senhor. I do remember *that*. A young man came in and said he had found it on a beach.'

'What did you tell him?'

'I told him simply: "Post the letter and keep the money."'

'An admirable order of priorities. Do you know who he was?'

'No idea. A visitor, I suppose.'

'Which beach did he find it?'

'I think he said Arrifana. Perhaps he was part of your wager, eh? The English are very – how do you say? – *sportive*.'

'Very,' Carter agreed without enthusiasm. 'I often wish it were otherwise.'

The village of Carrapateira stands at the mouth of a wide dried-up river. To the left on the main road, going south, flat land like paddy fields stretches towards the hills. A pagoda-shaped building gives an added eastern appearance. When he saw it, Carter immediately thought of Burma and the Golds and their action at Mandalay.

To the right lay a vast sandy expanse of beach, reached by a track bounded on either side by cactus plants. A morning wind was whipping the sand to a fine abrasive mist where the track divided. One branch led to the beach, and the other up a hill. Carter took this road. It ended on the cliff-top in a grey outcrop of rock scattered with gorse and herbs. Here, throughout the summer, patient locals would squat on Saturdays and Sundays with enormously long fishing-rods, their lines dangling down to the sea against the harsh grey granite of the cliff-face. Picnickers' cars and caravans were usually parked one behind the other, rocking on their springs, as the strong Atlantic wind came in from the sea. Now only one small Renault was parked here, prudently facing the road. Mr de Silva climbed out as Carter approached. Carter beckoned him into his own car.

De Silva stood for a moment cautiously, watching him. Carter appeared to be alone, but that did not mean that he was on his own. A lifetime of side-deals, of offering different services to different people – a runner here, an adviser there, sometimes a petty blackmailer or a contact man – had made de Silva wary. So he shook his head.

'I like the open air,' he explained. 'I have spent too much of my time cooped up in offices.'

This was not the real reason, of course. He had spent very little of his time in offices but, as a cautious man, he felt safer outside the confines of a stranger's car.

Carter nodded towards de Silva's Renault.

'I see you've brought Gamba with you. As a guard dog?'

De Silva smiled.

'Not exactly. I'll let him out for a walk.'

'Won't he go home?'

'Only if I tell him. Otherwise, he stays by me. He's pretty loyal.'

'I wish I could say the same for humans,' said Carter. 'You're wondering how I got your number? It's not in the directory.'

Carter did not know whether it was or wasn't, but he realized he had been right when de Silva showed surprise.

'How *did* you get it, then?'

'From a mutual acquaintance. He didn't have much to say for himself when we saw him on the slab in Lagos mortuary.'

'I don't understand you.'

'Name of Bridges. Remember? He posted a letter to his widow before he died. Not a long letter. Just your telephone number and one word: Fortissimo. Mean anything?'

'No. I don't think so.'

'You have a good memory, Mr de Silva?'

'Not especially so, no.'

'I think you should cultivate it, then. If you concentrate, you will discover what it means.'

Carter's right hand shot out and gripped de Silva's jacket lapel. He turned him around easily, pressed him back against the bonnet of his car. The wind lifted de Silva's thin hair. His tie flapped wildly like a pennant. His eyes stared wildly in two directions. Far beneath them, in a mist of spray, heavy Atlantic waves pounded the empty beach.

'It means survival, so far as you are concerned. And what else?'

'There's no need for violence, Mr Carter.'

'There hasn't been any – yet. And when your memory comes back there won't be any. Now, why should a dead man write to his wife giving her your telephone number?'

'I have no idea. Please let me go. Let us conduct this discussion in a more civilized way, Mr Carter. You are not in the Army now.'

Carter released his hold.

'I haven't got all day to argue the toss with you,' he said. 'So let's get straight to the heart of things. First, what exactly is your job in the British consulate?'

'A sort of liaison man, if you like,' Mr de Silva explained. 'I have a lot of contacts. I can help people who need a restaurant licence, say, or a planning application. If there's a death, I can smooth some of the formalities for the relatives. That sort of thing. In a purely freelance capacity, of course.'

'Of course. Who else do you work for in the same freelance capacity?'

'Anyone who finds my services of use.'

'Mr Serrafino? Which of your services does he find of use?'

'Really nothing. Nothing important at all.'

'Are you sure?'

'I know.'

'So why should Bridges ask his wife to ring you? It seems he hadn't time to write a proper letter. Just a codeword and your phone number.'

'I have no idea.'

'Then, find one. Now.'

Carter turned slightly to one side so that de Silva could see his fist clench. De Silva swallowed. This big man could break his jaw with one blow, and then what would happen to him? He saw himself in a Portuguese hospital ward, wired up, unable to speak, unable to eat, being fed from a drip. He swallowed again.

'All right,' he said. 'It can only mean one thing. Mr Serrafino has found what he is looking for.'

'Gold?'

De Silva nodded very quickly.

'Gold,' he agreed hastily – so hastily that Carter guessed he had reached the wrong conclusion.

'Or what else?' he asked.

'What else is there? I don't know, Mr Carter.'

Carter raised his fist slightly and slowly. Again, de Silva saw the movement and read his intentions. Already he could feel the splinters of bone, his mouth filled with broken teeth and salt blood. He was suffering future pain by proxy. How true Shakespeare had been to write that cowards die many times before their death.

He held up his right hand in surrender. The wind had suddenly blown away his breath, and he felt very weak. His heart fluttered like a caged bird in his narrow chest. How little need he say? What would this English idiot believe?

'I will tell you, Mr Carter,' he said at last, with all the sincerity he could muster. 'I think Serrafino's on to something more valuable than gold.'

'Like what?'

'I don't know. It's no good trying to punch me because I just do not know. If I did, I would have capitalized on it. Right?'

'You could be. What's that got to do with Bridges' death?'

'Maybe he discovered what it was.'

'Why should he? How was he involved?'

'I heard he was in Arrifana.'

'You saw him yourself?'

'No. But I have informants. Maybe he took a trip south by boat and fell off.'

'Or was pushed?'

'I don't know. This is just a supposition, of course, Mr Carter. The matter could be dangerous if you dug too far.'

'To you – or to me?'

'To both of us. Mr Serrafino is a hard man.'

'Do you know Mrs Kent?'

'I have her acquaintance, yes.'

'Seen her recently?'

'A couple of days ago.'

'What is her occupation, exactly?'

'Mr Carter, I have to tell you, she was my wife.'

'How do you mean – *was*?'

'I mean in the sense that she no longer is my wife. I divorced her. Desertion.'

'When?'

'This year.'

'She told me her husband's name was Kent. That this was the only thing he had ever given her.'

'Women are not always truthful, Mr Carter, when it comes to matters of this sort. I gave her rather more. The promise of British citizenship. In anticipation of this she called herself Mrs Kent. She thought that Kent was probably a more – shall I say? – English-sounding name than mine.'

'She was not born in England, then?'

'She wasn't, Mr Carter. But, above all else, she wanted to be English. My wife was born in Sofia.'

Carter remembered Celia's slightly foreign accent when she came to see him in Arrifana and had been terrified in case anyone saw her.

'Partly because of work I have done from time to time for the British government,' de Sylva went on, 'I was able to secure her the promise of British citizenship.'

'But she hasn't got it yet?'

'It has been definitely promised.'

'And then she left you?'

'That is so, Mr Carter. But why all these questions? Why is my life – or hers – of any interest to you?'

'Because, Mr de Silva, I am very sorry to bring you bad news. Celia Kent – or Celia de Silva – was killed last night. Shot dead. Outside my house in Arrifana.'

'Shot dead? But by whom? Why?'

De Silva's voice sounded hoarse with horror and disbelief. Words trembled indecisively on his tongue. One eye regarded Carter closely, the other stared blankly at the sea.

'If I knew, I would tell you. But I don't. What I do know – or, rather, suspect – is that you could also be in some danger, Mr de Silva.'

'Me? But why me – and who from?'

De Silva's haggard face showed his anguish. His hands were shaking. Carter felt sorry for him, a player in a game outside his league, the little fellow in a big man's world. De Silva wiped his forehead with his handkerchief, dabbed his lips. The wind flattened his shirt to his thin body.

'Come with me to the Nautilus – where we first met,' Carter suggested gently. 'I'm calling there in any case, and a drink would set you up. Set us both up, come to that. Then maybe we can have a talk about Mr Bridges and his message – and your wife.'

'Thank you, but no. Not today. Not now. Your news has been a heavy blow to me. Even though we were divorced, we were still on friendly terms. I tried to make her happy, Mr Carter, but to try was not good enough for her. She was a perfectionist. Success was all. Like Oscar Wilde said, women worship success. I like a drink, Mr Carter. She could not abide alcohol. She had a saying, "When the wine's in, the wit's out." '

'She made her views clear at our first meeting,' Carter replied. Each drink killed so many brain cells, she said. How many, exactly? Was it thousands or millions? Maybe if he hadn't drunk so much throughout the summer he'd be making a better go of finding who killed her and where her body was now. And also the reason why de Silva had not asked him either question – or even how he knew she was dead. Did de Silva already know the answers – or did he simply not care?

'If you won't drink with me,' Carter said. 'At least call in and see me. And as soon as you can. I'm in most evenings. But don't use the phone. It's tapped.'

He gave de Silva his address in Arrifana.

'I will do that,' de Silva promised, breathing more easily, colour returning to his cheeks. 'I give you my word.'

Carter crossed to his car.

'Staying here or coming down behind me?'

'I'll stay on for a few minutes,' said de Silva. 'I want to consider what you have told me, think what I'm going to do. I will visit you, I promise, Mr Carter.'

Carter climbed into his car, drove down the ridged bumpy track between gorse-bushes tossing their yellow flowers in the rising wind. He glanced in his mirror as he drove; de Silva was still standing facing the sea. From the set of his shoulders, he appeared dejected; down, if not quite out.

De Silva half-turned to watch Carter's car descend, trailing a frond of dust, and then move like a swiftly diminishing bright bead towards the main road. He wanted to be sure that Carter had actually left. Then he leaned on the bonnet of his Renault, feeling the comforting warmth from the engine through the thin stuff of his suit. He was in no hurry to leave. He had nowhere particular to go, no one he wanted to see – and it could be that the Englishman was right, and people might want to see him. In all these unexpected circumstances, it would be prudent to stay away from his house for a few days, and also very easy to arrange. He had friends who owed him favours. He had, of course, no intention of visiting Carter; he wasn't sure whether Carter believed his story about Celia Kent. It would be best to keep out of everyone's way for a few days. Then, when Serrafino had sailed away, he would surface. Eventually, someone would pay him a lot of money for the information he had to sell.

The thought was comforting; and yet, as he approached the car and saw Gamba jumping up and down excitedly in the passenger-seat expecting a walk, a doubt grew in his mind. De

Silva nodded to the little dog soothingly, as much as to say: I will let you out in a minute, but I have more important things on my mind. And he had; the most important matter that could occupy any man's mind: survival.

It was useless carrying in his head all this dangerous knowledge he had amassed. It needed to be written down, or recorded somewhere. Then it could be used as currency or collateral. It was impossible to sit in the car in this windy place and write, but he had a tiny tape-recorder.

He climbed in behind the wheel, pushed Gamba off his lap, took the Pearlcorder from the dashboard locker, checked that the cassette was new, and began to dictate. The wind rocked the car on its springs and Gamba whined, not understanding this delay in taking him for a walk. When de Silva finished dictating, he removed the cassette, slipped it into its transparent plastic case, no larger than two postage stamps, put the recorder back in the locker, and looked at Gamba.

'All right,' he said. 'It's a walk for you. A long walk. Home. You understand?'

The dog wagged its tail and began to jump up and down excitedly on the front seat. De Silva opened the first-aid case he always carried in the car, took out a strip of sticking plaster. With this he bound the cassette in its minute case to Gamba's collar, then climbed out of the car. Gamba jumped after him. De Silva stroked his head.

'Home,' he said. 'Home.'

The dog ran around the car two or three times, sniffing the ground, then gave a little bark of excitement, and set off.

De Silva saw with approval that he did not follow the zig-zag track but ran direct through the dried grass. He watched him out of sight, then climbed back into his car and drove down the hill very slowly. He thought of many questions he should have asked Carter. From Carter's answers he might have learned exactly how much he knew, what he suspected. But he had lost his opportunity. He didn't like that. His living had been made by recognizing all opportunities, not letting one pass by. Perhaps he was getting old or the strain was beginning to tell?

He leaned across the dashboard to switch on his radio; music would cheer him up.

He was tuning to Lisbon, and momentarily had his eyes off the road, when some latent instinct, sharpened by years of serving many masters, warned him of danger. De Silva braked violently and stopped within feet of a brown Allegro parked across the road.

He cursed the driver under his breath. Probably some stupid courting couple who had gone into the bushes, or out-of-season tourists who had parked their car carelessly to find a better view from the cliffs, never imagining another car was parked even higher up. The Allegro certainly hadn't been there when he arrived. He jabbed his horn button irritably. The beep-beep sounded thin and empty against the wind, like the bleat of a sheep. He climbed out of his car and shouted: 'Anyone about? You're blocking the way.'

'I know,' a voice replied behind him. 'That's why we stopped.'

De Silva turned quickly. Franz and two of the other divers were standing six feet behind him on the track. Arms folded, they regarded him with amused contempt.

'Well, move your car, then. I can't get past otherwise.'

'We want to talk with you,' Franz told him.

'Right. But move the car first.'

To de Silva's surprise, they all walked down to the Allegro. Franz climbed in behind the wheel, started the engine. Then he began to reverse up the hill. De Silva's mind raced at the speed of his terrified heart, for he suddenly realized that Franz wasn't going to drive off the road at all. He was simply going to back the Allegro into his car, and then he would be totally trapped. How the devil had they followed him here? Did they know about Celia – or about Bridges' message?

As Franz revved the engine, de Silva started to run up the track. The surface was fluffy with soft sand, and the smooth leather soles of his city shoes would not grip, and were in any case totally unsuited to speed. He slipped and stumbled, and he heard someone shout behind him, and then the increasing beat of younger feet pursuing him. If he could reach the top of the cliff, he knew a secret way down to the beach that would bring him on to a lower footpath. Then he would be within sight and sound of a friend's house, and he would be safe.

He ran on desperately, panting for breath, and suddenly the footsteps behind him ceased to follow him. He did not dare to turn his head, for this would slow him down, so he did not know that Franz had simply moved to one side to pull tight a loose strand of piano wire he had covered with sand with just such a chase in mind. Now this trip-wire leaped up across the track, taut as a violin string, just ahead of him and less than a foot above the ground. De Silva caught his foot in it, tripped, stumbled, lost his balance and catapulted forwards.

As he fell he could see the rocks several hundred feet beneath, streaming with foaming water. He lay on the ground, inches from the edge of the cliff, gasping for breath.

'You must take more care,' Franz advised him sarcastically. 'You might have fallen over, like the Englishman Bridges. You need us to look after you.'

De Silva screamed in protest as they picked him up and carried him down to their car, but the wind swept away his cries for help. A few seabirds circled cautiously overhead, disturbed by his shouts, but they soon glided back to their nests; the noise did not endanger them.

The Germans dumped de Silva in the front seat, next to Franz at the wheel. As the car bumped down the track, the radio telephone buzzed. Hans picked up the receiver. A voice said: 'Subject driving green BMW is approaching São Sebastião.'

'Keep out of sight,' Hans told him brusquely. 'We will make contact.' He replaced the handset.

De Silva shouted desperately: 'Help! Help! I've been kidnapped! Help!'

'Shut up,' ordered Franz roughly. 'There's no one to hear you. Save your breath to tell us how much Carter knows – and what his real job is.'

'I know nothing about him,' replied de Silva. 'Nothing.'

The car reached the main road, and he looked out at cork forests stretching to infinity on either side. There was no help there, no one who would see or hear him; or, if someone did see him waving his arms to attract attention, they would ignore him, put him down as simply another drunken foreign tourist.

Perhaps, if he told these divers a little, they would let him go, or at least not hurt him? He could not bear the prospect of physical violence. De Silva began to talk, hesitantly at first, and then with a rush as he began to realize the full horror of his predicament, one man against three.

He kept going back over each incident he described, repeating himself, adding and subtracting motives, thoughts, finally saying almost anything that came into his tortured mind because he felt that while he talked they would not hurt him. This had worked with Carter, so why couldn't it work with them? Speech was his insurance against violence.

He was so concerned with amplifying what he had already said, dredging for new words of explanation, with his mouth dry and his throat hoarse, that he did not see Franz glance in the rear-view mirror and then give a slight nod to Hans in the back seat.

De Silva felt the tiny jab of the hypodermic through the sleeve of his shirt like the harmless bite of an insect, and when he brushed his arm and turned and saw the spine of the needle with the bead of fluid still weeping at its point, like a tear of mourning, the poison was already in his bloodstream.

Franz stopped the car outside the hospital, put on a pair of sunglasses and golfing-gloves and went into the outpatients' department. The waiting-room was crowded. Patients sat on benches ranged around the whitewashed walls. Those too ill to sit lay full length, with worried relatives by their side, mopping perspiration from their faces. Franz nodded to an orderly who was counting pills into a round cardboard carton for a patient, and then pointed to a collapsible wheelchair under a window.

'For an emergency,' he explained in English. 'He can't walk.'

The orderly nodded permission. Some tourist, no doubt. Well, he could wait his turn like the rest. Franz wheeled the chair out to the car. Hans and Irwin lifted de Silva carefully into it. His head lolled forwards over his chest. They rearranged him so that his head lay back and then they closed his eyes. Franz pushed him slowly into the outpatients' department.

'What's the matter with him?' the orderly asked without much interest, handing over the pills.

'Fell and hit his head, playing golf. We were asked to bring him in as we had a car. Never seen him before. Don't even know his name. Hang on, I'll get his papers for you.'

Franz went out of the building, climbed into the car and drove away. The orderly waited for a few moments and then went outside to look for him. The street was empty. He shrugged his shoulders. Tourists! He crossed to de Silva still sitting in the wheelchair, head back. Odd, the man had not moved. The orderly lifted one of his eyelids, and then felt his pulse. His face suddenly wrinkled with alarm. He ripped open de Silva's shirt and applied a stethoscope to his chest. He could hear no heartbeat, register no breathing. Mr de Silva was dead.

Miranda paused as she walked across the beach at Arrifana while Tom Jim bent down to pick up a smooth white pebble. She saw with surprise that he already held half a dozen like it in his hand.

'What do you want them for?' she asked him.

'Don't you remember?' he replied reproachfully.

'Remember what?'

'With Dad. When we were at the seaside last time. He could throw them and make them skim on the water. I want to do that, too. He promised he'd show me how.'

They walked on towards the sea.

'Can you do it, Mummy?' he asked her.

'I'll try.'

He handed her a pebble, warm from his hand. Miranda threw it hesitantly at the water. The stone disappeared instantly.

'That's no good,' Tom Jim said scathingly.

He tried himself, with no better results, until he had used up all the pebbles. Then he wiped the palms of his hands on the sides of his trousers.

'Do you think Uncle Tony can make them skim?'

'You must ask him.'

'Or Mr Khan?'

'I don't know. I think, possibly, they both can. Maybe they could teach you.'

They would, too, if they were here, she felt certain of that. But Akbar Khan had driven off early that morning, soon after Carter had left for the post office in Aljezur, explaining he had a business appointment in Evora, east of Lisbon, several hours' drive away. Without either of them here, Miranda felt lonely. Yet, as a widow, loneliness was something she had better adjust to; and the quicker the better.

Tom Jim's voice scattered her thoughts.

'Do *you* like Uncle Tony, Mummy?'

'Uncle Tony? We knew each other years ago,' she said, avoiding a direct answer. 'Before I met Dad.'

'You think Dad's in heaven now?'

'I think he's happy,' his mother assured him gravely.

'Wasn't he happy here with you and me?'

'Of course he was,' she said at once.

'I wonder what he is doing *actually*? At this very moment?'

'It's difficult to say,' she said. 'But I expect he is interested in what we are doing. You and me.'

'Do you think he can see us? We can't see him.'

'I just feel he's watching over us, somehow.'

'I think you are right, Mummy. I feel like that, too,' he said gravely. 'I'm glad he's happy.'

Tom Jim held out his hand. She gripped it, her eyes filling with tears at her son's concern.

They walked on.

Jack was never really happy with me, she thought, and I wasn't happy with him. We should have parted years ago. No doubt we would have done so if it hadn't been for Tom Jim. I wonder if he knew that we didn't really get on? They say children notice everything.

Theirs had been an attraction of opposites. She was a contemplative person who loved music and painting and conversation; Jack was a man of action. A doctor friend had described their two types of personality as cautical and thelamic. One was activated by direct physical response – you met an insult with a blow – the other with a more reasoned and diplomatic reaction.

Jack had been the first man she had met who thought in such simple direct terms. For him, people and things were either good or bad, their motives black or white. There was no grey in between, no middle ground of compromise or extenuating circumstances. His viewpoint made life appear very simple, clear-cut, compartmentalized. But when she knew him better she realized too late that this approach offered him no lasting solution to anything other than the simplest problems. He might silence criticism by an angry retort or the threat of violence, but that silence was only temporary. The criticism was not answered, nor was it stilled. And what in the beginning could have been resolved by a soft answer, a willingness to agree that the other person had a point of view, however mistaken that might be, gradually became a bitter point of contention, a kind of cruel game with each side eager to score points.

Jack's work had taken him overseas more and more, and they were both secretly glad of this. She felt disloyal at the relief she felt each time she waved goodbye at the airport, knowing that for the next two or three weeks she and Tom Jim would be on their own, safe from sudden bursts of temper over trivial causes, or irrational attacks on people her husband had suddenly decided he did not like.

She thought it likely that most marriages began with an attraction of opposites, as the magnet is initially drawn to the iron, and when or if that early attraction faded the partners could be left in a curious, unhappy, unsatisfactory limbo land. She and Jack could each see the other's good points, but better from a distance, when they were apart. Together, their characters rubbed raw. Death of a marriage partner often seemed to canonize them in the mind of the one left alive, but she was too honest to pretend that she had loved Jack. She would miss him of course, for they had shared years together, and she had borne his son, but that was a loss time would certainly heal, and in the end to have lost, never to have loved, was better than to love and lose.

She was still young, of course, and people would say she should marry again. In the meantime, she had a degree in politics, philosophy and economics – but so had probably hundreds of thousands of other women of her age. It was not a very unusual or marketable commodity. Like other friends whose marriages had failed, she might face a future of writing applications for jobs advertised in the Sunday newspapers, waiting for replies that did not arrive. Another marriage appeared on the surface to be the easier answer, but after her experience with Jack she knew that this presented infinitely greater problems. Most men of her age, or just a little older, were already married. And, if they weren't, there was usually a reason, either sexual or selfish. Why should she think she might succeed where others had failed or turned them down?

She thought of Tony Carter, Akbar Khan. She was disappointed in Carter. At Oxford he had appeared so confident of his own career, so sure he would succeed, and yet within a few years the dream appeared to have faded. He had been working all summer as a children's swimming instructor in a second-rate holiday complex. Now he was in charge of a handful of East German divers seeking some sunken gold treasure. The difference between promise and performance was immeasurable, and yet she could not quite understand where Carter had failed. He was headstrong, of course, and outspoken, but these were characteristics that could be controlled by a wife or girlfriend. Perhaps with someone who could counsel patience, who would help him to assess the merits and pitfalls of several courses of action open to him, he might have made different decisions. Or was this simply a frequently held feminine point of view about any man who had attracted them, even superficially? And did Carter still attract – or did he only present her with a challenge? Confucius might have been accurate when he said that the road to success was filled with wives pushing their husbands along but, for this to apply, the husband had to be willing to be pushed in what his wife believed was the right direction. Perhaps Tony Carter, like her husband, would resent her pressure, misjudging advice for criticism.

And Akbar Khan, what about him? She had only met him a few times in company with Jack or Tim Rowley or Tony Carter; he was pleasant and friendly but he had put on weight, and she had hardly recognized him when he had first called at her house only days before. She could not see a future with him in some African state, embroiled in politics of left and right, black and white, and was certain that she held no attraction for him. But where *could* she see a future for herself?

She paused on the long shining beach, looking out at *Quendon*. Tony Carter should be back soon. Then tomorrow he would go on duty, whatever these duties entailed. She wondered about the gold lying for nearly fifty years beneath that shining sea. One bar of that gold could solve all her problems. Two would make her wealthy. But she had as much chance or hope of finding any gold as of walking on the water out to the ship. As she stood, she saw a man walk down the far end of the beach. Two other men held a motorboat steady while he waded out into the water and climbed aboard. He was plump, small, bald. This must be Mr Serrafino, whom Carter had mentioned.

Miranda didn't like the look of him, even from a distance; but, then, there was no reason why she should. He was simply another rich, ageing man of little physical appeal. Without his wealth, he would be grotesque, but gold had a rare glitter of its own. The rich man's jokes were always funny.

Tom Jim turned to his mother.

'That's the owner of *Quendon*,' he told her. 'Or at least he's hired it.'

'How do you know?' she asked him.

'Mr Khan told me. I don't think he likes him.'

'What makes you say that?'

'He told me to keep away from him. Said he was a bad man. I don't like the look of him, either, Mummy.'

'Doesn't mean to say he is bad. After all, he's given Uncle

Tony a job. Maybe there is some good in him. And he can't help his appearance.'

Why did she always have to take an opposing view? she asked herself. Did she really like an argument, or was it simply to assert her own personality, to prove she had a personal opinion and was not simply her husband's echo? Well, that was past now: she was her own woman, no one else's. And even that was not so agreeable as it had appeared when she was a wife and not a widow.

'Anyhow, he's going,' said Tom Jim.

'What do you mean, going?'

'I was listening outside the café early this morning. He was there with several divers from the ship. He told them to pack up, they were leaving tonight.'

'You're certain?'

'I know, Mummy.'

'You shouldn't listen to other people's conversations. Did he notice you?'

'No. I crouched down on the ground, very small.'

'If he is a bad man, he mightn't like you listening to what he was saying.'

'I know that, Mummy. That's why I was crouching down on the ground.'

Miranda smiled.

'Well, don't do it again. You are absolutely *sure* they are going?'

'Of course.'

'I wonder if Uncle Tony knows.'

'Well, you can tell him.'

'He's not here.'

'He will be soon,' said the boy, looking at his watch.

'You like him, don't you?'

'Yes. And he's promised to bring me a present.'

'That's very kind of him. Do you know what it is?'

'No. But it will be something nice. He's a nice uncle, Mummy.'

seven

CARTER DROVE SLOWLY down the main street of São Sebastião, looking for a place to park. Although the summer season was over, cars were still jammed bumper to bumper on each side of the road. Many retired people found it cheaper and infinitely more agreeable to rent flats and houses for a month or two in the early autumn than to stay in Britain or Germany or Sweden. He saw an alley near the Nautilus bar, backed into this, switched off his engine. He wanted to collect the envelope of money he had left with Manuel.

The door to the Nautilus bar was propped open with a wedge; the barman had been swabbing the marble floor. His face brightened as he saw Carter.

'Brandy Alexander, senhor?' he asked hopefully.

'The same. And one for you.'

'Thank you, senhor.'

They walked up to the bar together. Manuel lifted the flap, went behind it for the brandy and crême de cacao and a shaker.

'Been away for a few days, otherwise I would have called in earlier for those pictures I left with you,' Carter explained.

'No problem, senhor. They are still all right. Perhaps a little cold, eh? But that shouldn't affect your friend, though.'

They raised glasses to each other.

'I will have them now while I remember,' said Carter.

Manuel opened the refrigerator door, took out an envelope.

'Have you another envelope I can put them in?' Carter asked him. 'As you say, they do feel a bit chilly.'

'Of course.'

Carter scribbled a note on the back of a menu while the barman searched for a thick manila envelope. Carter put the note in the new envelope with the money, sealed it up, addressed it to the manager of his bank in Lagos. He did not want to carry so much cash around in his pocket; his training had taught him that the mail was a safer place. He paid for the drinks, turned to leave. Manuel was reluctant to see him go; he did not have too many customers so late in the season, and nothing puts off a potential drinker more than seeing a bar is empty.

'Funny thing,' he said conversationally, hoping to delay Carter's departure. 'Someone was asking for you only a few minutes ago.'

'Who?'

'A man rang up. Didn't give his name. Said he was a friend. Wondered if I had seen you. He must want to get in touch with you pretty badly.'

'What makes you say that?'

'I have been over this morning to that bar opposite where you used to live. He'd telephoned there, too, but they didn't know where you were. Perhaps he is your friend worrying about those pictures, eh?'

'Perhaps. Did he sound Portuguese?'

'No. Nor English. But, well, foreign. Perhaps German or French?'

'And you say it was just a few minutes ago?'

'Only moments before you came through the door, senhor.'

Carter made up his mind, handed the barman a thousand-escudos note.

'Do me another favour, will you?'

'If I can.'

'I would be obliged if you could post this letter for me. The post office is right at the far end of town and it's difficult to turn my car with all those idiots parked on both sides of the road.'

'Of course,' said the barman. 'As a matter of fact, I was on my way down there when you arrived. I was going to see my brother-in-law, the Fiscal, who lives next to the post office. His wife has just had a baby. A boy.'

'Give him a drink from me.'

'He will be very pleased to accept. But the fact is, he is feeling sad. He may be posted away shortly.'

'Why's that?'

'Because nothing ever happens here, senhor. No accidents, not even a punch-up. Nothing for a Fiscal to do all through the summer.'

'Some would say that's a good sign,' said Carter.

'Possibly, senhor. But it helps promotion, if you show you are busy. And, as a father, he will need the money. I know that. I have two children, and a third is expected.'

Manuel picked up the envelope. As he busied himself with a bunch of keys, locked the safe and the cash-register, a moving shadow darkened the frosted glass of the front door. A car stopped. A door slammed. The car moved on. There should be nothing odd in that, yet to Carter there was. Some basic animal or chemical reaction tightened the hair on his scalp. He crossed the bar, looked out through the one small plain pane of glass the door contained. Franz and Irwin were outside, waiting for Hans, who was walking back from where he had parked the car.

'I will see you, senhor,' said the barman, picking up his keys.

'I hope so,' said Carter. 'In the meantime, I would like to change drinks. I'll have a Bloody Mary.'

'Please mix it yourself, senhor.'

The barman placed a silver tray, with bottles of tomato juice and Worcester sauce, a pepper-pot and salt-cellar, on the counter in front of Carter.

'That's real Russian vodka,' he said. 'Not your local stuff.'

He walked towards the door.

'Leave it open,' said Carter. 'We might have some customers. And when you see your brother-in-law, bring him back. He needs cheering up and I'd like to drink his health here.'

'I will be delighted,' said the barman. 'And so will he.'

And so, with any luck, will I, thought Carter.

Franz stood to one side as Manuel came out of the door. Then he entered the bar, followed by Hans and Irwin. They walked slowly, like cowboys in a Western, Carter thought as he shook some pepper into his tomato juice. The pouring-holes were clogged; Bloody Mary was not the most popular drink in the Nautilus. He unscrewed the top and then turned on his stool to face the newcomers.

'Alone?' asked Franz.

'For the moment, yes. Will you join me for a drink? Let bygones be bygones, and so on.'

'I will never drink with you,' retorted Franz shortly. He kicked the wedge away from the door. It swung shut on a heavy spring.

'There's no one to serve a drink, anyway,' Hans pointed out.

'There's me,' said Carter.

They came up to within six feet of him and stood watching him, thumbs in their belts.

'If you won't drink, why come into a bar?' Carter asked, hoping his concern did not sound in his voice.

'We happened to see your car,' Franz explained.

'I'm surprised. It's not parked outside.'

'It was pointed out to us.'

'Ah.'

So he had either been followed or someone was already in town and watching him. Carter looked at them all in turn. Irwin blushed.

'We would like to ask you some questions,' said Franz.

'About what?'

'A man called de Silva. You met him on the cliffs at Carrapateira.'

'What about that?'

'That's what we want to know.'

'What business is it of yours?'

'That is our affair. Are you going to tell us?'

'Nothing much to tell. I met him in the bar here a few days ago. He was waiting to see the widow of an Englishman who had been killed falling down a ravine. Mr de Silva said he was working for the British consulate. So that's your answer. Now let me ask you a question, Irwin. Where did you get that ring on your finger?'

'Bought it in an antique-shop in Lagos.'

'Not so,' said Carter.

'What the hell do you mean – "not so"?' asked Franz angrily, elbowing Irwin aside so that he could come closer to Carter to swing a punch. 'Are you calling my friend a liar?'

'Yes. And maybe a murderer. That ring belonged to the Englishman I mentioned who was killed near Castelejo. You probably know more about that than I know about de Silva. Perhaps we should exchange information.'

He leaned back against the bar as though pleased with this proposal, and his hand went out casually towards the tray. Franz lunged at him. Carter saw the blow coming, seized the pepper-pot and threw its contents into his face. Franz screamed with surprise and pain as the pepper blinded him. Carter jumped off the stool, picked up the bottle of Worcester sauce and drove it like a ram into Hans' face. The glass splintered. He screamed and staggered away as the sharp vinegary fluid burned his eyes like acid. Carter hit him on the side of his head with a bar-stool. Hans collapsed on the floor.

'Don't hit me!' cried Irwin. 'Don't hit me.'

He ran back a few paces and stood, staring at Carter in terror. Carter ignored him. Franz was blundering around like a blinded beast, arms flailing. Carter tripped him and, as he fell, brought down the stool on the back of his head. He did not move. Now Carter turned to Irwin. He took Mrs Kent's pistol from his back pocket, cocked it, pointed it at Irwin's stomach.

'Talk,' he told him roughly. 'Where did you get that ring?'

'He gave it to me.'

He pointed at Franz.

'Why should he?' began Carter, and then realized.

'Next time,' he said, 'find yourself a stronger protector. Was he in Castelejo?'

'Yes.'

'Doing what?'

'He had to meet someone.'

'The Englishman?'

'I don't know. He was away for a whole morning. When he

got back, he gave me this ring. He told me he'd bought it in an antique-shop in Lagos. Then he told me the truth.'

'If I had a daughter, I'd give her the advice I'm giving you now. Never believe what *any* man tells you. Ever. What about de Sylva? Why the interest?'

Hans was regaining consciousness. He started to groan and claw at his lacerated face. Carter planted the stool across his shoulders, sat on it.

'I don't know anything about that,' said Irwin nervously.

'No? Well, think how you'd feel dead – or with a face like his.' He nodded down at Hans. 'I'll give you three. One.'

Irwin said nothing. He was mesmerized by the gun, seeing death and eternity in its tiny muzzle.

'Two.'

Irwin found his voice, shrill and terrified and hoarse.

'I don't know,' he said desperately.

'Three.'

Carter swung around and fired at the broken sauce-bottle on the floor. The glass shattered into tiny frosted diamond fragments. Irwin stared at them in horror.

'That's what your face will look like, and the nearest plastic surgeon is two hundred miles away in Lisbon. For the last time, who is de Sylva?'

'He was a contact man. Mr Serrafino used him to find out things. Who he should approach for permissions or licences. What the opposition were doing.'

'Was? Isn't he still?'

Irwin swallowed nervously, looked at Franz and Hans on the floor.

'I don't speak English very well,' he said at last. 'I don't know anything more about him.'

'What opposition, then?'

'Honest to God, I don't know. Possibly others are after the same loot. People will do almost anything for gold.'

Carter picked up the cocktail-shaker, tossed it in his hand as though testing its weight.

'Don't hit me,' cried Irwin. 'I beg of you, don't hit me!'

'I wouldn't spoil the shaker,' said Carter thoughtfully.

A shadow darkened the frosted-glass door. Manuel came in with his brother-in-law, who wore the grey uniform of the Fiscal Guard, with polished Sam Browne belt and revolver in a black leather holster. Both men were beaming. Carter palmed Mrs Kent's pistol into his back pocket.

'Ah, senhor,' said Manuel's brother-in-law as he approached Carter. 'How kind of you to ask me to drink with you. It will be my pleasure.'

'As they say in England, let's wet the baby's head,' said Carter expansively. 'After all, your country and mine are the world's oldest allies.'

'How true, senhor. It is good to remember such things in these days when friendship and loyalty are rare virtues. I will have a Scotch whisky, if I may.'

'A treble for Father,' Carter told Manuel. 'Whatever you want for yourself. An *agua mineral* for me.'

Both men had reached the bar now and stood looking down in amazement at the two East Germans on the floor in a pool of brown sauce, like dried blood.

'What has happened, senhor? Who are these men?'

'I can tell you, but later. They attacked me.' Carter explained. 'They came in, started to become abusive, then the bigger one hit me without any provocation, and the other fellow thought he'd have a go. Mr Irwin here was a witness. That is what happened, isn't it?'

'Yes,' agreed Irwin reluctantly, hoping his two colleagues could not hear his treachery.

'Violence to a foreign visitor means arrest in Portugal,' explained the Fiscal Guard gravely. 'Especially violence to a British subject.'

'An ally?' Carter handed him the whisky.

'Of course, senhor. Always.'

'Here's to your son's long life, good health and future wealth,' said Carter, raising his glass. 'And may he, like us, continue to foster friendship between our two peoples. As you say, always.'

He paused and added, almost as an afterthought: 'And possibly your actions here will influence the decisions of those who decide such things, and allow you to continue your service in São Sebastião.'

'I will drink to that,' replied the Fiscal, and did so.

'They asked me about a Mr de Silva,' Carter continued. 'I first met him here a few nights ago. Remember, Manuel?'

'Of course, senhor. José de Silva usually comes in when he is in São Sebastião. I saw him this morning. When he heard I was going out to see my brother-in-law, he offered to take Gamba for a walk.'

'Did he say where he was going?'

Manuel shook his head.

'I met him about an hour ago on the cliff-top at Carrapateira,' said Carter. 'When I left him he seemed in good form. But when I asked Mr Irwin here about him he said he *was* a contact man. Not is, remember, but *was*. The past tense. I hope nothing's happened to him.'

'It's unlikely,' said Manuel. 'I think José can look after himself.'

Carter turned to the Fiscal.

'If I may suggest it, I'd call your station and order a truck to haul these characters away. It might be an idea to stop at the hospital to look at their cuts and bruises. We don't want any foolish talk of police brutality.'

'A good idea, senhor. I know the orderly in the outpatients' department. He owes me a favour. He will help me.'

Akbar Khan stopped his car in the square outside the church of St Francis in Evora, climbed out and stood for a moment stretching his arms and legs after his long drive. This was his first visit to a city that had been old when the Romans arrived nearly 2000 years previously on their way north to France and Britain. After them, over many centuries, came the Visigoths, the Moors and, latterly, armies of tourists. The Romans had left the most enduring marks of all these invaders: wide streets, cool squares, an aqueduct that still towered above surrounding buildings. Their temple to Diana was so well built that the locals used it as a municipal slaughterhouse during the nineteenth century – which, thought Akbar, said more for Roman construction standards than for Portuguese architectural appreciation.

When the Moors took over, they ruled until the twelfth century. Then the Christians captured Evora, led by an outlawed knight, Gerald the Fearless, who climbed the city walls at midnight using a ladder of lances. He had earlier seduced the Moorish governor's daughter, and on his instruction she unlocked the city's main gates for his men. Akbar thought sadly, as he contemplated the church, that no one seemed to know the end of the matter. Did Gerald's bravery mean the end of his banishment? Did he marry the girl – or did he just ride away and leave her? Life was full of unsatisfactory loose ends, unfinished business. People were used, betrayed, abandoned, often for the wrong reasons; sometimes, it seemed, for no reason at all.

As he crossed the cobbles, and climbed the steps to the church, one of the giant bells boomed in the tower. He recalled the African belief that mission bells do not ring to summon the faithful to prayer so much as to mark the swift passage of time and the approach of eternity; so little done, so much to do.

He pushed open one of the heavy wooden doors, and walked inside. A marble tessellated floor of black and white tiles stretched ahead like a giant chessboard. On either side candles lit in memory of the dead fluttered in black metal holders, hung with white wax. The scent of incense was strong, and the quietness of the church was accentuated by the heavy tick of a clock. Above him, the roof soared up on curved arches. Masons, carpenters, painters, craftsmen of many skills, had given their best work over the best years of their working lives to fashion this house of God as a mark of love and faith. And now so few believed in anything, Akbar thought; not even in themselves.

He walked on towards the side-chapel known as Capela dos Ossos – the Chapel of Bones. The letter he had received from a business-house in Lisbon dealing with the export of Portuguese figs had suggested this meeting. He had met the man who signed the letter as William Best only once before, in a flat off Sloane Street in London, when Mr Best had informed him of the sudden death of Akbar's father in West Africa, and the unexpected problems about the succession.

Best had not appeared to have anything to do with figs then. Indeed, Akbar Khan had been told before their meeting that he was a specialist in African affairs, by which Akbar assumed that the Foreign and Commonwealth Office meant political rather than romantic ones. Perhaps Mr Best had other interests in trade – or perhaps he was involved in what was generally referred to with studied vagueness as Intelligence or Security. Akbar Khan thought that this was most likely, but he liked and trusted the man, and since Best had taken the trouble to trace him to Portugal he felt he owed him the courtesy of this meeting.

Akbar followed painted signs to the Chapel of Bones. The air felt chill inside this chapel, for it was virtually a gigantic tomb, one of the largest in the world. He paused at its entrance, surprised at the sight that greeted him. Six giant square pillars supported a curved and painted roof, and at the base of each pillar black chains prevented visitors from approaching the walls too closely. This was as well, for the walls were not built of stone or brick, but constructed entirely from human bones laid one upon another, ends pointing outwards: bones from legs, arms, rib-cages, spines, with hundreds of skulls. The pillars were decorated with femurs and tibias laid parallel, skulls piled one above the other on each corner. The frieze on the proud arches they supported was made not of gold leaf, but again of human skulls. Eyeless sockets gaped at him from all sides. There seemed something accusing in the sightless stare. What right had he to be alive and in good health? He recalled a tombstone inscription he had seen as an undergraduate in a country churchyard near Oxford: 'Pause, stranger, and think of me. As I am now, so you will be.'

A voice spoke softly behind him.

'Mr Khan, I must apologize for suggesting such a gloomy meeting-place.'

'Why are they all here? Where did so many bones come from?' asked Akbar as he shook hands with William Best.

'There was a terrible pestilence or plague in Evora in the thirteenth century,' Best explained. 'The whole city was virtually wiped out. There weren't enough men left alive with strength to dig graves for the dead who just lay where they fell.

'When the plague finally burned itself out, the corpses were skeletons, all flesh gone. The survivors decided not to bury the bones but to incorporate them into this chapel as a reminder that the city had once transgressed the laws of God and He had visited it with His wrath. Do you read Portuguese, Mr Khan?'

'Unfortunately, no.'

'Then I will translate what is written above the arch as a reminder of our own mortality.'

Mr Best cleared his throat.

' "Our bones await your bones," ' he said. 'Interesting thought. And undeniably true.'

'Agreed,' said Akbar. 'But surely our business is with the living? What do you want to see me about so urgently, and why couldn't we discuss it on the phone or meet in Lisbon? It is nothing to do with figs, I take it.'

'You take it correctly, but one has to be careful,' Best replied. 'I'm on my way back to Madrid and this struck me as being a halfway house. Also, out of season, it is totally deserted. There is no chance of our being overheard.'

He paused. They walked the length of the chapel to the altar and the gold wall behind it, turned and walked back. Under the domed roof their feet echoed like the tap of metronomes and the tick of the clock.

'It's about the situation in your country,' Best continued. 'You are aware of the strong and bitter feelings your uncle still holds with regard to the succession? Despite all efforts to make him change his views?'

'I am.'

'He still insists that he should be ruler, for he was your father's only brother.'

'That feeling must be shared by many younger brothers,' said Akbar. 'I sympathize with it and I'm sorry my uncle is so upset. But there is nothing I can do about it.'

'There appears to be something *he* is trying to do about it, and most actively. We believe he has considerable influence among several disaffected former members of your late father's cabinet.'

'I know. My father sacked them in short order for incompetence, corruption and laziness.'

'Three good reasons to us, Mr Khan, but no doubt not entirely satisfactory to the persons concerned.

'To get to the point of the matter. This so-called Emperor Odongo, who has been deposed from *his* golden throne, has been persuaded to help your uncle. He has no hope whatever of getting back to power in his own country, so his offer of help would be entirely academic unless he can offer something his opponents now in power simply cannot match.'

'Like what – eternal life?'

'He would, if he could. But if Odongo could prove to them that he could seize *your* country, and give them a share in all revenues from minerals, oil and uranium we are spending so much money trying to extract in commercial quantities, then he would be in with much more than a chance of getting back his golden throne. He would be in to win.'

'But how *can* he do that?'

'By offering your uncle aid. Then, when your uncle becomes ruler of Abukali instead of you, Odongo has his reward.'

'But, as you say, Odongo is finished. His people have thrown him out. They are sick of corruption. He is down and almost out, lucky in my opinion even to be alive. If he tries to make any comeback, the relatives of all the people he's murdered in his prisons and shot against walls, will tear him to pieces.'

'If,' said Best grimly. 'One of the smallest words in the English language, but one of the most important. *If* they are in any position to do as you say, yes, I agree. But Odongo will see to it that they won't be. There is a ship with a vital part to play in Mr Odongo's plans anchored off Arrifana at this very moment.'

'You mean *Quendon*?'

'Yes. Have you any idea what it's doing there?'

'It's hired out to an expedition trying to bring up gold from a ship lost in the Spanish Civil War. At least, Portuguese government licences have been issued for such a purpose.'

'Ah, yes. The operative words are, as you say, "at least". Another question. Have you seen any of the men aboard that ship?'

'Yes, I have. Not actually in the ship, but in the local café, walking across the beach. That sort of thing.'

'You would recognize them again?'

'Certainly.'

'Well, look at these pictures.'

Best took a folder of colour photographs from an inner pocket. Akbar examined them under the eyeless gaze of a dozen skulls in an alcove. The pictures had obviously been taken in haste and without the subjects knowing they were being photographed. One man leaving a black glass and stainless-steel building; another shutting the door of a car; a third at a bus-stop; a fourth lighting a cigarette in the street.

'I have seen the man near the car,' Akbar said. 'He was in a fight with a friend of mine the other day. He got the worst of it.'

'Then your friend must be quite tough. He is Franz Halstein. Know anything about him?'

'Only that he is a diver.'

'He's rather more than that.'

Best turned over the photograph; on the back was typed a six-line caption.

'Read what it says here,' he said. 'Then you will know what we are up against.'

Akbar did so, handed back the photograph in silence.

'Now,' said Best. 'Are you a student of geography, Mr Khan?'

'No. Why? Should I be?'

'Not necessarily. But let me explain a basic underwater

181

feature of this Portuguese coast which, if you had been a geographer, you would have already known. There is no continental shelf off Portugal, as there is off most of Europe. If you go to Sagres, the most westerly point of Europe, you will see all manner of big ships – liners, warships, tankers – coming in very close to shore simply because the water is so deep. If the expedition in Arrifana *is* actually searching for gold within a mile of the coast, they would need to carry infinitely more complex equipment than the ship has at present aboard. Generally speaking, a man in a wetsuit can only descend to a depth of about 132 feet, maximum. Below that, he would run into difficulties, and need a diving bell, a decompression chamber, or he would get the bends when oxygen returns to his blood. *Quendon* is not carrying any sophisticated diving equipment of this kind.'

'How do you know?'

'We have reason to believe what I have told you.'

'What sort of reason?'

'Someone who was aboard the ship informed us.'

'Who?'

'Please, Mr Khan.'

'Where is that person now?'

'I'm not at liberty to say, Mr Khan. But I can tell you that this source is unfortunately no longer able to supply us with information – which is why I seek your help.'

'You mean, they've gone away? Or they are dead?'

They stopped their walk beside an entire skeleton hanging on a wall. Centuries of dust darkened fissures of bone, wisps of hair still sprouted from the skull. Best nodded gravely towards the macabre sight and did not reply to either question.

'So what is *Quendon* doing off Arrifana if they are not diving for gold?'

'That is a question that is causing Her Majesty's Government some concern. Let us consider all the possibilities. We know there *was* a ship, *El Medina*, said to be carrying gold for Russia, that went down somewhere off that coast in 1938. But these people have no equipment to raise heavy bars of gold from such a depth. So they could be using this story so that they will be given official licences and permissions to dive, which is only a cover in their search for something else entirely.'

'What do you mean? Drugs?'

'I think not. They're after bigger fish than even the profits from heroin could supply. There *is* something of value at the bottom of the sea, but perhaps not where they are searching for it. You may be aware, Mr Khan, that this ship has cruised up and down the coast, I am told for refuelling purposes. They went south as far as Sagres a few days ago, and then up as far north as Lisbon a few days before that. But on neither occasion did she enter port for refuelling, which was given as the reason for these trips.'

'So what do you think she is doing?'

'What I think she is doing, Mr Khan, is something altogether more dangerous and terrible than searching for the richest treasure this world can offer. If they find what they seek, they could turn your country into a wasteland peopled only by the bones of the dead, like this chapel.

'It would be so terribly ravaged that not in your lifetime or mine would anything grow, or any animal or person be able to live within its frontiers.'

'I just don't understand you, Mr Best. What could they find under the sea that could possibly be capable of doing this?'

'Let us continue our perambulations and I will explain it all to you in the simplest possible terms. . . .'

eight

TOM JIM RAN to meet Carter as he climbed out of his car.

'I've got something to tell you!' he cried excitedly.

'And I've got something to tell *you*,' said Carter. 'I have brought you a present.'

'You said you would. I knew you would. What is it, Uncle Tony?'

'Nothing very much, really. There wasn't a great deal of choice in São Sebastião. Maybe your mother won't like it, but I hope you will.'

'I *know* I shall. And it's my present, not hers,' Tom Jim pointed out.

'Of course. Well, here it is.'

He handed the boy a catapult.

'You select a stone like this,' said Carter, picking up a round flat-sided pebble. 'Hold the wooden part of the catapult in your right hand and pull back the elastic slowly. And then – bang! . . .'

He released the elastic. The pebble hit a metal litter-bin with a boom like the Rank Organization's gong.

'You can change direction quite easily,' Carter explained, showing the boy how. 'But never point it at anyone and don't ever shoot any stones near windows. It's a funny thing, but they'll always hit windows even when you don't aim directly at them.'

'My Dad could make stones bounce on the water,' said Tom Jim gravely. 'Will this help me do that?'

'Of course,' said Carter. 'But I think we should really work as a team of two. I'll show you how to aim, and you watch me for a signal to fire. Then we won't have any accidents.'

'What's the signal, Uncle Tony?'

'I'll hold up the first finger of my right hand, like this. You watch me. I may not hold it up *exactly* like this, because that's too obvious, and this is a secret signal only between us. So I may scratch my ear. Or I may touch my nose, or stroke my chin. OK?'

'OK.'

They shook hands gravely.

'Now, let's have a run-through. But, first, what's your news?'

'I was outside the café this morning, and the men were talking about the ship sailing.'

'What men?'

'Mr Serrafino was telling the divers. It's leaving tonight.'

'You sure?'

'He seemed certain,' said Miranda, who had now walked from the house to meet Carter.

'But they haven't found the gold yet, have they?'

'I know nothing about that. But Tom Jim is absolutely adamant that's what he heard. And he isn't one to exaggerate.'

The little boy ran into the house excitedly with his catapult.

'I'll go and see Serrafino,' said Carter. 'I must find out exactly what's happening, in case he's trying to clear out without paying me. He owes me a lot of money. Where's Akbar?'

'He left after breakfast.'

'Left? For good?'

'Oh, no. Said he'd a business meeting in Evora.'

Carter walked up the hill to Mr Serrafino's house. An old man was feeding chickens in one of the shacks by the side of the track, and nodded a greeting as Carter walked past. The evening wind made telephone wires sing like giant violin strings, and the half-completed estate had a desolate, deserted appearance. All the houses appeared empty, shutters closed, gates locked.

He pressed the bell outside Mr Serrafino's front door. Its ring sounded hollow, like an echo in a cave. Carter peered through the windows. Metal trellises had been drawn across the glass panes, although the outside shutters were still open. He banged on the door, squinted through the letter-box, then walked around the house. Every door was locked. Mr Serrafino was not at home. Of course, he could be in Aljezur or somewhere else and expected back at any moment, but somehow Carter did not think so. There was no sign of any servant, no tea-towels out to dry on the frame in the kitchen courtyard, not a spade or a sprinkler left out in the garden. Clearly, Mr Serrafino was not expecting to return for some time.

As Carter came down the hill the old man with the chickens called him. Carter stopped. The old man shook his head and waved one arm across his body in a gesture to show no one was there. Carter nodded his thanks and walked on to the caravan the expedition had been using as an office. No one replied to his knock on the door. He then banged as loudly as he could on the doors of several adjoining houses, where he knew the divers were billeted. Again, there was no reply. Everyone had left; no doubt about that. He looked out towards *Quendon*. There was no movement on the ship's deck that he could see, nor any sound from her engine. If *Quendon* was to sail, she would probably leave at dusk, without lights, hoping to slip away unseen. But why the devil *should* they sail off? What about the rest of his contract?

He hurried down the hill to his house. Akbar had just arrived; he looked tired and worried.

'I've something to tell you,' he called to Carter from his car.

'Later,' replied Carter. 'That ship's sailing tonight.'

'You sure?'

'Tom Jim overheard it. I've been up to Serrafino's house and the office and banged on the doors of houses where the divers are staying. They're all shut up. Deserted.'

'Where's it bound for?'

'How the devil do I know? But I intend to find out.'

'How?' Miranda asked him.

'Take the speedboat and see if Serrafino's aboard. After all, he has to pay me, whether he wants me to do the job he hired me for or not.'

'Maybe they're just sailing out for a day or so, like when they went to Sagres?'

'In that case, no hassle. On the other hand, it seems they may be clearing out altogether.'

'What if he won't see you – or if he isn't there?'

'I'll have a butcher's around *Quendon* and try to discover what I can about their plans.'

'When they know you are aboard? Don't be an idiot.'

'They won't know.'

'How are you so sure – if you're going out to see Serrafino? They won't let you nose around,' said Miranda doubtfully.

'They will, because they won't know I'm there. Akbar will see to that.'

Until it was dark enough to carry out his plan, Carter stayed on the beach, showing Tom Jim how to aim his catapult, how to measure distance with his eye, how to choose the best pebbles for the most accurate shot. He enjoyed this, but he also had a secondary motive for being on the beach, within sight of *Quendon*. If Mr Serrafino was aboard, as he assumed, and saw him engaged in such harmless activity, he was unlikely to think that Carter suspected he was about to run out on him.

As the dusk deepened he and Tom Jim went into the house. While Miranda put Tom Jim to bed, Akbar and Carter changed into dark-blue jeans and long-sleeved blue shirts. Carter also wore a peaked blue yachting-cap. Then they set out along the sand to the edge of the sea, where the speedboat bobbed at her buoy thirty yards out. They waded through the shallow water, climbed aboard. Akbar crawled forward under the floor decking and lay flat on the ribs of the hull, hearing the cluck and slap of the water on the other side of the thin fibreglass skin.

Carter then dropped down behind the wheel, turned on the petrol and ignition, pressed the starter button. The Volvo inboard/outboard started with a roar, bubbling water from the exhaust. He let the engines warm up, and then cast off and turned the bow towards *Quendon*.

He came alongside, cut his engines and secured the painter to the hanging ladder. Then, putting a pencil torch into his back trouser pocket, he climbed up on deck. Lights were already lit; cabin windows glowed behind drawn chintz curtains.

Ruskie was on duty.

'Forgotten something?' he asked him.

'No. I want to see Mr Serrafino.'

'He's not aboard.'

'He's not in his house, either. Do you know where he is? It's very important.'

'No idea. Haven't seen him all day.'

'I hear you're sailing tonight.'

Ruskie shrugged.

'News to me,' he said shortly.

'I'll see if there's anyone else who can help,' Carter told him, and went down the companionway into the bowels of the ship. The air felt warm here, overlaid with the strong amalgam of hot oil and dried salt peculiar to small ocean-going ships. A radio was playing in a mess room. Carter glanced in through uncurtained windows as he walked past. The divers were sitting, reading, smoking, playing cards, drinks at their elbows. He walked the length of the ship to the stern, turned around and came back on the port side to the bow. Then he climbed up on deck, leaned over the rail, looking down at the reflections of the portholes in the dancing dark water, wondering about his next move. Ruskie called down to him from the bridge.

'Satisfied? He's not here, you know.'

'OK,' Carter replied. 'Maybe he's turned up at his house. Good night.'

Ruskie did not reply. Carter climbed down the companionway, jumped into the speedboat that dipped and rocked with his sudden weight. Above and behind him, the hull of the ship soared like a sheer black cliff. He could still hear music, now thin and metallic and remote, from the radio. He hoped he was unseen in the deepening gloom, but he could not afford to take any risk, so he crouched down by the driver's seat as Akbar came out from under the decking. Carter handed his peaked cap to him, then climbed on to the companionway and stood flat against *Quendon*'s hull.

Akbar switched on the ignition, revved the engines ostentatiously, turned the speedboat's searchlight towards the shore and set off slowly. Immediately, a bigger searchlight blazed out from the bridge. The beam traversed the sea, held the speedboat. Akbar did not look back. The searchlight picked out his blue long-sleeved shirt, the peaked yachting-cap. From that angle and in that light, Carter thought he seemed a reasonable look-alike. The man operating the searchlight presumably thought so, too, for the light went out. The speedboat now accelerated towards the shore, the rasp of her exhaust echoing from *Quendon*'s hull.

Carter waited for several minutes, listening to the slap of water against the ship's bulk. Then, very slowly and with infinite care, to prevent any of the wooden rungs of the ladder banging against *Quendon*'s side, he climbed up on deck. Here, he waited for a count of ten in the shadow of the cabins in case anyone was patrolling the decks. They appeared empty, so he walked forward slowly, his eyes gradually growing accustomed to the darkness. He slid open the nearest door, closed it silently behind him, and went down a metal companionway, past engines bright with polished brass and copper and shining green paint. Beneath shielded ceiling lights, a man was whistling to himself as he lubricated a bearing from an oil-can. Carter waited until he moved out of sight, then walked on into the heart of the ship.

The smell was now overwhelmingly of rusting salty metal, and his way was lit by small overhead circular lamps protected by wire mesh. He walked carefully along a metal catwalk, fearful of making any noise, until he reached the stern. Here, the inside of the hull streamed with condensation and huge rudder chains black with grease lay slackly like gorged serpents in the oily bilge. There seemed nothing for him to discover, so he came back towards the bows along another catwalk. This led past fuel-tanks, then a store with tools, spanners and oil-cans fitted according to size on one wall, and ended at a watertight door with four handles, one in each corner.

Carter tried them all, gently at first, then with more force. To his surprise, after the poor maintenance he had noted earlier on deck, they turned easily on oiled threads. He opened the door, and stepped inside a small hold. He immediately had the unpleasant sensation of being in an iron airless tomb beneath the surface of the sea. He put out both hands and touched a rough-welded metal edge; and then a curved surface. Both felt cold with condensation. He waited in case anyone else might also be in the hold, but he could hear nothing except the faint suck of the sea on the other side of the hull.

He took the pencil torch from his pocket. The walls were shining as though with sweat. He turned the tiny beam on the metal he had touched and was surprised by what he now saw. The hold contained what appeared to be grey-painted oil-drums, small boilers and old-fashioned heating radiators, welded together with steel bars into blocks of metal about six feet square. He tried to move one, but it was far too heavy.

He sniffed them closely and smelled salt. One bore a trace of seaweed, like a damp green beard. They had been in the sea recently, but where? Could these be the gold-containers that Serrafino had mentioned? He walked around the hold, shining his torch on them from different angles, in the hope that he might discover a clue to their contents. How incongruous that this rusting metal could contain a treasure worth millions.

To one side of the metal casings lay two reels of fine steel hawser. Carter calculated that they each contained several hundred feet of wire, well greased and still damp from the sea, and fitted with three-pronged grappling-hooks. They must have used these hooks to haul up the casings, he thought. But unless the ship had more sophisticated diving equipment than he had seen, no diver could survive at anything like the depth the length of these hawsers would represent. Maybe the ship had sailed slowly around the area, trawling for the casings? In that case, why did they need divers at all?

As he pondered these questions, he sensed rather than heard a faint movement behind him and instantly switched off his torch. Then he heard the clanging resonance of a heavy metal door closing and the squeak of a key. Someone had locked the watertight door behind him. He was trapped.

The hairs on the back of Carter's neck stiffened, and he felt sweat trickle down between his shoulder-blades. Then he heard what he had dreaded most of all: the sound of breathing. Was someone in the hold with him?

Carter held his breath in case this other person might be able to follow him in the darkness by the sound of his breathing. But he could only do this for a matter of moments, before he had to open his mouth, expel the air and breathe in again, as slowly as he could. There must be another door if only because each compartment he had seen so far had a way in and a way out. But how to find it? He did not dare to use his torch again, but the thought tormented him: if someone had been in the hold all the time, why hadn't he made himself known? Or had he come in behind him and then closed the door, ready to discover what Carter was searching for, how much he knew?

He fought down a rising tide of panic as he realized that there might not be a handle inside the second door, that he could be trapped in a steel room until his captors chose to release him.

Slowly and with infinite care, Carter felt along the soaking walls until his fingers touched a horizontal lever on a second watertight door, and he pushed down on it. The lever moved so easily that he almost lost his balance. Relief all but overcame him. He put his weight against the door, pushed it open slowly on oiled hinges. He was out in a dark companionway, where the cold air tasted like iced wine, the wine of freedom. Then he realized that this was no wind from the sea; he must be inside the ship's cold store.

He closed the door carefully behind him, and his breath fanned out like fog; white rime coated the walls. In the glow of his torch he could make out sides of beef and pork, covered with sheets of protective muslin, hanging from sharpened hooks in the ceiling. They swayed gently with the slight motion of the ship. Huge deep-freezes and refrigerators hummed on either side of him, green lights glowing above their doors.

He hurried between them to reach a door at the far side of the store, for in his shirt and jeans the chill struck to his bones. Then something made him pause. The green light on the last deep-freeze was not alight. This meant that it had not reached its operating temperature; something unusually large must have been put inside recently. He paused, trained always to observe the unusual, the unexpected, why one man in a marching column would be out of step, why one warning light out of six was not lit. He took a pace forward, meaning to put the matter out of his mind, and then turned back, and on impulse opened the door.

On a white slatted tray, wrapped in a sheet of gauze like the carcasses dangling from the roof, lay the body of Mrs Kent. Under the gauze, frozen to her flesh and bound with strips of bandage around her ankles and thighs and chest was a heavy metal bar.

Carter drew back in horror, and then, overcoming his distaste, reached out and touched her face through the mesh. Her body could have been in the cabinet for several hours, perhaps even for a day. They must be planning to dump it in the ocean when they were many miles offshore. The metal bar would make certain it sank instantly, and predatory fish would do the rest. But why – when Mr Serrafino had said he regarded Mrs Kent as a daughter? Was her body being carried aboard his ship without his knowledge?

Carter closed the deep-freeze door, hurried through the cold store, let himself out of the spring-loaded door at the far end. Once more he was in a narrow corridor, lit this time by a single overhead bulb. He stood, eyes closed, to accustom himself to the dimness. As he opened them, the gloom exploded into light. A battery of lamps blazed down from the ceiling, blinding him.

Two men he had not seen before stood facing him. Each carried an iron bar of the size and shape Carter had just seen strapped to Mrs Kent's corpse.

'Just checking up,' said Carter as calmly as he could. His voice, booming and echoing against acres of sheet metal, sounded as hollow as his claim.

'I think *we* are doing that,' a familiar voice corrected him.

He turned. Mr Serrafino was smiling at him. His bald head glistened like a bladder of melting lard.

'Get him up on deck,' he ordered the men briefly.

The two men nodded to Carter. He followed them along the catwalk, up the companionway, to the deck.

'Into this cabin,' said Serrafino.

'What the hell *is* this?' asked Carter indignantly. 'You ask me to check everything on this ship, and now you frog-march me off.'

'Hardly, Mr Carter. I have not asked you to check anything aboard this ship. Your duties are specifically concerned with the discipline of the divers. You have no business whatever in any other part of the ship.'

'I had to familiarize myself with the vessel.'

'That is not in our agreement,' said Serrafino. 'Now, what were you really doing down there?'

'I have just told you.'

'Please do not waste my time with such absurd explanations. You were spying, Mr Carter, looking for someone or something that is none of your concern. I find this conduct totally out of keeping with the duties for which I hired you and for which I am paying you handsomely. In fact, I find your behaviour totally unsatisfactory.

'First, on the very evening I engage you at a high fee, you come creeping around my house after dark, looking for what? Next, you pick a fight with my most senior colleague. Then you tell me that Mrs Kent is dead, and when I come to investigate this astonishing claim I can find no trace of her whatever, alive or dead.'

'You didn't look very far. Her body is in a deep-freeze on the other side of that door.'

'Please, Mr Carter, spare me such rubbish. Answer my question. What were you doing down here with a torch in the dark?'

'I couldn't find the switch,' Carter retorted.

'Fortunately, we have surveillance equipment on board. So,

while you couldn't find the switch, we found you, and followed you.'

'So that's it, then,' said Carter. 'Now shall we all go home?'

'I think not.'

'Why not?'

'Because, Mr Carter, I am unexpectedly forced to abandon this whole quest for sunken gold. The meteorological authorities say that the weather is worsening. My divers report that already the currents are stirring up the sand. Underwater visibility is too poor to continue.'

'So you are paying me off?'

'Our contract is for four weeks. You have barely served four days. I will, of course, honour the contract. So will you. And until your time is up, or I choose to release you, you will stay aboard ship.'

'You didn't even have the courtesy to tell me you were leaving.'

'I did not have the opportunity. I understand that you were away – in my time – seeing someone no longer in my employ. De Silva. Probably trying to find out something else that was none of your business. Why, Mr Carter?'

'Mr de Silva told me he works for the British consulate. In fact, he told me of the death of a friend of mine. Jack Bridges.'

'Mr de Silva worked for *me*. But now he will not work for anyone again.'

'Why not?'

'Because he is dead. You met him, I understand, on a cliff-top in Carrapateira?'

'I did.'

'And less than an hour later his body was delivered to the outpatients' department of Lagos hospital in a wheelchair by someone who answers your description.'

'Are you serious?'

'Deadly.'

'How do you know this?'

'Because Franz, and two of his most senior colleagues, Hans and Irwin, were arrested on some ludicrous charges after *you* had attacked them in a bar in São Sebastião. They were taken to the hospital for treatment and to their amazement were then accused of bringing in poor de Silva's body. They were, of course, released. Fortunately, the only orderly who could have identified them had just gone off duty.'

'Fortunately for whom?'

'For them. Otherwise they could have been jailed indefinitely awaiting trial. But not, perhaps, so fortunate for you. Franz is especially angry. This is the second time you have attacked him.'

Mr Serrafino moved to one side. Franz and Hans stepped out of the darkness into the blazing pool of light.

'Search him,' ordered Mr Serrafino.

Franz found Mrs Kent's pistol and handed it to his employer. Then he produced a pocket handkerchief, Carter's American Express card. Mr Serrafino shrugged them away.

'You are unlikely to charge up your experiences with me,' he said contemptuously and handed them back to Carter. Then he nodded to Franz and Hans. Franz hit Carter first, so quickly he had no chance to avoid the punch. He staggered against a bulkhead and struck the back of his head on a handle of the watertight door. He reeled, momentarily dazed. Hans kicked him in the stomach. Carter went down on the catwalk. Then time dissolved in a red, roaring tide of pain as boots and blows rained on him. Dimly, as though from across a vast chasm, he heard Mr Serrafino's voice, faint but entreating.

'Don't kill him. He's got to stand trial for de Silva's murder. Don't kill him.'

Mercifully, Carter fainted.

He swam back to consciousness through raw layers of pain, and the taste of his own blood on his tongue. He was lying on a red carpet that moved slightly with the long slow roll of the ship. He opened his eyes slowly and could make out a ceiling with a light, a chest of drawers, a bed, but his eyes would not focus properly, and he saw all these homely things through a vague pink mist, and recognized none of them. Where the hell was he?

Slowly, feebly, he crawled to his feet. A door was open, and he went through it, steadying himself with both hands against the walls as he walked. His fingers, ground by Franz's boots, left smudges of blood on the paintwork. The door led into a tiny bathroom. This contained a bath, with two huge nickel-plated taps, one marked *Sea-Water*, a lavatory pan and a small, curved washbasin. Above the basin was a large wall-mirror and a shaving-mirror on an expanding chromium-plated trellis. One side had a flat face, the other was concave to magnify the shaver's chin. Two small hand-towels, newly ironed, were draped over a rail.

Carter filled the basin with cold water, doused his head in it, then drank greedily from the cold-water tap. There were no glasses. He dried his face and hands on a towel and examined his bruises in the magnifying mirror. His upper lip was split and he had a black eye and purplish bruises on his temples. He flexed his shoulder and arm and leg muscles carefully, breathed deeply; nothing seemed broken. He came back into the cabin, and sat down on the bed. There was no chair and the bed was bolted to the floor. He could see nothing he could conceivably use as a lever to try to force the door, or that might serve as a weapon.

He stood up and tried the doorhandle. As he had expected, it was locked and the door fitted perfectly in its frame; he would need a jemmy to prise it open, and he did not even have a penknife. The cabin possessed one round porthole with a glass cover screwed back in the open position outside. A strong mesh of half-inch metal bars protected the aperture. He seized the bars with both hands, like a monkey in a zoo, and pulled. He could not move them even a fraction of an inch, and the effort only gave him a headache.

Far beneath Carter's feet, he heard the thrum and boom of an engine starting, and then the screech of anchor chains being reeled in. He peered out of the porthole and saw a light on shore swing steadily from right to left. The ship began to move, turning slowly out to sea. Gradually, the light slid away out of sight. Others replaced it, and then the intermittent beam of a lighthouse, and finally a patch of indigo sky pricked by stars.

The ship dipped and rose with the Atlantic swell and settled to a steady rolling rhythm. They were at sea.

Akbar scanned *Quendon* through his night-glasses. The decks appeared deserted, but a few lights burned in portholes. He could see no sign of Carter. If Carter had seen Mr Serrafino and was sailing willingly, then Akbar was certain he would somehow have sent word to him of his intentions. He had not done so, which led Akbar to believe that he must be sailing unwillingly. He could have been discovered or he might simply have been trapped in a hold or a cabin by a self-locking door.

As *Quendon*'s speed increased, she trailed a wide phosphorescent wake behind her. Akbar checked his watch. Carter had been aboard for twenty minutes. He waited for another ten in the hope that Carter might have dived off the far side of the vessel and would come into view, swimming ashore. Then he had to admit that his friend was not coming back. Alive or dead, he must still be aboard.

In which direction would *Quendon* sail? Akbar thought it most likely that she would head west out of sight of land, and perhaps beyond the range of coastguard radar, before she turned either north or south. By first light, she would be many miles away. He walked slowly up the beach to the house. As he came through the front door, the telephone rang. Miranda picked it up. A voice spoke excitedly in her ear.

'He's not here,' she said. 'But a friend has just come in who knows where he is. I'll pass you over.'

She held her hand over the mouthpiece as she turned to Akbar. 'Man called Manuel. Says he runs the Nautilus bar in São Sebastião. Wants to get hold of Tony. Says it's very important.'

Akbar took the receiver.

'Perhaps I can help you,' he said. 'I am a close friend of Mr Carter. He isn't here at the moment, but I'll take a message.'

'He was in my bar at lunch-time,' Manuel explained. 'There

was an argument, a bit of a fight with three East Germans. And he did my brother-in-law, the Fiscal, a good turn.'

'I'm glad to hear that, at least,' said Akbar. 'What's the message?'

'It's about my dog, Gamba. José de Silva took him for a walk. He has just come back.'

Manuel paused.

'But the message?' Akbar repeated.

'José de Silva tied a micro-tape cassette to the dog's collar. I have played part of it. Mr Carter is mentioned. It is very important I reach Mr Carter. My brother-in-law thinks so, too. That's the message.'

Akbar glanced at his watch.

'I'll be with you as soon as I can. Keep the bar open until I arrive.'

He replaced the receiver.

'What's that about?' asked Miranda.

'Something that apparently affects Tony.'

'Where *is* Tony, anyhow?'

'Still aboard *Quendon*.'

'Aren't you waiting to pick him up?'

'There's no point. She's just put out to sea.'

'You mean, he's a prisoner?'

'I don't know. He may be stuck below decks and just can't get out. He may get free somehow, of course, and try his luck swimming in farther down the coast.'

'That seems to me what Jack must have done. I think he was aboard that ship against his will, and then somehow escaped and swam to the shore.'

'He might have gone there uninvited and then been discovered,' suggested Akbar, remembering what Best had told him in the Chapel of the Bones.

'Then, how could he swim to the shore?'

'Perhaps he outwitted them or maybe they deliberately allowed him to go free at the one point on the coast they reckoned a strong swimmer could reach the shore. But someone was waiting for him on the beach.'

'You mean, to kill him?'

'Yes.'

'But why not do that aboard ship?'

'Because you can fake an accident so much more easily from a cliff-top. If a body's washed ashore, all sorts of checks are made about ships passing at the time, with currents and tides and so on.'

'But why should Jack have been aboard at all?'

Akbar did not answer. This was not the time to tell Miranda what he had learned in Evora. He had wanted to tell Carter, to alert him, but he had simply not had the chance. Carter had been concerned about seeing Serrafino, and when Akbar had wanted to get him on his own, for what he had heard must be for Carter's ears only, Carter had said he had promised to teach Tom Jim how to aim accurately with his catapult.

'What are we going to do about Tony?' Miranda asked. 'We can't just do nothing.'

'We'll find out where the ship is going and follow her. She must stop eventually. Then we go aboard.'

'But how can we possibly follow a ship that size? They'd see us miles away, even if we had a boat big enough for the open ocean, which we haven't. The speedboat would be useless.'

'I'll tell you how we'll do it when you've pulled poor Tom Jim out of bed and packed your things and his. We're all driving to the airport at Faro as soon as you're ready.'

'But that's miles away – and in the opposite direction.'

'An aircraft will only take minutes to fly fifty miles out to sea. *Quendon* won't have travelled much farther by dawn. A big swoop by air south of Sagres or north around Lisbon and we'll soon pick her up.'

'And then what?' Miranda asked sceptically.

'We check the direction she's heading, north or south. Then we land at the nearest airport for a bath, a change of clothes, a good meal, and take off again to make sure we don't lose her.'

'What aircraft is going to do this for us? Be reasonable, Akbar. It all sounds fine, but no airline flies about in this way to help two or three passengers. They go direct from Faro to London or Lisbon.'

'But we are not going by airline, my dear.'

'What are you talking about, then?'

'My own plane. My own pilot.'

'You mean, you have your own aircraft at Faro?'

'I do. One of the benefits of being rich, Miranda – and there are many – is that you don't ever have to bow to the whims of others. If an airline doesn't fly where I want to go, my own plane takes me.'

'I never realized that you were so rich.'

'Let's hope that Mr Serrafino doesn't, either.'

Miranda packed clothes for herself and Tom Jim in a suitcase, and then woke him up gently, and dressed him.

'We are going to take a journey to meet Uncle Tony,' she explained. 'In Uncle Akbar's own plane.'

'He's got a Cessna,' said Tom Jim, all sleepiness vanishing at the prospect of excitement. 'He was telling me about it. I've never been in a Cessna.'

Akbar carried the cases to the car. Miranda and Tom Jim followed. They were about to climb in when suddenly Tom Jim gripped Miranda's hand and looked at her anxiously.

'Whatever's the matter?' she asked him.

'I must go back. I've forgotten something.'

'We'll be back in a day or so. We can get it then. It can't be that important.'

'But it is , Mummy. It's the most important thing. It's the present Uncle Tony gave me. My catapult.'

The turning of a key in the cabin door awoke Carter. Hastily, he swung his legs out of bed, and tried to pull on his shoes before the door was fully open, but he was too late. Franz and Hans were inside the cabin before he could stand upright. Hans carried a tray with a jug of coffee, a cup, several slices of bread, a plate and a jar of jam.

'There's no knife,' Carter complained.

'Use the teaspoon,' Franz replied. 'It's plastic.'

They went out and left him. The coffee steamed invitingly and, despite his predicament, Carter felt hungry. He sat down on the edge of the bed, pulled the tray towards him. Sunshine reflected from the glittering sea outside and threw a dappled circle of light on the ceiling. From the angle, he calculated they must be sailing almost due south, but at what speed he had no idea. Presumably they must now be somewhere off the northwest coast of Africa.

The two men came in again, picked up the tray. Carter jumped at Hans as he held the tray, but Franz was ready for the movement and tripped Carter easily. Hans put down the tray carefully as though he had all the time in the world. Then, as Carter struggled to straighten up, Franz kicked him hard in the stomach.

The two men smiled at each other, and went out of the cabin. Carter waited until he heard the key turn in the lock, and then stood up, walked slowly and painfully into the bathroom and was violently sick. He lay down on the bed to try to devise some way he could escape. He was allowing his muscles to do the work of his mind, and that could never be successful. He should be following the old army saying: Sweat saves blood, and brain saves both. Then, surprisingly, he slept. When he awoke, he still felt bruised, but more cheerful, even optimistic; although why he should, he had no idea. He did fifty press-ups on the floor to keep in trim. Outside, it was already dark, and soon the sky was only an ink circle framed by the porthole. When the door opened for a second time, Franz and Hans set down a tray with a mug of water, and some beef hash, again with a plastic spoon, useless as a weapon. Carter ate gratefully, then had a bath and went to bed.

The light in the cabin was kept on all night. Every now and then, he stirred briefly from an uneasy sleep to see a strange, disembodied face peering through the porthole at him, to make sure he was still there. At about six o'clock next morning, Carter awoke and dressed. Far away, in the bright sky, he heard the drone of an aircraft engine. He crossed the cabin and peered out of the porthole. A tiny blue and silver plane, looking like a tropical bird, swooped and turned as though delighted to be free. Then it headed away. He thought: If I had been quick, I might have signalled an SOS to the pilot with a mirror. But of course this presupposed that the pilot would even see the flashes, that he would also understand Morse, and that he would do anything about it. More important, Carter had no mirror.

There was a shaving-mirror on the bathroom wall, though. A guard was standing six feet away, leaning on the ship's rail, also looking up at the aircraft. As it flew away, he stared down at the sea. Carter wondered what he could be watching so closely. Then he saw the blue-steel glint of a shining shape in the water; then another, and a third, and finally a whole school of dolphins. They rolled and dived and stuck their pointed noses up into the air, forcing clouds of spray from blow-holes on top of their sleek heads.

Carter went into the bathroom, filled the washbasin with cold water, soaked the towels. Then he removed the toilet-paper container from its bracket on the wall and carried it back into the cabin. He glanced carefully out of the porthole. The guard was still staring at the dolphins. Carter shook out the separate sheets of paper on to the carpet beneath the porthole, crumpled them up, and went back into the bathroom. Now he gripped the shaving-mirror firmly by its long trellis and ripped it from the wall as quietly as he could – a push in one direction, a pull in another and away it came. Carter carried the mirror back into the cabin under his shirt, just in case the guard should look in and see him, but the man was still leaning on the rail, absorbed by the antics of the dolphins. Carter crossed to the bed, arranging the bolster and pillow in the centre, fashioning them as best he could into the shape of a sleeping man, and covered them carefully with a sheet. Then he sat on the carpet near the door and angled the mirror towards the pile of paper tissues under the porthole. He directed the rays of the sun on to the paper, and slowly pulled the mirror back until what had been a wide circle of light dwindled to a dazzling dot of halfpenny size.

For a moment, nothing happened. Then gradually the paper wrinkled and turned brown at the heart of the light, and Carter held his breath, willing the guard not to move. Where the light had been brightest, a hole appeared and spread rapidly, ringed with flame. Carter held the mirror steady until the hole grew wider and the flames rose higher. He lifted the end of the sheet from the bed and held this across the burning paper. The flame was doused momentarily, and then the linen caught alight.

Carter waited until it was burning strongly and went into the bathroom and wrung out the two towels. He wrapped one around his mouth and nose. The other he spread carefully over the blazing paper and sheet. The flames died down with a hissing like a nest of angry serpents, and the cabin quickly filled with steam and acrid white smoke. Carter's eyes smarted, and even with the towel around his face he began to choke for breath.

He waited for a count of twenty, then cried: 'Help! Help! Fire! *Help!*'

He crouched down by the side of the bed, out of guard's line of vision from the porthole, and heard an exclamation of surprise and annoyance outside. A face appeared momentarily, framed in the porthole and wreathed in smoke, and he heard a whistle blow and feet beat an urgent tattoo on the wooden deck.

The room was now thick with smoke. Carter waited behind the door. Two men came in at a rush: Franz and Hans. Franz carried a big red cylindrical fire-extinguisher. He banged its nozzle on the floor to break the seal, and directed the white spray of foam at the hump on the bed. Hans, holding a handkerchief to his face, ran across the room to pull the sheet from the bed with his other hand. As he bent over the bed, Carter jumped on his back, drove both knees into his kidneys and, looping his towel over Hans's face, pulled with all his strength. Hans screamed, one hand trapped beneath the towel, then Carter felt the man's neck snap like a twig. His body sagged, his knees gave way. Hans fell back on the floor.

Dimly, through the fog of smoke, Franz saw Hans fall, and with a shout of rage and alarm swung the jet of foaming chemicals at Carter's face. But Carter had dropped on both knees, so that the white reeking stream sprayed harmlessly above him on to the far wall. He clenched his fists together and drove them up into Franz's stomach. Franz reeled from the brute force of the blow and momentarily his grip on the fire-extinguisher slackened.

Now Carter gripped the red cylinder and pulled. In a natural reflex action, Franz clasped it more tightly to him. Then Carter suddenly forced it towards Franz's body. Franz lost his balance and fell over on to his back. Foam swirled out into the air like a white candy-floss fountain.

Carter slipped on the sodden carpet and nearly fell. Franz, throwing the extinguisher away, seized him by the front of his shirt and head-butted him. Carter staggered back against the wall, gasping for air, and reeled through the open door, on deck. Choking waves of smoke and acrid-smelling foam billowed out behind him.

He could hear whistles blow and feet pound along the deck beneath him. Within seconds, the other divers would come charging up the companionway and his bid for freedom would be over before it had properly begun. He had only seconds in which to escape. Franz also realized this and raced through the doorway after him. Carter threw out his right foot and tripped him. Franz fell heavily and slid, with the force of the fall and his weight, across the deck, and hit his head on the scuppers. Carter seized him by a leg and an arm, heaved him up and rolled him through the railings. Franz shrieked in alarm and despair as he dropped towards the sea.

Carter allowed himself a quick glance over the wooden rail. Several men on the deck below had stopped running and were staring over the rail at the spot where the body hit the sea, watching for it to surface. Franz was also wearing blue jeans and a blue shirt, and in the brief view they had of his falling body Carter hoped they thought that he had made an escape attempt.

As though in a slow-motion dream, he saw a small sailing boat drift past, diamond-shaped sail stretched against the sun like a drumskin; then a very long blue canoe with a red outrigger. One man sat in the stern, controlling the rudder; another sat amidships near the engine. Neither glanced at *Quendon*.

Half a mile beyond these, Carter could see a low green coastline, like a long marsh, with buildings and electric pylons, but between the ship and this shore the tide was running strongly. They were entering the mouth of a huge river; the deep blue Atlantic was already behind them. Strong swimmer as he was, Carter knew he could never reach land against the force of that current; no one could.

He ran around the deck to the port side. Here, the current was just as strong, but a curious change took place in the surface of the water about two hundred yards from the land. It was as though an invisible line stretched down the centre of the river. On its near side, the water was rough and dark with depth, racing with all the force of the turning tide. On the far side, nearer the north shore, the water seemed strangely calm and brown, the colour of weak tea. This must mean that a sandbank lay in mid-stream, and beyond it the sea was shallow. Perhaps a mile farther on, lay the land, where buildings gleamed white as teeth in the sun, and car windscreens heliographed messages along a shore road.

Deep below Carter's feet in the heart of the ship, a telegraph clanged, the note of the engines changed. The whole ship shuddered. They were slowing down. The noise broke the spell of inaction. He had to jump now, or not at all, for it would take *Quendon*'s captain half a mile to slow sufficiently to lower a boat and pick up Franz. As the ship's propellers reversed, churning the water into a brown lather, the school of dolphins swam from the disturbance to calmer water on Carter's side of the ship. He climbed on to the top rail and dived.

He hit the water cleanly, as he had taught so many children to do throughout that summer, and went deep before he risked turning, for he had dived from a height of at least fifty feet. As he came out of the dive and began to surface, he could gradually make out the dark torpedo shapes of the dolphins against the translucence of the sea's surface. Then he was head and shoulders above the water and so close to them he could smell the oily fishiness of their slippery skins.

They circled around him, moist, sleek bodies turning, diving, half-leaping from the sea. Their black gambolling bulk would give him some cover from any lookouts aboard ship, but not much and not for long. He took a deep breath, dived again, and swam for as long as he could with his bottom sticking up out of the water, as he had demonstrated so often to the more advanced swimmers in Tim Rowley's pool. He calculated that his blue jeans would make it almost impossible for anyone to pick him out from the dolphins at a distance. The real risk would arise when they rescued Franz and realized that he had also jumped into the sea – or even before that, if the dolphins suddenly decided to swim away. He could not hope to keep pace with them for more than a few yards. Left on his own, he would be a floating target.

The dolphins moved slowly over the sandbank, and by swimming with all his strength Carter could just keep up with them. Then they drew ahead easily, and he was on his own. He turned on his back to look at *Quendon*. The ship appeared to be stationary. A lifeboat had been lowered, and in a blue haze of exhaust smoke this was chugging back to where Franz had last been seen to pick him up. Carter swam underwater for as long as he could towards the shore, surfaced briefly for air and went below again. He kept up this sequence, up and down, up and then down again, until his lungs were almost bursting, and blood roared in his ears. When he surfaced, even the sea seemed red, and exhaustion gripped his bruised body like an iron clamp.

He trod water for a moment to regain his strength and saw with dismay that all his efforts had only just brought him across the sandbank. He was now in the centre of the calmer browner water and still a depressing distance from land. The current was infinitely stronger than he had anticipated.

He heard shouts behind him, and looked back towards the ship. As he did so, he heard a crack like a distant firework and two sudden splashes of water appeared, first to his left, then to his right. It took Carter seconds to realize that these were bullets. He had been seen and recognized and was under fire. He dived again and swam on, more wearily, more desperately, towards the shore. The current seemed even stronger now, or maybe he was so much more exhausted, for he could barely make any progress at all; he was simply maintaining his position against a powerful tide that constantly threatened to sweep him out to sea. But at least he was over the sandbank. The captain would be unlikely to risk his vessel here, but of course he had no need to do so, for now Carter had been spotted *Quendon*'s lifeboat could easily pick him up. Carter had dived and swum to no avail; recapture must only be a matter of time.

nine

AKBAR PEERED OUT of the circular side-window as his Cessna banked and turned. He directed his bonoculars at *Quendon*.

'She's stopped for some reason,' he reported to Miranda in the seat beside him.

'Perhaps they have to take on a pilot?'

'Not with a vessel of that size, so long as she keeps clear of the sandbank, which is easy enough to do. They've lowered a boat. What the hell is going on?'

Tom Jim aimed his catapult at the ship, as though gauging the range. Then, with a sigh of regret, he slipped it back into his trouser pocket.

'Perhaps Uncle Tony's escaped?' he suggested hopefully.

'Unlikely,' said Akbar. 'I know the Gambia river quite well. The current is very strong. If Tony's in the water, he'll never be able to reach the shore.'

'Maybe that's what they hope?' said Miranda, remembering her husband.

'Possibly. But, if so, why have they stopped? Why have they lowered a boat? Surely it can only be to pick him up?'

Carter rested, treading water again. Small local craft, of the type he had seen from the ship, drifted past with yellowish sails that looked as though made from animal membrane, rounded by wind into the shape of half-balloons. Other boats were longer and brightly coloured, with complex designs: squares, circles, eyes, the shapes of birds.

He had never seen such boats before. Their hulls appeared to be made from single tree-trunks on which was built a canoe-shaped superstructure. One passed him a hundred yards away, going out to sea, and then he heard the put-put of an engine approaching from behind. He turned and prepared to dive again, for he half-expected to see *Quendon*'s lifeboat. Would Serrafino shoot him or simply hit him over the head with an oar and let the racing current do the rest?

But he was wrong. Instead of a lifeboat, one of these curiously long boats was coming in from the sea, making slow progress against the tide. He could see five men sitting one behind the other, with a rolled-up pile of fishing-net. None of the men had seen him. Carter waved to them frantically, then dived, and swam beneath the boat and surfaced on the far side. Now the helmsman saw him and waved.

'How are you today?' he called cheerfully in English.

'Help me!' shouted Carter in reply. The boat slowed, and the bow wave fell away as the helmsman throttled back.

'Don't slow down!' Carter yelled, for this could reveal his exact position; Mr Serrafino would guess that he had been picked up. The man looked surprised, but accelerated. Carter swam alongside the hull. Using his last reserves of energy, he reached up, gripped the warm wet wood, and slowly hauled himself aboard.

The floor of the boat was covered with a pyramid of silvery fish, gleaming like dagger blades in the sun. He could see that originally the boat must have been designed for a team of oarsmen, one sitting behind the other, as in a racing skiff. But a hole had been cut in the centre and fitted with a hollowed-out section of a tree-trunk, caulked to stop leaks. This hole now contained the outboard engine. Even in the extremity of his exhaustion, Carter admired such mechanical ingenuity.

'Who are you, then?' the helmsman asked him without much interest or surprise. 'A tourist?'

'Yes. A tourist.'

'You American, Spanish man, German?'

'No. English.'

'Good. England very good country. I have cousin in Streatham. You know of Streatham?'

'Yes. I know of Streatham.'

'Maybe you know my cousin, then?'

'Maybe. If not, I hope to meet him.'

'I give you his address. You swimming, man?'

'I was.'

'Why you wear clothes to swim, man!'

Why indeed? Carter warmed to these friendly people and could think of no answer that would sound in the slightest bit convincing. If he admitted he had jumped from a ship, they might take him back, thinking that this was what he wanted. To tell them the whole truth would be disastrous, for most people doubt anything outside their own narrow spectrum of experience. Carter shook his head, shrugged his shoulders as though too tired to answer.

'Maybe those clothes keep you warm in the water, eh?'

The helmsman roared with laughter at the idea. Carter grinned.

'Maybe,' he agreed.

'Where you going, then?'

'Land.'

'Banjul?'

Carter nodded. He had no idea what the man meant. Was Banjul a place – or was this simply a query in some local tongue as to his well-being?

'Your first visit The Gambia?' asked the helmsman. 'You like it here, man?'

Carter nodded. So that was where he was; in Britain's first and last colony in West Africa; the smallest independent country in the African continent, the closest of all English-speaking Commonwealth countries. And, of course, Banjul was the post-independence name for the main port. In Carter's schooldays this had been Bathurst, after the third Earl of Bathurst, who was British Colonial Secretary when The Gambia first became a colony. Carter felt he should have known this. But, then, he should have known lots of things, and he was tired.

'Where do we land?' he asked.

'The fish-market. Where you going? You stay local hotel?'

'What's the best?'

'Atlantic very good.'

'I'll try that.'

Carter nodded towards *Quendon*, now steaming ahead slowly, half a mile away.

'Where will that ship dock?' he asked casually, as though it was of only passing interest.

'Down beyond,' said the man vaguely. 'Past the ferry.'

The helmsman turned the long boat against the tide and headed in towards the shore. The river suddenly grew shallow and muddy. Skeletons of old and rotting fishing-boats, long since left to sink at their moorings, raised curved and mossy ribs from the water. The helmsman steered in carefully between these hazards, switched off his engine. Two men jumped ashore, made fast the boat as they bumped against a long stone quay.

On one side, under a rattan screen that shaded them from the pitiless sun, several men were carving the hull of a similar boat from the trunk of a single gigantic tree. Along the quayside, rows of flat sardine-like fish, gutted and filleted, were neatly spread out on the ground to dry in the sun. From the smell, some had been drying for days. In a concrete shed a diesel engine pounded away with a noise like a beating heart; smoke drifted up from its exhaust in a black spiral to the hot and windless sky.

Carter held up one hand to shade his eyes from the blaze of sun on water. He felt immeasurably weary. The helmsman climbed up on to the quay, waved a greeting to some friends, then began to help his companions to unload their catch. A young man in a wheelchair began to propel himself towards the quay from the cooler shadows of a building.

'Thank you for picking me up,' said Carter. 'I would like to give you a present.'

'No matter,' said the helmsman, shaking his head.

'It's a great matter to me,' Carter replied vehemently. 'But I'm sorry, I've no money on me. Where can I find you – when I can get to a bank?'

'We here every day 'bout this time. You know many people in Banjul?'

'No. But I have a friend to the east. In Abukali. Akbar Khan. His father was ruler apparently.'

'Oh, yes. You know Akbar Khan? He has a house here.'

'Where is it exactly?'

'Somewhere in Fajara. Not sure just where. On the beach.'

A policeman in khaki uniform approached them to look over the catch. Carter shook hands with the crew, set off towards the town. The concrete quay soon gave way to red dust, the colour of earthenware tiles ground to powder. Farther on, this merged into a pavement of crushed seashells. He came out of the fish-market, paused for a moment to get his bearings. To the left, a sea-wall had been strengthened with dozens of crashed cars; their red, blue and green bodies, hammered flat, gleamed incongruously above the water. Beyond this lay shacks and shanties and open fields. The main part of the town must lie to the right.

He set off along the only road. Dogs prowled hopefully in dusty gutters on either side, watching him with wary, yellow eyes. Outside a flat-roofed house, a man rocked himself to and fro in a hammock, one end tied to a tree, the other to a doorpost. Two plump middle-aged men in freshly laundered white robes cycled by him importantly, suitcases strapped on their rear mudguards. He passed shabby colonial-style port buildings with green verandas and blue and white enamel notices for Manager, Pilots, Harbour Master. Here chickens pecked in the dust and men wearing brightly coloured woolly hats fed cement into a mixer. Dust hung about them in a grey halo. Farther on, other men toiled in the shafts of trolleys, piled high with sacks of grain, and a goat dragged its tether listlessly from one patch of dusty grass to another.

Almost unexpectedly, the little buildings fell away and he was facing the docks. A woman washed clothes in a bucket by the side of a guardhouse under a running tap. The drain was filled with soap suds. An advertisement for a soft drink read:

'Fanfare. It's a bottle of fun.' I could use some, Carter thought. That's what's been missing in my life over the past few months. Fun.

Through the gate, he could see ships loading and unloading, hulls towering like sheer black cliffs against the pre-war single-storey buildings.

He paused for a moment. If he went direct to the British High Commission – assuming that he could find this – and explained he had seen a body in the deep-freeze of a ship in harbour, they might believe him or, again, they might not. But with his unshaven and battered appearance, wearing a shirt and jeans soaked in sea-water and now drying on his body, they might understandably view his allegations with some reserve. And by the time he had persuaded them, almost certainly Mrs Kent's corpse would have been removed, possibly in one of the containers he could see already being swung ashore by a crane – if, indeed, it had not already been dumped overboard miles out at sea.

It would be more productive to watch Mr Serrafino come ashore and discover where he was going, and whether he would unload the metal containers Carter had seen in the hold.

A West African in khaki drill-uniform, with a rifle slung over his shoulder, approached him slowly.

'You want anyone?' he asked.

'Just looking,' said Carter.

'You need a pass to come in here, man.'

'Where can I get one?'

'At the office. Inside.'

'Well, then, I'll go to the office.'

'Not possible without a pass, man.'

Carter smiled in spite of his predicament. Then he saw two Europeans in sweatshirts and jeans coming out between stacked wooden crates on the nearest dock.

'Do me a favour,' said Carter quickly. 'Ask these two for *their* passes.'

He dodged hastily to one side, for he had recognized Franz and Kurt. But they had also seen him and shouted, and began to run towards him, past the guard. Behind them, Carter saw other divers also start in pursuit.

He ran along the main road, keeping in the shadow of the houses where he could, jumping over open drains thick with purple bubbling refuse, and sleeping dogs. It was very hot. Birds dozed by the dozen on overhead telegraph wires; buses were parked with their doors and windows open to catch any breeze. He could see no place to hide, and not knowing the layout of the town he dare not risk running into any of the narrow alleys that branched off the street in case they led to buildings and he would be trapped.

They were gaining on him. He could hear them shout in English: 'Stop him! Stop that man!'

Locals came out of doorways and from shops to stare at the hunters and the hunted. Carter was tiring. His swim had exhausted him and the brief rest in the fishing-boat had not restored his energy. As though in a fearful dream, he saw signs above doorways: 'African Home Stores'; 'Curriculum Centre, Ministry of Education'; 'Seagull Home Stores'. A gang of men working in the road with a pneumatic drill cheered him as he ran, more slowly now than when he had started.

He passed a row of containers from the docks, red, blue and yellow, dumped at the roadside; trucks abandoned without their wheels; pyramids of sacks spilling salt – but nothing that offered any place to hide or double back on his tracks. Yet he had to find an escape from this straight road within seconds, or it would be too late, for he was running blindly, without any real aim, and his pursuers were barely thirty feet behind him.

Shops passed in a blur. A photographic studio. A window crammed with Japanese transistors. A man in a caftan squatting on a trestle-table to cut a bale of cloth with scissors the size of shears. A cheerful West African woman on a stool with a basket of peanuts in her lap – and then, behind her, he saw a small opening in a mud wall. Carter dived down this hole, barely two feet wide.

It led to an equally narrow catwalk covered with slatted-iron links, taken from a wartime airfield. On either side lay open drains where brown chickens scratched in the muck for scraps of food. Beyond these drains, jammed so close together they almost touched, were stalls stacked with bolts of cloth for suits, curtains, overcoats. Mounds of fleshy yellow fish crawled with flies. Other stalls had piles of mangoes, oranges, bananas, cheap watches. A sign offered 'Special Gunpowder China Tea'. Then he saw a notice, 'Prince Albert Market, Opened 1854', and slowed to a walk; it was difficult to run with so many people jostling him and pushing out from stalls to seek his custom.

The market appeared to be vast, and under a single roof of corrugated iron. Ahead, Carter caught brief glimpses of the glittering river through gaps in merchandise. Behind him, above a babble of voices and music from transistors, he could still hear faint cries: 'Stop!', 'Stop thief!'

He turned left down the first intersection, ran along the first catwalk on the right, and was immediately lost in another maze of stalls.

Big men, little men, fat men and thin, some wearing kaftans and round black Muslim caps and gold-rimmed spectacles, others in suits or jeans, looked at him curiously as he raced past. He dived to the left. Then he saw Franz ahead of him, walking slowly, looking along each of the bisecting alleyways. Franz looked up, saw Carter, and shouted to his colleagues.

Carter turned back, dodged into the first alley on the right, and stopped between two stalls, hoping he was out of sight from whoever could look from one end of the alley to the other. One stall was covered with little piles of black hair, for wigs. The other was empty except for a bowl of smoking incense powder that gave off a sweet soothing scent.

A woman squatted at his feet, oblivious of pursuers and pursued, frying slices of rancid meat on a metal plate the size of a dustbin lid over an open fire. Carter felt sick with the conflicting smells and, worse than either, a terrible sense of failure and futility.

Had he escaped from the sea only to be caught so easily on land? He *must* think of a plan, a way out, but he could think of nothing. Blood beat in his head like a drum.

He heard a shout behind him again, as his pursuers sighted him, and forced his way between the two stalls to yet another catwalk. On either side of him now, rows of treadle sewing machines clattered away as tailors made suits, shirts, skirts. They did not even look up as their deft fingers fed the cloth under the flickering jabbing needles. Then, ahead of him only yards away, he saw Franz and again Franz saw him.

'Got you!' Franz shouted triumphantly, and began to run towards him. Carter turned, and raced the other way. Too late he saw that this alley ended in a concrete wall, hung with bright metal photograph-frames. He was trapped.

Franz was shouting to the others now. Kurt and Ruskie had joined him. They pounded down the catwalk towards Carter, hemmed in by stalls piled high with tea-cosy hats and plastic sandals. The stallholders were also shouting, but whether in anger or encouragement he was too tired to care. Franz was barely twenty yards away now. Fifteen. Ten. It was all over. . . .

And then, directly in front of them, a man in a wheelchair propelled himself from a side-alley none of them had seen.

He was a young West African, legs wasted, arms and shoulders grotesquely muscled from his exertions. He stopped directly in front of the running men and deftly swung his chair around by its wheels to block their path.

Franz was running too fast to stop. He tripped and went headlong over the chair. Carter raced towards him as Franz struggled to his feet, hit him a left and a right to the jaw. Franz went down heavily, slipped sideways off the catwalk into the bubbling, stinking gutter. The West African in the wheelchair now shouted to the nearest stallholders, who seized staves, sticks, a pole from the inside of a bale of cloth to belabour the three East Germans. Under their ferocious attack, they turned and fled.

Carter, trembling with fatigue and reaction, approached the man in the wheelchair.

'Thank you,' he said, realizing how absurdly stilted and inadequate the words sounded.

The man smiled. His teeth were very white in his brown friendly face.

'You are Akbar Khan's friend?'

'Yes. How do you know?'

'They told me at the fish-market. I go there most mornings. Help tot up the catch. My uncle was steering the boat that picked you up.'

Carter remembered the young man in the wheelchair on the quay.

'I saw you there,' he said. 'But who are you? Why did you come to my aid?'

'I'm Joseph Mokomba. Akbar Khan has been a very good friend to me. He gave me this chair.'

He patted the chromium arms proudly. 'All the way from London. Especially made for me. If it hadn't been for him, I would just be a beggar on the street corner. His friend is my friend.'

The stallholders now went back to their stalls, grinning to each other. Excitement was better than passively waiting for customers.

'Why are those men chasing you?' Joseph asked Carter.

'It's really too long to explain here. They held me aboard ship but I managed to jump. That's how I met your uncle.'

'You know your way around Banjul, man?'

'Never been here in my life.'

'Then, I'll guide you. That's why I followed you. To see if I could help you. Where are you going now?'

'Any hotel where I can get a change of clothes and something to eat. Your uncle mentioned the Atlantic. Where is it?'

'Very near, but those men will be waiting for you outside the market. I cannot help you much in the open. It is different in here.'

He turned to a stallholder squatting on piles of red, blue and yellow woollen hats, spoke to him. The man nodded, clambered off the pile, handed Carter a dark-brown kaftan and a blue hat.

'Put them on,' Joseph told him.

'I can't pay you,' Carter said to the stallholder.

'Joseph will bring them back,' the man replied at once. 'Say you are trying them for size, eh?'

'Pull the hat right down over your ears,' Joseph advised Carter. 'Then keep your head down and push my chair. Don't on any account look up. You should be safe enough.'

Joseph gave him muttered directions as they moved through the bustling market: first left, second right, straight ahead. They came out into Russell Street, then around a dusty recreation-ground with a war memorial to the men of the Royal West African Frontier Force in two world wars, past a drinking-fountain in pink stone. The crowds were thick on the streets. Cars hooted impatiently and bullock carts moved in their slow and stately way.

Carter kept his head down as Joseph had advised, for out of the corners of his eyes he could see Franz, shirt and trousers still drenched with muck, and then four other divers. They were all standing on the far side of the road, watching the entrances of the market.

'Straight ahead,' said Joseph. Carter pushed him past a Texaco petrol station and a café, then down a road towards the river by the side of the Royal Victoria Hospital, then along Marine Parade to the hotel.

Outside, a fountain played in an artificial pond. To the left of this a number of yellow taxis waited in line, drivers lying asleep on mats spread out beneath the trees. A uniformed doorman came down the steps slowly as they approached.

'You take off the kaftan and hat now,' said Joseph. 'I'll give them back.'

'You probably saved my life,' said Carter.

'Then I have returned Akbar Khan's gift. Because, my friend, with this chair he saved *my* life.'

'I've no money to give you,' said Carter. 'But I will get some in a moment.'

'I don't want money,' replied Joseph simply. 'I did it out of friendship.'

He shook hands, then bent forward, gripped the wheels of his chair and propelled himself smoothly away down the hotel drive.

Carter crossed to the reception-desk. The clerk looked at him enquiringly. Carter was unshaven, in filthy clothes, his hair plastered to his head with sweat; not the sort of guest that any hotel would welcome.

'You have a reservation, sir?'

Carter pulled out his American Express card.

'As of now, I hope.'

The man examined the card.

'Do you have any luggage, sir?'

'That's coming on.'

The clerk gave him a room number and a key.

'The third floor, sir.'

Carter went up to his room, phoned room service for a razor, had a shave and a bath. Then he ordered brandy and ginger, coffee, eggs and bacon, and sat down on the veranda overlooking the swimming-pool and the river. He had just started breakfast when the telephone rang in the room. He went inside to pick it up.

'I was wondering when you would arrive,' said Akbar.

'Where the hell are you?'

'About three miles up the road at Fajara. I have a house there.'

'So I've heard. But I don't even know where Fajara is.'

'You soon will. I'll send a car.'

'I have only the clothes I stand up in, and they're filthy.'

'Not to worry. I have a full wardrobe here. We're about the same size. I can give you anything you want.'

'I'd rather have an explanation. How you knew I was here.'

'You'll have that, too. In the meantime, I look forward to seeing you. So do my other two guests: Miranda and Tom Jim.'

Carter put down the telephone, lifted the brandy and ginger to drink to his good fortune. Then he caught sight of himself in a long mirror on the far wall above the dressing-table. He had lost weight since Arrifana. He looked tougher, leaner, harder.

It would be madness to go back now to those days and nights when he looked at the future through the bottom of an upturned glass. He had told himself often enough that this and this and this would be his last drink. Now this must be the last time he said that; this must also be that last drink. He toasted himself symbolically in the mirror, then carried the full glass into the bathroom and slowly, deliberately, poured the drink away into the basin. Then he rinsed out the glass, went out on to the veranda. The sun was shining, and the world suddenly looked very good.

Mr Serrafino waited by the Customs post in the port authority building at Banjul. It was very hot. A fan slapped the air ineffectually above his head. He felt drops of perspiration trickle slowly down his back, and he mopped his forehead with a silk handkerchief. The Gambian customs officer pored over the typed list.

'Scrap iron,' he said at last. 'That's all you wish to import? Old oil-drums and boilers and heating radiators?'

'Yes. The weights and origins and so on are all there on the form.'

'No duty to pay, then, sir.'

'Thank you,' said Mr Serrafino.

'Thank *you*, sir. Welcome to The Gambia. It is good to see you English people trading here.'

'My pleasure,' Mr Serrafino answered him. He signalled to the driver of a truck parked in the shade of the building. The truck moved forward; a net of ropes held the blocks of metal drums and radiators firmly in place.

'You know the route,' Mr Serrafino told the driver. 'We will cross the frontier into Menaka before that border closes. All the documents are stamped and in order. I'll follow right behind you in the car.'

He heard a sudden commotion to one side and turned, frowning at the interruption. Franz came racing up to him. Mr Serrafino regarded his stinking clothes with disgust; flies were already crawling greedily over the stains.

'We saw the Englishman, Carter,' Franz explained breathlessly.

'Where?'

'Here. At the dock gates. We chased him. He got away in the market.'

'Was he alone?'

'Yes.'

'Well, he can't go very far. The market's a rabbit warren of criss-cross paths and only two ways out.'

'I know. The others are watching for him.'

'Good. If he went in, he has to come out before dusk. That's when it closes.'

'And when we get him?'

'Bring him along,' said Mr Serrafino. 'I will organize a truck to wait opposite the main entrance. You can pack him into it without much trouble, surely.'

Mr Serrafino gave a signal of command with his right hand. A Mercedes pulled out from a side-street opposite the docks. Mr Serrafino climbed in behind the driver, and frowned. The car was not air-conditioned. He ordered the driver to open the sun-roof and the two front windows. He felt he had been in hot, wearying climates for too long – Burma, West Africa, Central Africa – but another two days at the most, and all this discomfort would be behind him. Ahead stretched a life of ease, a world of white houses with striped awnings over their windows, swimming-pools kept at a constant temperature, wines from a dozen countries. There was nothing sensual or sexual in his plans; Mr Serrafino had no use for women and no need of boys. He felt totally safe and supremely secure in himself. He was his own man – and that was how it would always be. He sank back on the soft leather cushions, pondering the pleasures of independence and the prospect of immeasurable wealth.

'Checking out already?' the Atlantic Hotel receptionist asked Carter.

'I'll probably be back. But, in the meantime, as the advert says, this'll do nicely.'

He paid the bill with his American Express card, and then climbed into the Jaguar that Akbar had sent for him. As he settled into the seat beside the driver, Carter felt relaxed for the first time since he had met Mrs Kent in São Sebastião, and he tried to find any convincing reason for this totally irrational feeling of well-being. Could it be because, at last, he felt he was not alone, that he now had allies by his side? Possibly and partly, yes. But he had to admit, if only privately to himself, that the real reason was that soon he would be seeing Miranda again.

The road shimmered under the midday sun. On either side stretched a strip of dust two yards wide. Beyond this, on the left, he saw areas of thick grass and feathery trees, and then the rich soft green of miles of mangrove swamps. Dark mangrove roots sprouted upwards from the ground, like rows of blackened stakes. On the other side, between the road and the sea, they passed two cemeteries with some gravestones the size of doors, others draped with flowers. The driver slowed to pass a giant baobab-tree that almost blocked the road. Its trunk was thick and fat, yet its thin upraised branches looked as though they should really be roots and the whole tree had been turned upside down. The trunk was painted with white horizontal stripes as a warning to motorists.

'Why don't they cut that down?' Carter asked the driver.

'Very good tree, sir. That's why. We make fibre from its bark, boil its leaves to eat as vegetables. And baobab seeds contain tartaric acid, which flavours our drinks. You want medicines for headache, heartache, you name it? Then you can pulp bark and roots for that. Not many trees give you shelter, food and drink – and medicine if you eat and drink too much!'

'Any more even half as good here?'

'Oh, yes, some, sir. One palm-tree gives oil – and palm wine. Another is so strong even sea-water won't hurt it, so they use it for building wharves and landing-places. Then the cottonsilk has seeds full of kapok for mattresses. Its trunk is so wide we make planks out of it. You know what we use them for?'

'No idea.'

'Coffins. I tell you, sir, we have many fine and useful trees hereabouts. But I tell you one very sad thing. People in my country like to cook on charcoal fires, and since independence came in 1965 they've cut down a third of all the forests here just to get wood to burn. One tree in three, sir. Gone. Not ever coming back. So now there's very strong law against destroying any tree without Government's permission, or using tree wood for making fires.'

'I saw someone cooking on wood in the market,' said Carter, remembering the old woman in front of the incense stall.

'That would be broken bits of wood. Old packing-cases, crates, boxes, sir. Not new tree wood.'

'A good law,' said Carter.

'Oh, a very good law. But a bit late. Maybe it's all too late.'

'I hope not,' said Carter, thinking now of his own situation. 'I very much hope not.'

The driver approached a notice: *Police Check. Slow Down.*

Two policemen in khaki drill-uniforms, rifles slung over their shoulders, waited in the shade, watching the traffic. A third waved the car to a halt, examined the driver's licence, grinned cheerfully, waved them on again. A bridge with a sentry-box at each end, sandbagged and reinforced, spanned a creek; Carter saw the barrel of a machine-gun gleam behind the sandbags. They passed a village of huts made from oil-drums hammered flat and corrugated-iron fences. A hen nested in a hollow tree beneath advertisements for Long Life batteries and Silk Cut cigarettes. Then they swung away from the main road, and within minutes were in what appeared a totally different world: the suburb of Fajara.

Bougainvillaea cascaded in a mass of mauve and magenta and mustard flowers to conceal wire security fences twenty feet high. Palm-trees waved feather-duster branches elegantly above tamarisk hedges. Hibiscus plants lined drives and pathways with crimson, and sprinklers played on lawns. Through screens of bushes and shrubs Carter caught brief glimpses of large white houses, with sunshades down to shield wide windows. Smartly uniformed guards carrying truncheons stood sentry at front gates.

The driver turned into a red-surfaced drive, stopped under a huge portico. Akbar Khan came down the steps to meet Carter.

'You are quite right,' Akbar announced, regarding Carter's shabby appearance with a critical eye. 'You do need some new clothes. Badly.'

He led the way upstairs to his bedroom.

'Suits here; shirts, socks over here. Shoes in this cupboard. I'll see you downstairs when you're ready.'

Carter collected a pair of lightweight trousers, rope-soled canvas shoes, a T-shirt. Akbar Khan stood waiting for him on the terrace. Tom Jim was punting himself around the swimming-pool in an inflatable rubber boat. He waved a cheerful greeting. Beyond the wire fence, white rollers pounded the beach.

'I've still got it!' shouted Tom Jim gleefully.

'What?'

'The catapult you gave me. I've practised every day. I can make a stone skim twice – *and* hit a target every time. It's easy when you know how.'

'Everything is,' Carter replied. 'Now, I'll show you how to make it jump three times.'

He sat down in a rattan chair.

'What are you drinking?' Akbar asked him.

'Something soft. *Agua mineral* if you have it.'

'Not under that name, we haven't. We do have Julpearl or Fanfare.'

'I saw that advertisement in Banjul. I'll try a bottle of fun.'

'Thought you were a brandy man?'

'So did too many other people.'

'We'll have you a good Muslim yet. Teetotal.'

'Maybe you will; but, in the meantime, how the devil did you know I'd be at the Atlantic Hotel, here in Banjul, when we said goodbye off a beach in Portugal? I'd no idea myself where I was until I got here.'

'Put like that it does seem a remarkable piece of deduction,'

Akbar agreed. 'But when you didn't come back from *Quendon* I thought you must have decided to stay aboard for some reason. Either you were trapped below decks by an accident, such as a locked door, or, most likely, you'd been discovered and they were holding you prisoner.'

'Exactly what happened. They locked me up.'

'Quite so. Well, I felt I'd caused you enough trouble already, even if unwittingly. I couldn't very well leave you now, so I decided to follow the ship.'

'Follow the ship? How?'

'By aircraft. My own, actually. We flew from Faro. Before we took off, I checked with the local coastguard people, and they reported that *Quendon* was sailing south off Sagres, so we followed her. We landed several times on the way here, but I have a diplomatic passport so that was no problem. I had an idea that *Quendon* might be heading for Banjul, and I was right.'

'Your plane silver and blue?' Carter asked, remembering watching a small aircraft through the porthole.

'Right. So you must have seen me. Now, what happened to you?'

Carter explained.

'And you know how I managed to jump overboard, and was picked up by fishermen just when I thought I'd had it?'

'Joseph Mokomba told me. One of the pleasures of money is that you can buy most things you want. One of its privileges is that you can also do some good. Joseph is one of the few who's repaid everything I've tried to do for him. There's a saying in my country: "If you are unwise enough to help a lame dog, you must expect to be bitten." '

'And in mine, too, I don't doubt,' replied Carter. 'But what if I *hadn't* jumped? I'd still be aboard *Quendon* stuck in the docks, surely?'

'Probably not for long,' said Akbar. 'I have a number of good friends in The Gambia. We would have tried to ensure that your disembarkation was not delayed unduly.'

'So you mean I jumped into the river, risked my life with

tides, currents, crocodiles, sharks, serpents of the deep, bullets and God knows what else, when I'd have been better off staying on my butt in the cabin as a prisoner?'

Akbar laughed.

'You *might* have been killed, of course. Like Mrs Kent. And de Silva. Like growing older, that was the only alternative. So, considering everything, you acted for the best. Hindsight is always 20/20 vision. Which makes it dangerous for anyone to indulge in. You can only do what seems best at the time.'

'So what is best to do now? Do you think the metal containers I saw contain gold? If so, why bring it out here?'

'That's what we will have to discover,' said Akbar. 'I must tell you, I am informed that a truck has already picked up these containers described on the Customs forms as scrap iron. This was followed from the docks by a Mercedes with Mr Serrafino inside. The two vehicles have already passed through the town, going east. There is actually no other main road they *could* take, so this was not a very difficult deduction to make. The road follows the Gambia river, west to east. Everything bound for the interior that comes in by ship is unloaded in Banjul. To the north and south there's Senegal, and then farther to the east the vast countries of Mauretania and Mali, and my own very small Abukali. And, of course, Menaka.'

'Where that madman Odongo was deposed a few weeks back?'

'Correct. The road goes through the narrowest part of Menaka, and then reaches my country.'

'Where do you think Serrafino is heading?'

'Menaka or Abukali. I don't think he'd have much hope of finding customers for gold or much else in Mauretania or Mali. And his association with Odongo has been long and profitable. I'd lay two to one on Menaka.'

'Let's follow him, then. Get out on the road at once, otherwise we may lose him. There must be *some* other roads north and south he could take as well as this main road.'

'Oh, there are,' Akbar agreed. 'But when you have lived longer in Africa, Tony, you will realize that the pace of life is slower because the climate is against precipitate action. There is no need for the haste you find in cooler places.'

'Maybe there isn't for you, but there is for me. Apart from keeping me prisoner in his ship, Serrafino owes me ten thousand dollars. Not much, maybe, to someone with a house like this and his own aircraft, but it's still a tidy sum to me.'

'I understand your concern, but because we do not rush off immediately doesn't mean we won't go when it seems the best moment to move. Let me show you what I mean.'

Akbar nodded towards the corner of his garden that stretched down to the beach near the mouth of the Gambia river.

'What do you see on the river now?' he asked Carter.

'Three boats, like the one that picked me up. All going up-river.'

'And all travelling very slowly?'

'Hardly moving.'

'Understandably. Because the tide is running strongly against them. But, like you, their captains are impatient. They want to get their catch to market quickly, to be first if possible. So they waste nearly all the profit they hope to make from the fish on petrol, just to beat the current.

'There's your answer, Tony. If they considered the problem logically, they would realize that the tide was about to change. Within half an hour, say, it will be running in. Then it would carry them right up to the fish-market, virtually without petrol, sails or oars. In life, one has to make the best use of all natural facilities.'

'And you are?' Carter asked him sceptically.

'Let's hope so — at last. We haven't done much in that direction so far. In the meantime, here's Miranda. After all this is sorted out I want you to come with her and Tom Jim and spend a few days with me in Abukali. I'm having some aggravation from my uncle, who feels aggrieved I inherited the title of ruler instead of him. I would value your advice about this. He's been causing a lot of trouble, and there's enough already in the world without stirring up any more.'

'You intend to show him who is actually boss?'

'Yes, if not in such crude terms. Rather, where his best interests lie – and the interests of our country. We are a poor small state if we have to live simply on the produce of the land. We have no direct access to the sea, and that makes our products expensive. But, if we make the best use of minerals under our feet, we can raise the standard of life for everyone – not just for a few, as my uncle would like to do.

'I think that power, like wealth, brings special responsibilities – and temptations. I want to accept the former and avoid the latter. My uncle's priorities – like those of Odongo and Serrafino – are the other way round.'

Akbar Khan paused. Carter heard a car arrive outside the house. A door slammed, the car drove away. A man came out on to the terrace, looked about him. Akbar rose to greet him, turned to Carter.

'Tony,' he said. 'Meet someone who arrived from Madrid last night – not so dramatically as you. Simply by scheduled airline. William Best.'

They shook hands. Akbar turned to Miranda.

'I'm sorry we'll have to leave you for a short time. I want to ask Tony and William to help me over a small matter before we meet an interesting character. Tony already knows him, and William here believes he holds the answer to many of the questions that puzzle us. A man named Franz Halstein.'

ten

FRANZ WALKED DOWN the gangway of *Quendon*, carrying a suitcase in each hand. As Mr Serrafino had promised, a car was parked in the shade of a godown. Kurt called down to him from the deck of the ship.

'Have a drink tonight when you get back?'

'Of course,' Franz replied at once. 'Delighted.'

But he would not be coming back; all his belongings were already in the suitcases. When he had done what he had to do, he would catch the next flight from Banjul to Gatwick. By the following night he would be at home in Leipzig, with enough money in a Swiss bank to ensure that he need never work again — unless on some project that interested him. One more day. . . .

He crossed the dusty yard near the ferry terminal. Around him, yellow cranes dipped like the beaks of gigantic spindly birds, and pulleys squealed as bales of cloth and sacks of grain were hauled out from the deep holds of half a dozen ships. Franz climbed into the car. It was suffocatingly hot, and he opened both front windows before he drove out through the gates. He saluted the guard, turned right along the main street where only hours ago he had chased the Englishman Carter, past shacks and open drains and lines with tattered shabby washing hung out like flags of defeat.

His sharp eyes noted a shuttered warehouse with huge iron bars and padlocks across its doors. The men who owned that building and whatever it contained had doubtless spent a lifetime — as had possibly their fathers and grandfathers before them — amassing their wealth. Extraordinary to think that he could be rich in a matter of hours. It was simply a matter of timing, of knowledge, the taking of calculated risks. The whole thing was a scientific equation; nothing more, nothing less.

Mr Serrafino had engaged him because of his qualifications. Now he would present the papers he had prepared that guaranteed the value of what the drums contained to the man who had apparently engaged Mr Serrafino. One man had the money, another the idea, but he alone possessed the authority to link them, and without him the talents of the others were valueless. There had been some nasty moments with that idiot Englishman, Carter. A pity he had escaped, but the man's freedom would only be temporary. Where could be run to in a place like this?

Franz chewed gum as he drove along Independence Drive, past the sign *No Parking for Hackney Carriages*, then an upholsterer's shop where the owner slept on a sofa with its stuffing oozing out, surrounded by half-finished chairs and car seats. Then he was out of town, and approaching the police post. A constable in starched khaki bush-shirt and trousers and black peaked cap waved him to a halt.

'How are you today?' he asked him cheerfully.

'Fine,' said Franz shortly.

'Tourist?'

Franz nodded.

'Just enjoying the sun,' he explained, not wishing to appear discourteous in case the man delayed him; to be late could be disastrous. He handed over his passport and international driving licence. The man looked at them, then at him, handed them back, waved him on. As Franz crossed the bridge, a smell of rotting vegetation blew in from the swamps. He wrinkled his nose. You could never tell what deadly germs might be carried by the wind; that was the trouble with being a scientist. You knew too much, and those black lakes of stagnant water could so easily be a mass of bilharzia. The road swung to the left and right in easy curves. A second notice warned: *Slow. Police Check*.

Fifty yards on another policeman waved his swagger-cane for the car to stop. Franz pulled up obediently. The policeman pointed his stick off the road. Franz drove into a clearing, switched off his engine and waited. The policeman approached slowly, then banged imperiously on the roof of the car with his cane.

'Papers, please,' he said.

'I've already shown them up the road,' Franz replied, fumbling in his pocket for them.

'I'm sorry, sir. Only a routine check.'

The policeman looked at the passport and licence and frowned, pursing his lips.

'Everything all right?' Franz asked him nervously. It would be fatal if he was to be delayed by some bureaucratic folly. Everything depended on timing; he *had* to arrive on time. Franz kept concern out of his voice as he asked: 'What's the matter?'

'You are holder of this East German passport? You are Herr Franz Halstein?'

'Yes. I am.'

'Perhaps you would get out of the car, sir?'

'Of course. But why?'

Franz climbed out. The policeman swiftly leaned in through the window removed the ignition key, pocketed it.

'What's wrong?' asked Franz.

'Only that a couple of people would like a word with you, Mr Halstein,' said Akbar, handing back his passport and licence.

'Well, where are they?'

'Here,' said Carter, pushing aside the bushes that had screened him.

'You,' said Franz slowly. Then he glanced at William Best, who followed him out. His mouth tightened.

'We would like to know where you are going. And why,' said Carter. 'Especially, why.'

'What the devil is this? A hold-up?'

He turned to Akbar.

'If you must know, as a policeman, I have been paid off in Banjul port from a diving job. I am taking a look around your wonderful country, which I have never seen before, in a hired car. And then I return to my ship before it sails tonight.'

'You have not been paid off,' Best corrected him shortly. 'You're on your way to collect your pay-off. Open your bag.'

'*Are* you a policeman?' Franz asked Akbar, ignoring Best's request.

'No,' Akbar replied. 'But I don't think I'm too bad an actor.'

He handed the keys to Best, who opened the car boot, undid Franz's two suitcases and took out a British Caledonian airline ticket in the name of Mr Grundig.

'Since you tell us you are going back by ship, you won't need this,' he said, and tore the ticket into small pieces and let them flutter to the ground.

Franz looked from one man to the other, then jumped to one side and started to run. Carter put out his foot and tripped him. Franz fell flat on his face in the dust. Carter knelt in the small of his back, twisted his arms up in a Nelson hold.

'Answer one question,' he told him. 'What's in those metal cases in the back of Serrafino's truck?'

'Gold. You know that.'

'You took them out of the sea?'

'Of course. Before you arrived.'

Carter increased his grip.

'You're breaking my arm!' cried Franz.

'Then, don't waste our time. Once more, what's inside those cases?'

Franz shook his head.

'I've told you. Gold. That's the truth.'

'What is truth?' asked Akbar conversationally. 'That's the question Pilate asked. If he didn't know, how can we? But we all have our own theories, and mine is that you are not telling the truth, Mr Halstein. Whatever it is.'

He turned to Best.

'Put him in the car and we'll find out.'

Best had already opened the rear nearside door of Franz's car. Now he closed it again, came around to the other rear door, opened this and ostentatiously set the child's lock so that it could not be opened from the inside.

They man-handled Franz into the back of his car, closed the

door behind him. He seized the handle. It did not move. He pushed down on it and then pulled up with all his strength. The handle snapped in his hand. He threw it away.

'What the hell are you going to do?' he asked fearfully.

'Give you a test they used frequently out here long ago. Ordeal by fire. If you are innocent and speak the truth, you will come unscathed through the flames as they walked through the fiery furnace in the Old Testament story. But if you are not, my friend. . . .'

Akbar paused and shrugged his shoulders.

Carter raised the bonnet, picked up a large stone, smashed it on the carburettor. A smell of petrol filled the air. Best lit a spill of paper from his cigar-lighter, and threw this on to the engine. With a roar, a gout of flame shot six feet above the car. The windscreen cracked like a whip in the sudden rush of heat.

'You have perhaps two minutes before the petrol-tank goes up,' Akbar told Franz conversationally, as someone might remark that it was warm for this time of year, but the weather could change.

'It's at the back of the car,' he added. 'About a foot behind you. Now, what's in those drums?'

'I've told you,' began Franz in an anguished voice. An unexpected gust of wind blew flames through the shattered windscreen. They scorched the roof lining. He felt them singe his hair, his eyebrows.

'I'll tell you!' he shouted. 'I'll tell you! But let me out!'

'Afterwards.'

Franz began to shout against the crackle of bushes burning around the car, the smell of paint blistering on the bonnet.

'And that *is* the truth?' Best asked him.

'Of course it is. All the truth. For God's sake! Let me out!'

'In your own time,' Carter said easily. 'The far door isn't locked. Only this one.'

They moved away from the burning car as Franz leaped out through the other door. The front tyres were already alight and, as he raced between the trees, the petrol-tank exploded. He ran through the bushes out on to the main road. A police Land-Rover was cruising towards the clearing. It stopped. Two constables jumped out, and held him by the arms. Akbar took off his police cap and belt, put them in his own car concealed behind a clump of bamboo, and followed at a more leisurely pace. He consulted his watch.

'Thanks for being on time, Sergeant. I thought it would be a quarter of an hour. Actually, it has taken exactly twelve minutes. This tourist's car is on fire. An offence over here,' he explained to Franz.

'What the hell do you mean, an offence?'

Franz turned to one of the policemen.

'Officer,' he began, and then paused. How did he know whether they were genuine or not?

'Your car could set fire to this entire forest,' Akbar explained. 'It might burn for days, and spread for miles. There is a strict law in The Gambia that you cannot burn *any* tree – let alone a whole forest. And, Sergeant, I will be making charges of a more serious nature.'

Akbar produced his diplomatic passport.

'What kind of charges, sir?' asked the sergeant.

'Using this country as a base for terrorist operations against a friendly state – Abukali. Being involved in the murder of a British subject. Helping to conceal the body of another murdered person aboard a vessel now in Banjul port. Having a hand in the murder of a third person, a Portuguese subject. Does that answer your question, Sergeant?'

Odongo put on his black Homburg hat, adjusted it carefully in the mirror to the most becoming angle, as chosen by the British statesman he had seen on that newsreel so long ago. He would be wearing it soon on his triumphal return to his capital. The hat was his talisman, his ju-ju. It could never let him down. He came down the steps of his house to greet Mr Serrafino slowly and majestically in a way befitting an emperor.

He had seen the truck and the Mercedes arrive. The truck was parked to one side of the clearing, under the shade of a baobab-tree. The car was facing the road along which it had come. Mr Serrafino walked from it to meet Odongo and bowed gravely. He was not certain what mood the man might be in, and he wished to do nothing that could possibly upset him at such a delicate stage in their negotiations. If Odongo was suffering from one of his bad spells, he might postpone a decision indefinitely, and Mr Serrafino could afford no delays.

'You have brought what you promised?' Odongo asked him shortly.

Mr Serrafino nodded. He looked with distaste at Odongo's face, flushed with rum and vengeance. His wild yellow eyes were bloodshot. Flecks of dried saliva whitened the corners of his mouth.

'And you are certain it can do all you claim for it?'

'I have one of the greatest scientists in Eastern Europe following me in another car,' Mr Serrafino replied smoothly. 'He will vouch for that before anyone. He will also bring documents that will prove it in scientific terms to anyone able to understand them. Not you or me, maybe, Emperor, for we are not men of academic learning, but anyone in the West or in the Eastern Bloc who is will vouch for them immediately. That is this scientist's value.'

'It could also be our danger. When he leaves, will he tell anyone what we have done?'

'I think not, Emperor. He will never leave. Your guards will detain him.'

'Good. That is as I hoped.'

Mr Serrafino cleared his throat. The journey in the heat from the docks along a dusty road, and the strain of facing this psychopath, had momentarily robbed him of his voice.

'You have here,' he went on slowly, as he knew Odongo liked to be addressed. 'You have here, Emperor, a golden key to the kingdom of Abukali with all the wealth that awaits your orders to liberate it from the earth. On that truck is treasure beyond price, to make you the most powerful man in all Africa.'

'You speak truth, my friend,' replied Odongo, his voice thick with emotion. What would be sweeter than revenge? One thing: revenge plus power, and the certain knowledge that no one could stand against him. And yet, looking at these metal drums and castings roped together in the back of the truck, they seemed of no consequence or importance whatever. They bore an extraordinary resemblance to central-heating radiators he had seen in barracks in Aldershot where he had once been posted for an army course in his time as a soldier, and oil-drums in fuel depots of his own army.

But what did outward appearances matter? They were often deceptive. Was not the avocado pear rough and prickly outside but, when its skin was removed, full of soft sweet fruit? The spitting cobra had a skin unmatched for beauty, yet its poison could blind a man, and the venom of the lovely green mamba could kill as surely as a dagger blade. To some, Odongo realized, he might also appear as only another overthrown despot. But he knew the truth: he was on the verge of becoming the most important leader in Africa's history.

'I will address my people,' he announced and turned to give orders to an aide. Within minutes, a bugler sounded Assembly. From the shade of bushes and trees, men began to fill the clearing. All were armed, some with rifles or submachine-guns slung from their shoulders. Others had clusters of grenades at their belts. Many wore only underpants or loincloths. They gathered now in a wide circle with the rim of forest facing Odongo. He raised his Homburg to them in greeting, replaced it, tilted it to the correct angle, and began to speak.

'My soldiers,' he began and then paused. His voice was so heavy with emotion and pleasure at the thought of his approaching triumph after the misery and humiliation of defeat that he had to compose himself. His mind fumed with fantasies of the tortures he would inflict on his enemies and those who had deserted him. Already he could hear their cries for mercy and screams of pain mingle with the shouts of adulation from the thousands he had no doubt would loyally throng the streets of his capital to welcome his return to power. He felt so moved at the prospect that he did not know which sounds pleased him more. Tears rolled down his shining swollen cheeks and he made no attempt to wipe them away.

'This is the hour of destiny!' he went on at last. 'This is the moment when we regroup our followers and march to victory! Not only in our land, I tell you, but also in Abukali. I pledge to you that every man who has followed me into this fortress will receive a grant of fifty acres of land, and the equivalent of five thousand English pounds sterling *and* a pension for life, with the honorary rank of corporal.

'I speak to you, not only as your emperor, ordained by all the gods of field and forest, river and sea, but as a comrade-in-arms, who has carried a rifle for his king and emperor, as you have borne arms for me. Today, we rejoice! Tomorrow, we march!'

In a triumphant gesture, Odongo raised his Homburg hat in his right hand and waved it wildly. His audience cheered and stamped their feet. Mr Serrafino swallowed nervously as he approached Odongo.

'There is something else,' he began. 'I meant to tell you in private, but now I think it is something you may wish to make known.'

'What is it?' asked Odongo hoarsely, still waving his hat. He had not seen such exuberance for weeks. He must do nothing that could allow this enthusiasm to flag.

'I have learned that Akbar Khan will leave his house in The Gambia later today and drive to Abukali. This means, of course, that he has to cross your border. I suggest you order your men to fell a tree across the main road. Make it look like an accident so that he will have to take a detour that will bring him here. Then give him this ultimatum. Either he makes over Abukali here and now to you and your heirs – in front of your followers, of course – or you use what is in these containers. At once. No second chance. No delay. This is your hour, Emperor! Seize it and go forward to victory – and history.'

'You speak truth,' said Odongo greatly impressed. 'I will do as proposed. I, Odongo, have decided.'

He turned to his audience and held up both hands for silence. The cheering and stamping subsided immediately.

'I have just promised you control over the land of Abukali. Now my friend and blood brother here tells me that Akbar

Khan, who falsely claims authority over that country, is at this moment on his way to meet me here. In front of all of you, I will ask him to sign over the kingdom. And he will agree. The country of Abukali will be for you and your sons and your sons' sons to enjoy for ever!'

He paused, his mind fuddled with alcohol and oratory.

'It is I, Odongo, who has spoken,' he reminded them.

The men cheered and shouted: 'Odongo! Great is Odongo! Odongo!'

Akbar had no difficulty in crossing the frontier into Menaka; he simply showed his diplomatic passport, and the Immigration and Customs officials waved him through the barrier without even asking to see the other passengers' passports. They were not over-zealous in their duties. They had not been paid during the last months of Emperor Odongo's regime.

For a few miles from the border, the highway was straight and empty, with mangrove swamps on either side. Then it entered wooded country, and finally ran through the centre of a thick, dark forest. Akbar, at the wheel of the Jaguar, saw the tree down across the road first, and then the hastily painted warning sign, *Diversion*, with an arrow pointing to the left. He stopped the car, climbed out with Carter to examine the fallen tree. Miranda stayed in the back with Tom Jim.

'It's been half-sawn through at the bottom,' Carter told her as he got back into the car.

'Maybe the wind brought it down?' suggested Miranda hopefully.

'More likely a rope,' said Akbar. 'And directly across the road.'

'You think it's a trap?' Miranda asked.

'No doubt about it. But, bearing that in mind, as with the current on the Gambia river, let us follow the detour.'

Akbar turned the car along the crude track hacked into the forest.

'At the worst we're only going a few miles out of our way,' he said.

'And at the best?' Miranda asked anxiously, holding Tom Jim's hand tightly.

'That remains to be seen,' replied Carter grimly.

Akbar drove into a clearing packed with Africans. They watched as he stopped facing Mr Serrafino's Mercedes, which he had left in the middle of the road. On top of a small hill, a colonial-style house dominated the whole area. Carter's trained eyes noted weapon-slits in the walls, and hoped that Akbar was not overplaying his hand. Two men, one woman and a little boy would not stand much chance against these hundreds of scruffy, unshaven, armed men.

Mr Serrafino came down the steps of Odongo's house to meet them. He carried a fly-swat in one hand, and he was smiling. As far as he was concerned, this was almost the end of all his hardships. Within hours now, at the most, he would be away.

He was secretly surprised that Franz had still not arrived. Franz had always been most punctual, but there was obviously some simple explanation. He had most probably had a breakdown somewhere, and been temporarily delayed. Actually, it would not matter greatly if he did not arrive at all, so long as Odongo or Akbar did not ask for corroboration of the contents of the drums.

He thought that Akbar would be almost bound to agree with whatever Odongo proposed. He would have to make an instant decision, since the alternative was too terrible to contemplate. With any luck, Franz would not arrive before Mr Serrafino left. That would be best, for then he would not have to witness his murder. Odongo had a habit of prolonging these necessary but sometimes messy arrangements which Serrafino had frequently found distasteful. They brought back recurring images of that afternoon in the Arakan long ago. Murder might sometimes be necessary, and he accepted this as a business risk, but he did not enjoy the act of killing. Odongo did.

Mr Serrafino tapped on the roof of the Jaguar with his fly-swat. Everyone climbed out. Miranda and her son stood behind Akbar and Carter. Tom Jim gripped his catapult defensively.

'I didn't expect to see you again so soon,' said Serrafino, smiling at Carter. 'But I bear you no ill-will for all the trouble you have caused me.'

'I can't say the same,' Carter replied frankly. 'I didn't expect to see you, either; but, since we have met, there is the little matter of ten thousand dollars you owe me.'

'To the small-minded, all things are little matters,' retorted Mr Serrafino. He turned to Akbar Khan.

'The Emperor wishes to see you.'

'I am democratic,' Akbar replied quietly. 'I will see Mr Odongo at any time.'

'He will see you inside his house.'

'I will speak to him in front of all these people,' Akbar told him.

Mr Serrafino shrugged, and went back up the stairs to Odongo. He had hoped that this young fellow would agree to come into the house, where they could conduct negotiations in private, but he had nothing to gain by arguing in front of Odongo's followers, and it was important to start talking as soon as possible, in case Odongo's mood should change.

Odongo was waiting for him in the throne room. He had been drinking again, and some rum had trickled down his chin and stained his shirt.

'Is he willing?' he asked hoarsely.

'I haven't mentioned the deal yet,' Mr Serrafino explained. 'It was not opportune. He does not wish to come up here – I suppose he's frightened to do so. Understandably, when one considers your power and strength. He wants to meet you in front of all your people.'

He saw Odongo's hesitation and added quickly: 'It is good to do as he suggests. They will all then see how wise a ruler their emperor is.'

'You speak truth,' said Odongo, nodding. 'I will meet him outside.'

He began to search for his Homburg hat; he had put it somewhere only minutes earlier, but where? He must find it; every man needed his ju-ju. Without such a guardian, all manner of ill could befall him; without it, even an emperor went naked to face his enemies.

'Please, let us get this matter over with,' said Mr Serrafino anxiously. If they delayed, all impetus could be lost.

'My hat,' said Odongo hoarsely, not listening to him.

'You won't need it. The clearing is in the shade.'

'It's not that. It's my ju-ju.'

'An emperor needs no artificial ju-ju, no superstitious lucky charm. He is above that.'

Odongo grunted, unconvinced; but, bareheaded, he allowed Mr Serrafino to help him down the steps. The buzz of excited conversation that had arisen when Akbar Khan first climbed out of his car ended at once. Everyone stared silently as the man who had just made such glowing promises to them strode towards the new arrivals. There seemed something halting, almost reluctant, in his progress. Every now and then, Odongo smoothed down his wire-like hair uneasily with one hand.

'You wish to see me?' Akbar Khan asked him.

'Your uncle is unhappy at the thought that you may rule instead of him,' replied Odongo bluntly.

Akbar did not reply.

'I have brought you here to tell you that this will never come to pass.'

'I was already of that impression myself,' agreed Akbar.

'I, Odongo, have said he will not rule – but, then, neither will you. Instead, *I* will take over the country. It has been decreed by the ancient gods of forest and field and river and flood that I, Odongo, will be the next ruler of Abukali.'

Akbar shook his head.

'It has been decreed, if not by the ancient gods of forest and field, river and flood, but by the wish of the people, that you, Odongo, will be fortunate indeed to spend your days in exile. Thousands against whom you have given false witness, the relations of thousands more you have killed, will see to that. Is it not written, the voice of the people is the voice of God? They will speak with one voice, and from one memory. You are finished, Odongo. The days of your dictatorship are over. For ever.'

'Brave words,' replied Odongo. 'But look at those metal castings on that truck before you speak of matters about which you have no knowledge, young man.'

He waved his right hand, and at once the soldiers moved back hastily to the edges of the forest. Odongo beckoned Akbar to follow him towards the truck. As they walked across the clearing, a servant ran out after them from the house. He carried Odongo's Homburg in his hand. Odongo turned, embraced him, put the black hat on his head, grinning. His confidence surged back: now no one could beat him. He was invincible, above all men, unconquerable.

'You wait here,' Carter told Miranda in an urgent whisper. He had seen the change in Odongo's manner, the sudden new confidence in his walk, and knew it boded badly for them. 'If there's trouble, make for the house. You will be safer there.'

One of Odongo's soldiers heard him speak, detached himself from the crowd, and moved towards Carter. He was hung with bandoliers of ammunition; grenades were clipped to his belt. A sodden, unlit cigarette dangled from his mouth; he had not shaved that day. He carried a grenade-launcher by its sling and stood watching Odongo with bloodshot, mesmerized eyes. The soldier was so entranced by his oratory that he did not notice Carter now move closer to him and stand slightly to his left and slightly behind.

'You see these drums, these castings?' Odongo began rhetorically. 'You may think they are only worthless scrap metal, as my friend here, Mr Serrafino, declared to the Customs officials at Banjul port. Your English friend, Mr Carter, believes that they contain gold. I tell you they contain treasure more valuable than all the gold ever mined. They contain. . . .'

He paused, turning to Mr Serrafino for confirmation. His memory had suddenly deserted him; rum boiled in his blood.

Serrafino said quickly, like a stage prompter: 'They are packed with waste from nuclear generating stations in England and France. It is dumped at sea because the Europeans fear it is too dangerous to store anywhere on land. In the name of your emperor and your people, we have dredged it up from the ocean floor and brought it here to change the destiny of your country. The most famous scientist in East Germany is on his way to confirm this to you.'

'Was,' Carter corrected him drily.

Mr Serrafino looked at him, surprise and annoyance in his face changing to concern – and could it be fear?

'What do you mean?'

'We had a talk with Franz Halstein and persuaded him where his real interests lay. Then the local police decided they wanted to continue the conversation. There is a matter of hostile activities to Abukali. Involvement with two murders. The sort of thing police like to chat about.'

'What did Franz tell you?'

'Everything.'

Mr Serrafino's face suddenly lost its colour. Drops of perspiration trickled unchecked down his shining forehead.

'If I were a betting man – and, as you know, I'm not – I'd say you are in a no-win situation,' Carter continued, enjoying the other man's discomfiture.

'First, stealing atomic waste for terrorist purposes must bring you a heavy sentence. Probably life. If Odongo lets you live long enough to go on trial, that is. Another dubious possibility. And all the money in this world isn't much use if you're in the next world – or even still in this, in a cell.

'You will most likely be jailed here, of course. You are a Menakian citizen. Poor old Bob Astles wasn't tried in England, but in Uganda, because he gave up his British passport. Like you. I wouldn't think the Revolutionary Council in charge here would take a very lenient view of your activities. But that is only my opinion. Think about it. Come to your own conclusions.'

'I don't believe you,' said Mr Serrafino hoarsely. 'You're lying to get a way out of this. I know you are. I can see you are.'

Odongo's great booming voice overwhelmed their conversation. Flecks of saliva sprayed from his mouth as he spoke.

'I, Odongo, make you, Akbar Khan, the usurper of your

father's authority, an offer. Accept your uncle's sovereignty over the country of Abukali which you now wrongly claim. He will rule – with me to guide him.

'Refuse my offer, and within the hour my aircraft will take off with these containers to release them above Abukali.

'That will produce all the secondary effects of an atomic bomb. No explosion, of course, and no nuclear fission. But for at least a hundred miles around the dropping-area everything will be polluted. The earth will become a burned-out desert, covered with deadly atomic dust. Every living thing, every man, beast, bird and fish, all trees, plants, crops, will wither and die. Cultivation will cease. Water will be undrinkable. The land will be poisoned for ever. And you will be responsible, Mr Khan. You will have killed your own country.'

'A fearful prospect,' Akbar agreed soberly. 'But, if that does happen, how will you make any use of the mineral and other deposits you and my uncle are so keen to exploit? You may kill many people, and lay waste miles and miles of land, but you will also ruin your own hopes of a fortune.'

Odongo stared at him incredulously; he had not anticipated this. He turned to Mr Serrafino.

'Answer him,' he ordered sharply.

'The atomic waste will be dropped on the west of Abukali,' Serrafino explained. 'All mineral and other explorations are to the east. They will not be affected.'

'You give me a truly terrible choice,' said Akbar slowly. 'There is only one course open to me. The course of honour.'

He turned to Carter. His left eyelid drooped slightly. Carter glanced at the back of the guard standing in front of him. He appeared to be in a trance of wonder and admiration for his emperor. Truly, Odongo must have affinity with the gods of all the wild places, as he had always claimed.

Miranda stood a little to one side, her face pale with horror at the prospect of annihilation that Odongo had described. Tom Jim was in front of her; her hands were on his shoulders. Tom Jim could see from the faces of the grown-ups around him that something terrible was about to happen. He looked around the clearing, searching for any comfort, and then saw Carter looking at him.

Carter smiled reassuringly, nodded almost imperceptibly towards the rusty containers. Then, very casually, he stroked the side of his nose with the forefinger of his right hand.

Tom Jim grinned. This was a signal he could understand, and had been willing Carter to give ever since they had met in Fajara. He had even wondered whether Carter had forgotten all about their secret. Now Tom Jim knew that he hadn't, and his spirits soared. He put his hand into his trouser pocket, selected one of the smooth round pebbles he had hidden there without telling any grown-up, slipped the pebble into the catapult, pulled back the elastic and aimed. No one even noticed his action. Everyone was staring at Odongo, waiting for his next pronouncement.

Tom Jim's pebble hit a drum with a crack like a pistol shot. The sharp, unexpected noise in the silent clearing splintered the spell of silence. As the soldier in front of Carter swung his grenade-launcher into a firing position, Carter kicked him hard behind his left knee. The man staggered back, losing his balance. Carter tore the grenade-launcher from him as he fell, smashed the butt in the soldier's face, then jumped away from him and aimed it directly at the truck.

'For God's sake!' shouted Serrafino in terror. 'Don't shoot! You'll kill us all!'

'No one moves,' ordered Carter. 'Or that's just what I will do. Now, everyone – get back!'

With his left hand, he waved the nearest soldiers away from him. Miranda and Tom Jim sheltered behind him. Odongo stood staring in amazement, his moment of triumph turned to horror. Mr Serrafino felt his mouth go dry with fear. This lunatic could so easily kill everyone in the clearing – and from what Franz had told him it would be death of a most horrible kind. Their flesh would roll down in soft folds from their bones, eyes atrophy in their heads, blood congeal like jelly in their veins. He suddenly remembered the bungalow in Burma and the Japanese soldier driving his bamboo spike into the wounded

West African's jaw. He could see the man's beseeching look at him and remembered how he had turned away. He knew now how that man had felt.

'I beg you, don't shoot,' he implored Carter hoarsely. 'In the name of God, don't shoot.'

'You're mad,' said Odongo slowly, eyes narrowed, watching for the slightest weakening of resolve in Carter's face. 'Can't you understand that? Mad.'

He turned to an officer.

'Shoot that man,' he told him. 'I, Odongo, your emperor, order you.'

Carter raised the grenade-launcher to the level of his shoulders so that everyone could see his finger tighten slightly on its trigger.

'One shot and you all die,' he said. No one moved. The officer had raised his revolver on Odongo's command. Now he lowered it slowly, not looking at Odongo. As he did so, a sound like the rustling of a mighty wind spread through the clearing. Odongo's troops were beginning to back away into the greater safety of the forest. Their eyes were still on Carter and the muzzle of the grenade-launcher, as though by watching him they could somehow prevent him from firing until they were out of sight. The trees around the clearing stood very close together, and so many others had gathered in the open space that those behind soon began to cry out in protest as the men in front retreated and, in their haste to be away, forced them against the rough trunks and spike-leaved bushes. Others simply knocked down anyone in their way, heedless of the screams of those trampled underfoot.

'*Please!*' shouted Serrafino.

Carter took careful aim and pressed the trigger.

The grenade-launcher leaped in his grasp like a living thing. Grenades poured out with a stammering roar. Mr Serrafino fled for his car. Odongo followed him. Behind them, the containers on the truck erupted in a great white burst. A cloud of thick soft dust filled the air, and then started to settle slowly, drifting down from the tops of the trees, coating leaves and those still left behind who screamed in terror, for this was the dust of death. All Odongo's men ran shrieking into the forest, treading on the fallen, frantically hacking at anyone in their way with bayonets, rifles, clubs, shooting any who did not – or could not – get out of their way quickly enough.

Mr Serrafino jumped into his car, started the engine. As he raced away, rear wheels spinning in the dust, car slewing on full throttle, Odongo tore open the front passenger-door and dived in beside him. The top of his Homburg touched the roof. He grabbed frantically at the hat, but missed. It rolled away on its rim into the centre of the clearing.

Odongo gave a great shout of grief that changed to alarm as he saw Akbar's Jaguar blocking the only road. There was no room to pass. Serrafino cursed, and momentarily slackened speed.

'No!' yelled Odongo. 'Go right! Through the bamboo! There's another way. I'll show you.'

Serrafino swung the big car in a wide arc and accelerated into the clump of bamboos. He shut his eyes, put up one hand to shield his face as the Mercedes hit them head on. The car bucked, swerved, and then was through the tight lattice of thin green branches. Odongo's secret escape-route stretched ahead, so narrow that overhanging branches scratched and whipped both sides of the car as it gathered speed.

Mr Serrafino turned to Odongo and grinned with relief. They had escaped the holocaust of atomic dust, and the only witnesses against them had not. Everyone in Abukali would hear about this incredible day; he would personally see they did. And now, with Akbar removed, his uncle would have no opposition when he took power. Then Odongo would use the same blackmail and they would have the mineral wealth of the nation to divide between themselves. They had won. Against all opposition, against all odds, *they had won*!

But why was Odongo not sharing this triumph? It was his victory, too. Mr Serrafino's exultant smile faded as he saw dismay and terror grow on Odongo's face. His jaw had dropped in disbelief. He was mouthing words, screaming a warning, his forehead corrugated with terror, but no words came. In his moment of extremity, he was as dumb as the dead.

Mr Serrafino glanced back at the track ahead and then he saw what so horrified Odongo. The ant-hill blocking the road.

On either side large trees stood so close together that a walker could not have squeezed between them. There was no way round it and to reverse would be to die in the clearing.

The ant-hill towered nearly twenty feet high, like a castle in one of the fairy-stories Mr Serrafino used to read so patiently to Odongo. Through a space in overhead branches, the sun lit up the fearful apparition of earth formed into spires, turrets and pinnacles, its base pitted with holes each the size of a grown man's fist.

Restlessly swarming in and out of these gaping holes, smothering the cone-shaped hillock so that it appeared to have a heaving, breathing life of its own, were millions and millions of ants: black, red, white, brown; termites, workers, soldiers, scavengers; poisonous, deadly, dedicated.

Serrafino had no time to stamp on the brake pedal. The car hit the ant-hill head on, at full throttle. It swerved slightly. The rear tyres smoked and screamed as they spun uselessly in the soft surface of the track, boring the front bumper deeper into the tottering tower. Then, as clouds of ants were drawn like living dust into the air-intakes, the engine choked, faltered and died.

The car roof and windows were open, and the ant-hill tipped slowly and ponderously above the bonnet, darkening the sun. The two men heaved at both front doors, but the trees pressed so closely on either side that they would only open for a few inches. They were trapped in a metal tomb. Then the ant-hill tottered and broke into lumps of clogged earth held together with insect secretions, and fell directly through the open roof on to the men inside the car.

Mr Serrafino clawed at his bald scalp as ants by the million covered his head and shoulders. He gasped for breath as they swarmed into his mouth and nose, clogging his throat.

Odongo screamed in agony and terror as ants covered him

like a moving, many-coloured carpet, blinding him with a billion tiny stings.

By the time Carter and Akbar had reached the car, both men were totally covered by a throbbing, moving mass of ants. As they watched, sickened by the sight, the ants began an orderly retreat. Each held firmly in its pincers a minute morsel of human flesh. Like a victorious army, they were returning in triumph with their spoil to their queen, still hidden somewhere within her toppled kingdom, prepared to lick her to death as proof of their love and loyalty.

In the front seats of the car two cadavers, hung with shreds of flesh and clothing, leaned in despair against the doors. Carter bent down, picked up Odongo's Homburg. It was dented, the inside dark and damp with sweat. He threw it away; the ex-emperor's luck had run out at last. Above them, above the tallest trees, the vultures gathered, hoping to finish what the insects had begun.

Akbar led the way back to his car, now covered with white dust like frost. Miranda and Tom Jim were already inside. The clearing was totally deserted, but here and there in the forest someone trampled down or shot in the flight of Odongo's terrified supporters groaned in pain. Automatic rifles, grenade-launchers, machine-guns had been thrown away like the abandoned toys of an imbecile child of violence.

Akbar reversed the Jaguar, drove back in silence along the detour to the main road. On either side, they could hear Odongo's men, scattered in retreat, still crashing through the forest, desperate to escape the cloud of dust that drifted so gently down on to the leaves of all the trees.

For some time no one spoke in the car. Then Carter turned to Akbar.

'How were you certain those drums only contained flour?'

'I wasn't. But I relied on what Best had told me. As you know.'

'What did Franz hope to get out of it, then, if he knew the drums were harmless?'

'He is a very good nuclear scientist. He put a Geiger counter over all the containers, and couldn't get a reading. So he was convinced they were harmless. But, of course, he didn't tell Serrafino that. He felt that this vital knowledge gave him a lever over Serrafino. If he'd arrived in the clearing as agreed, then he could have used a bit of discreet blackmail on Serrafino to increase his share of the cake. Odongo would believe anything he liked to tell him about the contents of the containers. Serrafino had billed him as the best scientist in Eastern Europe, so he couldn't very well question his opinion. Serrafino would have been forced to increase his share – or lose his own.'

'How did Jack get involved?' asked Miranda.

'His mother was Portuguese, as you know, and he felt a great loyalty towards Portugal. Some of their security people weren't at all happy about Serrafino – given his record in Africa. They had doubts that he was really searching for gold, because he hadn't the right equipment. But he had reels of hawser and hooks – as you saw for yourself, Tony – and he could well be searching for something else. But what? They asked Jack Bridges to try to find out. Unofficially, of course. Such requests are always unofficial, in case anything goes wrong.'

'As it did here,' Carter pointed out.

'As it does so often. Bridges discovered what Serrafino was really up to, and told the Portuguese, who told Best's outfit. After all, the British and Portuguese have been allies for more than 600 years.'

'Our oldest allies,' said Carter, remembering Manuel's brother-in-law in the Nautilus bar.

'Quite so. It was arranged for decoy drums to be dropped fairly near Arrifana – the real stuff's miles and miles away, of course. Letters were sent here and there giving map coordinates, so that it would be easy for Serrafino's men to find out their position and trawl for them. No problem.'

'How did he know what was in these letters, though?' asked Miranda.

'The unfortunate Mr de Silva was allowed to look at them. He was very keen to say how he worked for the British and he was quite right. But he didn't really know the nature of all the work he was given. He did his best work, of course, thinking he was working for himself.'

'They didn't trust him?'

'Of course not. As I say, he worked primarily for himself. Probably we all do, but in his line of country that can be dangerous. When two sets of people hired him he would try to set them off against each other and so increase his value to both sides.'

'And in this case?'

'He simply increased the danger to himself. He got carried away, out of his class. You see, he helped Serrafino to get all the permissions and licences to dive, and if he'd stuck to that he'd be alive now. But he didn't. He was greedy and had too high an opinion of himself. The Russians became interested – quite understandably – when they heard Serrafino was trying to raise gold that belonged to them. They had been paid out insurance compensation, agreed, but that was nearly fifty years ago. They would much rather pay it back and have the gold instead, which would now be worth twenty or thirty times as much. They didn't have anyone on the spot to monitor events but they soon found someone.'

'Mr de Silva?' asked Carter.

'Exactly. His reports didn't add up to much when he discovered that Serrafino was not looking for gold. They became impatient and moved in one of their own people. Celia Kent. I don't know what her real name was, and it doesn't matter now. She had been here in Africa before, in case any of the faithful began to tire of the tedious teachings of Karl Marx. We've quite a dossier on her in Abukali, which I'll show you. She knew all about Serrafino's background, of course, from her time in Africa and she soon found out that de Silva was playing off every side. A tough lady.'

'A perfectionist,' said Carter. 'According to de Silva.'

'Indeed, yes. And a very dangerous, dedicated agent.'

'De Silva told me they had been married and divorced.'

'He told lots of people lots of things,' replied Akbar. 'But, like most of them, that's not true. It's all on the tape, in any case.'

'What tape?'

'Oh, of course, you don't know.'

He explained about Manuel's dog.

'Who killed her, then? Was that an accident?'

'Certainly not. De Silva calculated she was going to warn Serrafino that he had too many fingers in too many pies, so he took her out the only way he could in the time. He shot her. Then, according to Franz Halstein, he denounced her to Serrafino for doing exactly what he had been doing himself, playing both sides. They couldn't leave the body lying around, so they shipped it aboard *Quendon* to give her a burial at sea.'

'They were like those ants,' said Carter. 'All acting in self-defence, each believing that their own survival was at stake. They were correct, of course. But being right didn't save them.'

'On its own, just being right rarely saves anyone,' retorted Akbar. 'Now, before we get back and report to the worthy William Best, any more questions?'

'Yes. One that affects me most of all. Why did Serrafino hire me in the first place?'

'Mrs Kent suggested it.'

'Why?'

'She sold the idea to Serrafino that, as an ex-army officer, sea-green incorruptible, and short of cash, you could be a very useful fellow to have on his side if things went wrong.'

'How could they?'

'Easily. Serrafino's divers were a pretty rough crew. He paid their wages, agreed, but if they realized exactly what they were hauling aboard, and just what it could be worth in collateral or blackmail, he was a dead man.'

'And that was her only reason?' asked Carter.

'Her main one. I think she also thought you would owe her a debt for getting you the job. An introductory commission, if you like.'

'In cash or kind?'

'In help. Protection. She wanted to claim that favour when

she came down to see you after you telephoned Tim Rowley.'

'So all I've lost are a few days in my life and ten thousand dollars? I'll put that down as fees to what Serrafino called the University of Life.'

'I'd call it the University of Experience,' said Akbar. 'Post-graduate course.'

'It's certainly been an odd experience and, looking back, risky.'

'Of course. Everything worthwhile is. I would have thought that, as an army officer, risk is your career.'

'It was.'

'And will be. I think I'll need an officer – or even an ex-officer – to train the nucleus of a new defence force in my country. I'm looking for someone who would be commissioned directly into the Abukali Regiment and then later might quite reasonably transfer to a British regiment. Perhaps, who knows, the Golds?'

'Are you looking at him now?' asked Carter, grinning.

'I could be. But I tell you, Tony, it may be risky.'

Carter looked at Miranda. She was also smiling.

'Life is always risky,' she said softly.

'It can be fun, too,' Carter replied. And from now on that is what it would be. Like the advertisement in Banjul, a whole bottle of fun.

A small hand cautiously touched Carter's elbow. Tom Jim was looking up at him.

'Uncle Tony,' he said gravely. 'I'm sorry. I've got something terrible to tell you. I've lost the catapult you gave me. When I fired that stone and everyone started to shout and run, I dropped it.'

'And I have something to tell you,' replied Carter gravely. 'I picked it up. Now we can get down to something worthwhile. All of us.'

'Like showing me how to make a stone skim three times?'

'Absolutely like that. And much, much more.'

Castelejo – Arrifana, Portugal;
Banjul – Fajara, The Gambia

Hammond Innes

If you are looking for a tough action novel, of man against the elements, breathless but credible, out of the ordinary but authentic, you can't do better than a good Hammond Innes.

'Hammond Innes has a genius for conveying atmosphere.' *Daily Telegraph*

THE BIG FOOTPRINTS
THE BLUE ICE
CAMPBELL'S KINGDOM
LEVKAS MAN
THE LONELY SKIER
THE STRANGE LAND
THE WHITE SOUTH
WRECKERS MUST BREATHE
THE WRECK OF THE MARY DEARE
SOLOMONS SEAL
NORTH STAR
THE LAST VOYAGE
AIR BRIDGE
THE BLACK TIDE
ATTACK ALARM

and many others

FONTANA PAPERBACKS

Duncan Kyle

'One of the modern masters of the high adventure story.' *Daily Telegraph*

> GREEN RIVER HIGH
> BLACK CAMELOT
> A CAGE OF ICE
> FLIGHT INTO FEAR
> TERROR'S CRADLE
> A RAFT OF SWORDS
> WHITEOUT!
> STALKING POINT
> THE SEMONOV IMPULSE

FONTANA PAPERBACKS

Fontana Paperbacks: Fiction

Fontana is a leading paperback publisher of both non-fiction, popular and academic, and fiction. Below are some recent fiction titles.

- ☐ COMING TO TERMS Imogen Winn £2.25
- ☐ TAPPING THE SOURCE Kem Nunn £1.95
- ☐ METZGER'S DOG Thomas Perry £2.50
- ☐ THE SKYLARK'S SONG Audrey Howard £1.95
- ☐ THE MYSTERY OF THE BLUE TRAIN Agatha Christie £1.75
- ☐ A SPLENDID DEFIANCE Stella Riley £1.95
- ☐ ALMOST PARADISE Susan Isaacs £2.95
- ☐ NIGHT OF ERROR Desmond Bagley £1.95
- ☐ SABRA Nigel Slater £1.75
- ☐ THE FALLEN ANGELS Susannah Kells £2.50
- ☐ THE RAGING OF THE SEA Charles Gidley £2.95
- ☐ CRESCENT CITY Belva Plain £2.75
- ☐ THE KILLING ANNIVERSARY Ian St James £2.95
- ☐ LEMONADE SPRINGS Denise Jefferies £1.95
- ☐ THE BONE COLLECTORS Brian Callison £1.95

You can buy Fontana paperbacks at your local bookshop or newsagent. Or you can order them from Fontana Paperbacks, Cash Sales Department, Box 29, Douglas, Isle of Man. Please send a cheque, postal or money order (not currency) worth the purchase price plus 15p per book for postage (maximum postage is £3.00 for orders within the UK).

NAME (Block letters) _____

ADDRESS _____

_____

While every effort is made to keep prices low, it is sometimes necessary to increase them at short notice. Fontana Paperbacks reserve the right to show new retail prices on covers which may differ from those previously advertised in the text or elsewhere.